NEW YORK TIMES BESTSELLING AUTHOR

DIANA PALMER

A RANCHER'S KISS

Previously published as *Snow Kisses* and *Darling Enemy*

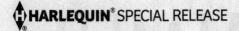

HARLEQUIN® SPECIAL RELEASE

Recycling programs
for this product may
not exist in your area.

ISBN-13: 978-1-335-54988-4

A Rancher's Kiss

Copyright © 2021 by Harlequin Books S.A.

Snow Kisses
First published in 1983. This edition published in 2021.
Copyright © 1983 by Diana Palmer

Darling Enemy
First published in 1983. This edition published in 2021.
Copyright © 1983 by Diana Palmer

This edition published by arrangement with Harlequin Books S.A.

For questions and comments about the quality of this book,
please contact us at CustomerService@Harlequin.com.

Harlequin Enterprises ULC
22 Adelaide St. West, 40th Floor
Toronto, Ontario M5H 4E3, Canada
www.Harlequin.com

Printed in Spain

CONTENTS

A prolific author of more than one hundred books, **Diana Palmer** got her start as a newspaper reporter. A *New York Times* bestselling author and voted one of the top ten romance writers in America, she has a gift for telling the most sensual tales with charm and humor. Diana lives with her family in Cornelia, Georgia. Visit her website at dianapalmer.com.

Books by Diana Palmer

Long, Tall Texans

Fearless
Heartless
Dangerous
Merciless
Courageous
Protector
Invincible
Untamed
Defender
Undaunted

The Wyoming Men

Wyoming Tough
Wyoming Fierce
Wyoming Bold
Wyoming Strong
Wyoming Rugged
Wyoming Brave

Morcai Battalion

The Morcai Battalion
The Morcai Battalion: The Recruit
The Morcai Battalion: Invictus
The Morcai Battalion: The Rescue

Visit the Author Profile page
at Harlequin.com for more titles.

SNOW KISSES

To the state of Montana,
whose greatest natural resource is her people.

CHAPTER ONE

THE ROAD WAS little more than a pair of ruts making lazy brown paths through the lush spring grass of southern Montana, and Hank was handling the truck like a tank on maneuvers. But Abby gritted her teeth and didn't say a word. Hank, in his fifty-plus years, had forgotten more about ranch work than she'd ever learn. And she wasn't about to put him in a bad temper by asking him to slow down.

She stared out over the smooth, rolling hills where Cade's white-faced Herefords grazed on new spring grass. Montana. Big Sky country. Rolling grasslands that seemed to go on forever under a canopy of blue sky. And amid the grass, delicate yellow and blue wildflowers that Abby had gathered as a girl. Here, she could forget New York and the nightmare of the past two weeks. She could heal her wounds and hide away from the world.

She smiled faintly, a smile that didn't quite reach her pale brown eyes, and she clenched her hands around the beige purse in the lap of her shapeless dress. She didn't feel like a successful fashion model when she was on the McLaren ranch. She felt like the young girl who'd grown up in this part of rural southern Montana, on the ranch that had been absorbed by Cade's growing empire after her father's death three years earlier.

At least Melly was still there. Abby's younger sister had an enviable job as Cade's private secretary. It meant that she could be near her fiancé, Cade's ranch foreman, while she supported herself. Cade had never approved of Jesse Shane's decision to allow his eldest daughter to go to New York, and he had made no secret of it. Now Abby couldn't help wishing she'd listened. Her brief taste of fame hadn't been worth the cost.

She felt bitter. It was impossible to go back, to relive those innocent days of her youth when Cade McLaren had been the sun and moon. But she mourned for the teenager she'd been that long-ago night when he'd carried her to bed. It was a memory she'd treasured, but now it was a part of the nightmare she'd brought home from New York. She wondered with a mind numbed by pain if she'd ever be able to let any man touch her again.

She sighed, gripping the purse tighter as Hank took one rise a little fast and caused the pickup to lurch to one side. She clutched the edge of the seat as the vehicle all but rocked onto its side.

"Sorry about that," Hank muttered, bending over the steering wheel with his thin face set into rigid lines. "Damned trucks—give me a horse any day."

She laughed softly—once she would have thrown back her head and given out a roar of hearty laughter. She might have been a willowy ghost of the girl who left Painted Ridge at eighteen, come back to haunt old familiar surroundings. This poised, sophisticated woman of twenty-two was as out of place in the battered pickup as Cade would be in a tuxedo at the Met.

"I guess you've all got your hands full," Abby remarked as they approached the sprawling ranch house.

"Damned straight," Hank said without preamble as he slowed at a gate. "Storm warnings out and calving in full swing."

"Snow?" she gasped, looking around at the lush greenery. But it was April, after all, and snow was still very possible in Montana. Worse—probable.

But Hank was already out of the truck, leaving the engine idling while he opened the gate.

"Drive the truck through!" he called for what seemed the tenth time in as many minutes, and Abby obediently climbed behind the wheel and put the truck in gear.

She couldn't help smiling when she remembered her childhood. Ranch children learned to drive early, out of necessity. She'd been driving a truck since her eleventh birthday, and many was the time she'd done it for Cade while he opened the endless gates that enclosed the thousands of acres he ranched.

She drove through the gate and slid back into her seat while Hank secured it and ambled back to the truck. He'd been part of Cade's outfit as long as she could remember, and there was no more experienced cowboy on the place.

"New York," Hank scoffed, giving her a disapproving glance. He chewed on the wad of tobacco in his cheek and gave a gruff snort. "Should have stayed home where you belonged. Been married by now, with a passel of younguns."

She shuddered at the thought, and her eyes clouded. "Is Cade at the ranch?" she asked, searching for something to say.

"Up in the Piper, hunting strays," he told her. "Figured he'd better find those damned cows before the snow hits. As it is, we'll have to fan out and bring them into the barn. We lost over a hundred calves in the snow last spring."

Her pale eyes clouded at the thought of those tiny calves freezing to death. Cade had come home one winter night, carrying a little white-faced Hereford across his saddle, and Abby had helped him get it into the barn to warm it. He'd been tired and snappy and badly in need of a shave. Abby had fetched him a cup of coffee, and they'd stayed hours in the barn until the calf was thawed and on the mend. Cade was so much a part of her life, despite their quarrels. He was the only person she'd ever felt truly at home with.

"Are you listening?" Hank grumbled. "Honest to God, Abby!"

"Sorry, Hank," she apologized quickly as the elderly man glared at her. "What did you say?"

"I asked you if you wanted to stow your gear at the house or go on down to the homestead."

The "house" was Cade's—the main ranch house. The "homestead" had been her father's and was now Melly's. Soon, it would belong to Melly and her new husband.

"Where's Melly?"

"At the house."

"Then just drop me off there, please, Hank," she said with a pacifying smile.

He grunted and gunned the engine. A minute later, she was outside under the spreading branches of the budding trees and Hank was roaring away in a cloud of dust. Just like old times, she thought with a laugh. Hank impatient, dumping her at the nearest opportunity, while he rushed on to his chores.

Of course, it was nearing roundup, and that always made him irritable. It was late April now—by June, the ranch would be alive and teeming with activity as new calves were branded and separated and the men worked twenty-four-hour days and wondered why they had ever wanted to be cowboys.

She turned toward the house with a sigh. It was just as well that Cade wasn't home, she told herself. Seeing him now was going to be an ordeal. All she wanted was her sister.

She knocked at the door hesitantly, and seconds later, it was thrown open by a smaller girl with short golden hair and sea-green eyes.

"Abby!" the younger girl burst out, tears appearing in her eyes. She threw open the door and held out her arms.

Abby ran straight into them and held on for dear life, oblivious to the suitcase falling onto the cleanly swept front porch. She clutched her sister and cried like a lost child. She was home. She was safe.

ADA

CHAPTER TWO

"I was so glad when you decided to come." Melly sighed over coffee while she and Abby sat in the sprawling living room. It had changed quite a bit since Cade's mother died. The delicate antiques and pastel curtains had given way to leather-covered couches and chairs, handsome coffee tables and a luxurious, thick-piled gray rug. Now it looked like Cade—big and untamed and unchangeable.

"Sorry," Abby murmured when she realized she hadn't responded. "I had my mind on this room. It's changed."

Melly looked concerned. "A lot of things have. Cade included."

"Cade never changes," came the quiet reply. The taller girl got to her feet with her coffee cup in hand and wandered to the mantel, to stare at a portrait of Donavan McLaren that overwhelmed the room.

Cade was a younger version of the tall, imposing man in the painting, except that Donavan had white hair and a mustache and a permanent scowl. Cade's hair was still black and thick over a broad forehead and deep-set dark eyes. He was taller than his late father, all muscle. He was darkly tanned and he rarely smiled, but he could be funny in a dry sort of way. He was thirty-six now, fourteen years Abby's senior, although he seemed twice that judging by the way he treated her. Cade was always the patronizing adult to Abby's wayward child. Except for that one magic night when he'd been every woman's dream—when he'd shown her a taste of intimacy that had colored her life ever since, and had rejected her with such tenderness that she'd never been ashamed of offering herself to him.

Offering herself...she shuddered delicately, lifting the coffee to her lips. As if that would ever be possible again, now.

"How is Cade?" Abby asked.

"How is Cade usually in the spring?" came the amused reply.

"Oh, I can think of several adjectives. Would horrible be too mild?" Abby asked as she turned.

"Yes." Melly sighed. "We've been shorthanded. Randy broke his leg and won't be any use at all for five more weeks, and Hob quit."

"Hob?" Abby's pale brown eyes widened. "But he's been here forever!"

"He said that was just how he felt after Cade threw the saddle at him." The younger woman shook her head. "Cade's been restless. Even more so than usual."

"Woman trouble?" Abby asked, and then hated herself for the question. She had no right to pry into Cade's love life, no real desire to know if he were seeing someone.

Melly blinked. "Cade? My God, I'd faint if he brought a woman here."

That did come as a surprise. Although Abby had visited Melly several times since she'd moved to New York, she had seen Cade only on rare occasions. She'd always assumed that he was going out on dates while she was on Painted Ridge.

"I thought he kept them on computer, just so that he could keep track of them." Abby laughed.

"Are we talking about the same man?"

"Well, he's always out every time I come to visit," Abby remarked. "It's been almost a year since I've seen him." She sat back down on the sofa next to her sister and drained her coffee cup.

Melly shot her a keen glance, but she didn't reply. "How long are you going to stay?" she asked. "I never could pin you down on the phone."

"A couple of weeks, if you can put up with me...."

"Don't be silly," Melly chided. She frowned, reaching out to touch her sister's thin hand. "Abby, make it a month. At least a month. Don't go back until you feel ready. Promise me!"

Abby's eyes closed under a tormented frown. She caught her breath. "I wonder if I'll ever be ready," she whispered roughly.

The smaller hand that was clasping hers tightened. "That's defeatist talk. And not like you at all. You're a Shane. We wrote the book on persevering!"

"Well, I'm writing the last chapter," Abby ground out. She stood up, moving to the window.

"It's been two weeks since it happened," Melly reminded her.

"Yes," Abby said, sighing wearily. "And I'm not quite as raw as I was, but it's hard trying to cope...." She glanced at her sister. "I'm just glad I had the excuse of helping you plan the wedding to come for a visit. What did Cade say when you asked if it was all right?"

Melly looked thoughtful. "He brightened like a copper penny," she said with a faint smile. "Especially when I mentioned that you might be here for a couple of weeks or more. It struck me at the time, because he's been just the very devil to get along with lately."

Abby pursed her lips thoughtfully. "He probably has the

idea that I've lost my job and came back in disgrace. Is that it?"

"Shame on you," her sister replied. "He'd never gloat over something like that."

"That's what you think. He's always hated the idea of my modeling."

Melly's thin brows rose. "Well, no matter what his opinion of your career, he was glad to hear you'd be around for a while. In fact, he was in such a good mood, all the men got nervous. Surely Hank told you that Hob had just quit? Too bad he didn't wait an extra day. Cade's bucking for sainthood since I announced your arrival."

If only it were true, Abby thought wistfully. But she knew better, even if Melly didn't. She was almost certain that Cade avoided her on purpose. Maybe it was just her sister's way of smoothing things over, to prevent a wild argument between Cade and Abby. It wouldn't be the first time she'd played peacemaker.

She glanced sharply into her sister's green eyes. "Melly, you didn't tell Cade the truth?" she asked anxiously.

Melly looked uncomfortable. "Not exactly," she confided. "I just said there was a man…that you'd had a bad experience."

Abby sighed. "Well, that's true enough. At least I'll be down at the homestead with you. He shouldn't even get suspicious about why I'm here. God knows, it's always been an uphill fight to keep peace when Cade and I are in the same room together, hasn't it?"

Melly shifted suddenly and Abby stared at her curiously.

"I'm afraid you won't be staying at the homestead," Melly said apologetically. "You see, my house is being painted. Cade's having the old place renovated as a wedding present."

Abby felt a wave of pure tension stretch her slender body. "We'll be staying…here?"

"Yes."

"Then why didn't you tell me when I asked to come?" Abby burst out.

"Because I knew you wouldn't come," Melly replied.

"Will Cade be away?" she asked.

"Are you kidding? In the spring, with roundup barely a month away?"

"Then I'll go somewhere else!" Abby burst out.

"No." Melly held her fast. "Abby, the longer you run away the harder it's going to be for you. Here, on the ranch, you can adjust again. You're going to have to adjust—or bury yourself. You do realize that? You can't possibly go on like this. Look at you!" she exclaimed, indicating the shapeless dress. "You don't even look like a model, Abby, you look like a housekeeper!"

"And that's a fine thing to say about me," came a deep but feminine voice from the doorway.

Both girls turned at once. Calla Livingston had her hands on her ample hips, and she was wearing a scowl sour enough to curdle milk. She was somewhere near sixty, but she could still outrun most of the cowboys, and few of them crossed her. She took her irritation out on the food, which was a shame because she was the best cook in the territory.

"And what do I look like, pray tell—the barn?" Calla continued, ruffled.

Melly bit her lip to keep from smiling. Dressed in a homemade shift of pink and green, her straggly gray hair pulled into a half bun, her garter-supported hose hanging precariously just above her knees, Calla was nobody's idea of haute couture. But only an idiot would have told her that, and Melly had good sense.

"You look just fine, Calla," Melly soothed. "I meant—" she searched for the right words "—that this isn't Abby's usual look."

Calla burst out laughing, her merry eyes going from one girl to the other. "Never could tell when I was serious and when I wasn't, could you, darlin'?" she asked Melly. "I was only teasing. Come here, Abby, and give us a hug. It's been months since I've seen you, remember!"

Abby ran into her widespread arms and breathed in the scent of flour and vanilla that always clung to Calla.

"Stay home this time, you hear?" Calla chided, brushing away a tear as she let go of the young woman. "Tearing off and coming back with city ways—this is the best you've looked to me since you were eighteen and hell-bent on modeling!"

"But, Calla…" Melly interrupted.

"Never you mind." Calla threw her a sharp glance. "Call her dowdy again, and it'll be no berry cobbler for you tonight!"

Melly opened her mouth and quickly closed it again with a wicked grin. "I think she looks…mature," Melly agreed. "Very…unique. Unusual. Rustically charming."

Calla threw up her hands. "What I put up with, Lord knows! As if that hard-eyed cowboy I work for isn't enough on my plate…. Well, if I don't rush, there'll be no peace when he comes in and doesn't find his meal waiting. Even if he doesn't come in until ten o'clock." She went away muttering irritably to herself.

Melly sat down heavily on the couch with an exaggerated sigh. "Oh, saved! If I'd realized that she was out there, I'd have sung the praises of your new wardrobe."

"Still hooked on her berry cobbler, I notice?" Abby

smiled, and for just an instant, a little of her old, vibrantly happy personality peeked out.

"Please tell him," Melly pleaded.

"And give him a stick to beat me with?" Abby asked with a dry laugh. "He's been down on me ever since I coaxed Dad into letting me go to New York. Every time I see him, all I hear is how stupid I was. Now he's got the best reason in the world to say it all again, and add an 'I told you so.' But he's not getting the chance, Melly. Not from me!'

"You're wrong about Cade," Melly argued. "You always have been. He doesn't hate you, Abby. He never did."

"Would you mind telling him that?" came the cool reply. "I don't think he knows."

"Then why was he so anxious for you to come home?" Melly demanded. She folded her arms across her knees and leaned forward. "He even had Hank bring up your own furniture from the homestead, just so you'd feel more at home. Does that sound like a man who's hating you?"

"Then why does he avoid me like the plague?" Abby asked curtly. She searched momentarily for a way to change the subject. "I sure would like to freshen up before we eat," she hinted.

"Then come on up. You've got the room next to mine, so we can talk until all hours."

"I'll like that," Abby murmured with a smile. Impulsively, she put her arm around Melly's shoulders as they went up the staircase. "Maybe we can have a pillow fight, for old time's sake."

"Calla's room is across the hall," Melly informed her.

Abby sighed. "Oh, well, we can always reminisce about the pillow fights we used to have," she amended, and Melly grinned.

It was just after dark, and Melly was helping Calla set

the table in the dining room when the front door slammed open and hard, angry footsteps sounded on the bare wood floor of the hall.

Abby, standing at the fireplace where Calla had built a small fire, turned just as Cade froze in the doorway.

It didn't seem like a year since she'd seen him. The hard, deeply tanned face under that wide-brimmed hat was as familiar as her own. But he'd aged, even she could see that. His firm, chiseled mouth was compressed, his brow marked with deep lines as if he'd made a habit of scowling. His cheeks were leaner, his square jaw firmer and his dark, fiery eyes were as uncompromising as she remembered them.

He was dusted with snow, his shepherd's coat flecked with it, his worn boots wet with it as were the batwing chaps strapped around his broad, heavy-muscled thighs. He was holding a cigarette in one lean, dark hand, and the look he was giving Abby would have backed down a puma.

"What the hell happened to you?" he asked curtly, indicating the shapeless brown suede dress she was wearing.

"Look who's talking," she returned. "Weren't you wearing that same pair of chaps when I left for New York?"

"Cattlemen are going bust all over, honey," he returned, and a hint of amusement kindled in his eyes.

"Sure," she scoffed. "But most of them don't run eight thousand head of cattle on three ranches in two states, now do they? And have oil leases and mining contracts...."

"I didn't say I was going bust," he corrected. He leaned insolently against the doorjamb and tilted his head back. "Steal that dress off a fat lady?"

She felt uncomfortable, shifting from one foot to the other. "It's the latest style," she lied, hoping he wouldn't know the difference.

"I don't see how you women keep up with the latest styles," he said. "It all looks like odds and ends to me."

"Is it snowing already?" she asked, changing the subject.

He took his hat off and shook it. "Looks like. I hope Calla's loading a table for the men, too. The nighthawks are going to have their hands full with those two-year-old heifers."

Abby couldn't help smiling. Those were the first-time mothers, and they took a lot of looking after. One old cowhand—Hob, the one who'd resigned—always said he'd rather mend fence than babysit new mamas.

"Who got stuck this year?" she asked.

"Hank and Jeb," he replied.

"No wonder Hank was so ruffled," she murmured.

A corner of Cade's disciplined mouth turned up as he studied her. "You don't know the half of it. He begged me to let him nurse the older cows."

"I can guess how far he got," she said.

He didn't laugh. "How long are you here for?"

"I haven't decided yet," she said, feeling nervous. "It depends."

"I thought spring was your busiest time, miss model," he said, his eyes narrowing suspiciously. "When Melly told me you were coming, it surprised me."

"I'm, uh, taking a break," she supplied.

"Are you?" He shouldered away from the doorjamb. "Stay through roundup and I'll fly you back to New York myself."

He turned, and her eyes followed his broad-shouldered form as he walked into the hall and yelled for Calla.

"I hope you've got enough to feed the hands, too!" he called, his deep voice carrying through the house. "Jeb's nighthawking with Hank!"

Jeb was the bunkhouse cook—some of the cowboys had homes on the ranch where they lived with their families, but there was a modern bunkhouse with a separate kitchen for the rest.

"Well, I'll bet the boys are on their knees giving thanks for that!" Calla called back. "It'll be a change for them, having decent food for one night!"

Cade chuckled deep in his throat as he climbed the stairs. Abby couldn't help but watch him, remembering old times when she'd worshipped that broad back, that powerful body, with a schoolgirl's innocent heart. How different her life might have been if Cade hadn't refused her impulsive offer that long-ago night. Tears formed in her eyes and she turned away. Wishing wouldn't make it so. But it was good to be back on Painted Ridge, all the same. She'd manage to keep out of Cade's way, and perhaps Melly was right. Perhaps being home again would help her scars to heal.

CHAPTER THREE

ABBY MIGHT HAVE planned to avoid him, but Cade seemed to have other ideas. She noticed his quiet, steady gaze over the dinner table and almost jumped when he spoke.

"How would you like to see the new calves?" he asked suddenly.

She lifted her eyes from her plate and stared at him, lost for an answer. "Isn't it still snowing?" she asked helplessly.

"Sure," he agreed. "But the trucks have chains. And the calving sheds are just south of here," he reminded her.

Being alone with him was going to unnerve her—she knew it already—but she loved the sight of those woolly little creatures, so new to the world. And she liked being with Cade. She felt safe with him, protected. Despite the lingering apprehension, she wanted to go with him.

"Well?" he persisted.

She shrugged. "I would kind of like to see the calves," she admitted with a tiny smile. She dropped her eyes back to her plate, blissfully unaware of the look Cade exchanged with Melly.

"We'll have dessert when we get back," Cade informed Calla, pushing back his chair.

Minutes later, riding along in the pickup and being bounced wildly in its warm interior, snow fluttering against the windshield, it was almost like old times.

"Warm enough, honey?" Cade asked.

"Like toast." She wrapped the leather jacket he had loaned her even closer, loving its warmth. Cade was still wearing his shepherd's coat, looking so masculine he'd have wowed them even at a convention of male models.

"Not much farther now," he murmured, turning the truck off onto the farm road that led to the calving pens, where two cowboys in yellow slickers could be seen riding around the enclosures, heads bent against the wind.

"Poor devils," she remarked, watching.

"The men or the heifers?" he asked.

"Both. All. It's rough out there." She balanced her hand against the cold dashboard as he stopped the truck and cut the engine at the side of the long shed. Cade was the perfect rancher, but his driving left a lot to be desired.

"Now I know how it feels to ride inside a concrete mixer," she moaned.

"Don't start that again," Cade grumbled as he threw open the door. "You can always walk back," he added with a dark glance.

"Did you ever race in the Grand Prix when you were younger, Cade?" she asked with a bright, if somewhat false, smile.

"And sarcasm won't do the trick, either," he warned. He led the way through the snow, and she followed in his huge footprints, liking the bite of the cold wind and the crunch of the snow, the freshness of the air. It was so deliciously different from the city. Her eyes looked out over the acres toward the distant mountains, searching for the familiar snow-covered peaks that she could have seen clearly in sunny daylight. God's country, she thought reverently. How had she ever been able to exist away from it?

"Stop daydreaming and catch up," Cade was growling. "I could lose you out here."

"In a little old spring snowstorm like this?" She laughed. "I could fight my way through blizzards, snowshoe myself to Canada, ski over to the Rockies…"

"…lie like hell, too," he said, amusement gleaming in the dark eyes that caught hers as they entered the lighted interior. "Come on."

She followed him into the airy enclosure, wrapping her arms tight. "Still no heat, I see." She sighed.

"Can't afford the luxury, honey," he remarked, waving at a cowboy farther down the aisle.

"Is that why it's so drafty in here? You poor thing, you," she chided.

"I would be, if I didn't keep the air circulating in here," he agreed. "Don't you remember how many calves we used to lose to respiratory ailments before the veterinarians advised us to put in that exhaust fan to keep stale air out of these sheds? Those airborne diseases were bankrupting the operation. Now we disinfect the stalls and maintain a rigid vaccination program, and we've cut our losses in half."

"Excuse me," she apologized. "I'm only an ignorant city dweller."

He turned in the aisle and looked down at her quietly. "Come home," he said curtly. "Where you belong."

Her heart pounded at the intensity of the brief gaze he gave her before turning back to his cow boss.

Charlie Smith stood up, grinning at Cade. "Hi, boss, get tired of television and hungry for some real relaxation? Jed sure would love to have somebody take his place—"

"Just visiting, Charlie," Cade interrupted. "I brought Abby down to see the newcomers."

"Good to see you again, Miss Abby," Charlie said respectfully, tipping his hat. "We've got a good crop in here, all right. Have a look."

Abby peeked into the nearest stall, her face lighting up as she stared down at one of the "black baldies," a cross between a Hereford and a Black Angus, black all over with a little white face.

"Jed brought that one in an hour ago. Damn...uh, dog-gone mama just dropped it and walked away from it." Charlie sneered.

"That's not his mama, huh?" Abby murmured, noticing the tender licking it was getting from the cow in the stall with it.

"No, ma'am," Charlie agreed. "We sprayed him with a deodorizing compound to keep her from getting suspicious. Poor thing lost her own calf."

Abby felt a surge of pity for the cow and calf. It was just a normal episode in ranch life, but she had a hard time trying to separate business from emotion.

Cade moved close behind her, apparently oblivious to the sudden, instinctive stiffening of her slender body, the catch of her breath. Please, she thought silently, please don't let him touch me!

But he didn't attempt to. He leaned against the stall and rammed his hands in his pockets, watching the cow and calf over her shoulder. "How many have we lost so far?" Cade asked the cow boss.

"Ten. And it looks like a long night."

"They're all long." Cade sighed. He pushed his hat back over his forehead, and Abby, glancing up, noticed how weary he looked.

"I'd better check on my own charge down the aisle here," Charlie said, and went off with a wave of his hand as the ominous bleating of the heifer filled the shed.

"Prime beef," Cade murmured, chuckling at Abby's indignant expression.

She moved away from him with studied carelessness and smiled. "Heartless wretch," she teased. "Could you really eat him?"

"Couldn't you, smothered in onions…?"

"Oh, stop!" she wailed. "You cannibal…!"

"How does it feel to be back?" he asked, walking back the way they came in.

"Nice," she admitted. She tucked her cold hands into the pockets of her jacket. "I'd forgotten how big this country is, how unspoiled and underpopulated. It's a wonderful change from a crowded, polluted city, although I do love New York," she added, trying to convince him she meant it.

"New York," he reminded her, "is a dangerous place."

She stiffened again, turning to study his face, but she couldn't read anything in that bland expression. Cade let nothing show—unless he wanted it to. He'd had years of practice at camouflaging his emotions.

"Most cities are," she agreed. "The country can be dangerous, too."

"It depends on your definition of danger," he returned. He looked down at her with glittering eyes. "You're safe as long as I'm alive. Nothing and no one will hurt you on this ranch."

Tears suddenly misted her eyes, burning like fire. She swallowed and looked away. "Do I look as if I need protection?" She tried to laugh.

"Not especially," he said coolly. "But you seemed threatened for an instant. I just wanted to make the point. I'll protect you from mountain lions and falling buildings, Abby," he added with a hint of a smile.

"But who'll protect me from you, you cannibal?" she asked with a pointed stare, her old sense of humor returning to save her from the embarrassment of tears.

"You're just as safe with me as you want to be," he replied.

She looked into his eyes, and for an instant they were four years in the past, when a young girl stood poised at the edge of a swimming pool and offered her heart and her body to a man she worshipped.

Without another word, she turned around and started back out into the snow.

CHAPTER FOUR

AS SHE WALKED toward the truck, huddled against the wind, her mind suddenly went backward in time. And for an instant, it was summer, and she was swimming alone in the pool at Cade's house one night when her father was in the hospital.

She'd been eighteen, a girl on the verge of becoming a woman. Her father, far too ill during that period of her life to give her much counsel, hadn't noticed that she was beginning to dress in a way that caught a lot of male attention. But Cade had, and he'd had a talk with her. She'd marched off in a huff, hating his big-brother attitude, and had defiantly gone for a swim that night in his own pool. There was no one around, so she had quickly stripped off her clothes and dived in. That was against the rules, but Abby was good at breaking them. Especially when they were made by Cade McLaren. She wanted him to look at her the way other men did. She wanted more than a condescending lecture from him, but she was too young and far too naive to put her growing infatuation into words.

She'd been in the pool barely five minutes when she heard the truck pull up at the back of the house. Before she had time to do any more than scramble out of the pool and pull on her jeans, she heard Cade come around the corner.

She was totally unprepared for what happened next. She turned and Cade's dark eyes dropped to her high, bare breasts with a wild, reckless look in them that made her breath catch in her throat. He just stood there, frozen, staring at her, and she didn't make a move to cover herself or turn away. She let him look his fill, feeling her heart trying to tear out of her chest when he finally began to move toward her.

His shirt was open that night, because he'd just come in from the corral, and the mat of thick black hair over the bronzed muscles of his chest was damp with sweat. He stopped a foot in front of her and looked down, and she knew that all the unspoken hunger she'd begun to feel for him was plain in her wide, pale brown eyes.

Without a word, he bent and lifted her. Very, very gently, he brought her body to his and drew her taut breasts against his chest, letting her feel the rough hair against her soft, sensitive skin in a caress that made her moan and cling to him, while her eyes looked straight into his and saw the flash of triumph in them.

He turned and carried her into the house, up the stairs and into his own bedroom, and laid her down on the bed. And then he sat there, with one hand on the bed beside her to support his weight, and looked at her again, letting his dark eyes feast on the soft, pink bareness of her body. She wasn't even aware of being wet, of her body soaking the coverlet. All she saw, all she knew, was Cade's hard, dark face and his eyes.

Finally, he moved and his fingers traced a pattern from her shoulder down over her collarbone. She held her breath as they kept going down, and she felt the slow, sweet tracing of them on the curve of her breasts—exploring, tantalizing with the light pressure—until they reached the burgeoning peak and caught it lightly between them.

She gasped, arching at the unexpected surge of pleasure, and his eyes looked straight down into hers.

"Hush," he whispered then. "You know I won't hurt you."

"Yes," she whispered back, as if the walls could hear them, her eyes wide with unexpected pleasure. "I...I want you...to touch me."

"I know." He bent, one hand still cupping her, and she lifted her arms hesitantly until they were around his neck. He looked into her eyes as his warm, hard mouth brushed hers, so that he could see the reaction in them. "Open your mouth for me, Abby," he breathed, moving his hand to tip up her chin, "just a little more...."

She obeyed him mindlessly and felt the delicious probing of his tongue between her lips, working its way slowly, sensuously, into her mouth. She gasped, moaning, and he eased down so that she could feel his bare chest against her breasts. She lifted herself, clinging, and for one long, unbearably sweet moment she felt his warmth and weight and the fierce adult passion of a man's kiss.

She thought she imagined a tremor in his hard arms before he suddenly released her, but when he sat up again he was as calm outwardly as if he'd been for a quiet walk. His eyes went down to her breasts and drank in the sight of them one last time before his big hand caught the coverlet and tossed it carelessly over her bareness.

"You wanted to know," he said gently, holding her hand tightly in his as if to soften the rejection, "and I've shown you. But this is as far as it goes. I care too much to seduce you just for an hour of pleasure."

She swallowed, studying his hard face, her body still tingling from the touch of his fingers, her mouth warm from the long, hungry kiss they'd shared. "Should I be ashamed, Cade?" she asked.

He brushed the damp hair away from her face. "Of what?" he asked tenderly. "Of wanting to know how it felt to be touched and kissed by a man?"

She drew in a deep, slow breath. "Not...by a man," she corrected. "By you."

The impact of that nervous confession was evident on his face. He hesitated, as if he wanted desperately to say something but thought better of it. His jaw tautened.

"Abby," he said, choosing the words carefully, "you're eighteen years old. You've got a lot of growing up to do, a lot of the world to see, before you tie yourself to one man. To any man." He toyed with the coverlet at her throat. "It's natural, at your age, to be curious about sex. But despite the modern viewpoint, there are still men left who'll want a virgin when they marry." His eyes met hers levelly. "Be one. Save that precious gift for the man you marry. Don't give it away to satisfy your curiosity."

"Will you?" she asked involuntarily.

"Will I what, honey?" he asked.

"Want a virgin?"

He looked strange at that moment. Thoughtful. Hungry. Irritated. "The biggest problem in my life," he said after a minute, with a flash of humor, "is that I want one right now." He bent then and kissed her briefly, roughly, before he stood up.

"Cade...?" she began, her hand going to the coverlet, the offer in her young eyes.

"No," he said firmly, loosening her fingers from the material. "Not yet."

"Yet?" she whispered.

He traced her mouth with a lazy, absent finger. "Make me the same offer again in about three or four years," he murmured with a faint smile, "and I'll drag you into a bed and make love to you until you pass out. Now get dressed. And don't try this again, Abby," he warned firmly. "It's the wrong time for us. Don't force me to be cruel to you. It's something I'd have hell living with."

Her head whirling with unbridled hope, she watched him walk to the door with her whole heart in her misty eyes.

"Cade?" she called softly.

He'd turned with one hand on the doorknob, an eyebrow raised.

"I'll hold you to that...in three or four years," she promised.

He smiled back at her, so tenderly that she almost climbed out of the bed and threw herself at his feet. "Good night, honey," he chuckled, walking out the door.

NEITHER OF THEM had ever mentioned it, or referred to it, in all the time since then. Shortly afterward she had left the ranch; she'd seen Cade only a few times in the intervening years. It was odd that she should remember the incident now, when her promise was impossible to keep. She'd never be able to offer herself to Cade now.

She opened the door of the truck and got in.

Cade was quiet on the way back to the house, but that wasn't unusual. He never had liked to talk and drive at the same time. He seemed to mull over problems in the silence, ranch problems that were never far away. In winter, it was snow and getting enough feed to the livestock. In spring it was roundup and planting. In summer it was haying and fixing fence and water. Water was an eternal problem—there was either not enough or too much. In May and June, when the snow melted on the mountains and ran into streams and rivers, there would be enough water for agriculture— but there would also be flooding to contend with. After roundup, the cattle had to be moved to high summer pastures. In fall, they had to be brought back down. The breeding program was an ongoing project, and there were always the problems of sick cattle and equipment breakdowns and the logistics of feeding, culling, selling and buying cattle. Cade had ranch managers, like Melly's husband-to-be, but he owned three ranches, and ultimately he was the one responsible to the board of directors and to the stockholders, as well. Because it was a corporation now, not just one man's holdings, and Cade was at the helm.

Her eyes sought his face, loving it as she'd loved it for four, long, empty years. Cade, the eternal bachelor. She wondered if he'd ever marry, or want children of his own to inherit Painted Ridge and the other properties he had stock in. She'd thought once, at eighteen, that he might marry her one day. But he'd made a point of avoiding her after that devastating encounter. And in desperation, she had settled for the adventure and challenge of modeling.

It had been the ultimate adventure at eighteen. Glamour, wealth, society—and for the first year or so it had almost satisfied her. She remembered coming home that first Christmas, bubbling with enthusiasm for her work. Cade had listened politely and then had left. And he'd been conspicuously absent for the rest of the time she was at Painted Ridge. She'd often wondered why he deliberately avoided her. But she'd been ecstatic over the glitter of New York and her increasing successes. Or she had been at first…

Cade seemed to sense her intense appraisal. His head suddenly turned and he caught her eyes as he pulled up to the house and parked at the back steps. Abby felt a shock of pure sensation go through her like fire. It had been a long time since she'd looked into those dark, glittering eyes at point-blank range. It did the most wonderful things to her pulse, her senses.

"You've been away longer this time," he said without preamble. He leaned back against his door and lit a cigarette. "A year."

"Not from the ranch," she countered. "You weren't here last summer or at Christmas when I was."

He laughed shortly, the cigarette sending up curls of smoke. "What was the use?" he asked coolly. "I got sick of hearing about New York and all the beautiful people."

She sat erect, her chin thrusting forward. "Are we going to have that argument all over again?"

"No, I'm through arguing," he said curtly. "You made up your mind four years ago that you couldn't find what you wanted from life anyplace except New York. I left you to it, Abby. I know a lost cause when I see one."

"What was there for me here?" she demanded, thinking back to a time when he wouldn't come near her.

But his face went cold at the words. It seemed actually to pale, and he turned his eyes out the window to look at the falling snow. "Nothing, I guess," he said. "Open country, clean air, basic values and only few people. Amazing, isn't it, that we have the fourth largest state in the country, but it's forty-sixth in population. And I like it that way," he added, pinning her with his eyes. "I couldn't live in a place where I didn't have enough room to walk without being bumped into."

She knew that already. Cade, with his long, elegant stride and love of open country, might as well die as be transplanted to New York. This was Big Sky country, and he was a Big Sky man. He'd never feel at home in the Big Apple. A hundred years ago, however, he would have fit right in with the old frontier ways. She remembered going to the old

Custer battlefield with him, where the Battle of the Little Bighorn was fought, and watching his eyes sweep the rolling hills. He sat a horse the same way, his eyes always on the horizon. One of his ancestors had been a full-blooded Sioux, and had died at Little Bighorn. He belonged to this country, as surely as the early settlers and miners and cattlemen had belonged to it.

Abby had wanted to belong to it, too—to Cade. But he'd let her get on that bus to New York when she was eighteen, although he'd had one hell of a fight with her father about it the night before she left. Jesse Shane had never shared the discussion with her. She only knew about it because she'd heard their angry voices in the living room and her name on Cade's lips.

"You never wanted me to go to New York," she murmured as she withdrew from the pain of memory. "You expected me to fall flat on my face, didn't you?"

"I hoped like hell that you would," he said bluntly, and his eyes blazed. "But you made it, didn't you? Although, looking at you now, I could almost believe you hadn't. My God, Calla has better taste in clothes."

She avoided his eyes, puzzled by the earlier statement. "I'm very tastefully dressed for a woman on a ranch," she threw back, nervous that he might guess why she was wearing loose clothing, why she couldn't bear anything revealing right now.

"Is that a dig at me?" he asked. "I know ranch life isn't glamorous, honey. It's damned hard work, and not many women would choose it over a glittering career. You don't have to tell me that."

How little he knew, she thought miserably. She'd chuck modeling and New York and the thought of being internationally famous if he asked her to marry him. She would have given up anything to live with him and love him. But he didn't know, and he never would. Her pride wouldn't let her tell him. He'd rejected her once, that magic night years before, even though he did it tenderly. She couldn't risk having him do it again. It would be too devastating.

Her eyes dropped to her suede boots. The boots would be ruined. She'd forgotten to spray them with protective coating, and she'd need to buy a new pair. Odd that she should think about that when she was alone with Cade. It was so precious to be alone with him, even for a few minutes. If only she could tell him what had happened, tell him the truth. But how could she admit that she'd come back to be healed?

"Hey."

She looked up and found him watching her closely. He reached out and caught a lock of her long hair and tugged it gently.

"What's wrong?" he asked quietly.

She felt the prick of tears and blinked to dispel them. It was so much harder when he was tender. It reminded her forcibly of the last time she'd heard his voice so velvety and deep. And suddenly she found herself wondering how she would react if he tried to hold her, touch her, now.

"Nothing's wrong," she said shortly. "I was just thinking."

His face hardened and he let go of her hair. "Thinking about New York?" he demanded. "What the hell are you doing here in April, anyway? I thought summer was your only slack time."

"I came to see Melly, of course," she shot back, her face hot and red. "To help her get ready for the wedding!"

"Then you'll be staying for a month," he said matter-of-factly, daring her to protest. How could she when she'd stated the lie so convincingly?

She swallowed. "Well…"

"I understood you were designing her a dress?" he continued.

"Yes," she agreed, remembering the sketches she'd already done. Over the past few years she had discovered that she enjoyed designing clothes much more than modeling them.

"My God, you're quiet," he observed, his eyes narrowing against the smoke of his cigarette. "You used to come home gushing like a volcano, full of life and happiness. Now you seem…sedate. Very, very different. What's the matter, honey, is the glitter wearing off, or are you just tired of going around half-naked for men to look at?"

She gasped at the unexpectedness of the attack and drew in a sharp breath. "Cade Alexander McLaren, I do not go around half-naked!"

"Don't you?" he demanded. He had that old familiar look on his face, the one that meant he was set for a fight. "I was up in New York one day last month on business and I went to one of your fashion shows. You were wearing a see-through blouse with nothing under it. Nothing!" His face hardened. "My God, I almost went up there and dragged you off that runway. It was all I could do to turn around and walk out of the building. Your father would have rolled over in his grave!"

"My father was proud of me," she returned, hurting from the remark. "And unless you missed it, most of the people who go to those shows are women!"

"There were men there," he came back. He crushed out the cigarette. "Do you take off your clothes for men in private, too, Abby?"

She lifted her hand to hit him, but he caught the wrist and jerked. She found herself looking straight into his narrowed eyes at an alarming distance. But worse, she felt the full force of his strength in that steely grip, and she felt panic rise in her throat.

"Let me go, Cade," she said suddenly, her voice ghostly, her eyes widening with fear. "Oh, please, let me go!"

He scowled, freeing her all at once. She drew back against her door like a cornered cat, actually trembling with reaction. Well, now she knew, didn't she? she thought miserably. She'd wondered how she'd react to Cade's strength, and now she truly knew.

"Remember me?" he asked angrily. "We've known each other most of our lives. I was defending myself, Abby. I wasn't going to hit you. What the hell's the matter with you? Has some man been knocking you around?" His face became frankly dangerous. "Answer me," he said harshly. "Has one of your boyfriends been rough with you? By God, if he has…!"

"No, it's not that," she said quickly, drawing in a steadying breath. Her eyes closed on a wave of remorse. "I'm just tired, Cade. Tired. Burned out. Too many long hours and too many go-sees that didn't work out, too many demanding photographers, too many retakes of commercials, too many fittings, too many temperamental designers…." She slumped back against the door and opened her eyes, weary eyes, to look at him. "I'm tired." It was a lie, but then, how could she possibly tell him the truth?

"You came home to rest, is that what you're telling me?" he asked softly.

"Is it all right?" she asked, her eyes searching his. "A whole month, and I don't want to interfere with your life…."

"That's a joke," he scoffed. His eyes went over the shapeless dress. "You don't know what a joke it is." He turned abruptly to open the door. "Let's go in. It's freezing out here. We can sit around inside for the rest of the night and watch your sister and Jerry climb all over each other."

He sounded utterly disgusted, and she laughed involuntarily. "They're engaged," she reminded him.

"Then why don't they get married and make out in their own house?" he growled.

"They're trying," she said.

He gave her a hard glare before he opened his door and went around to open hers. "The wedding can't be soon enough to suit me," he said. "The only place I haven't caught them at it is in a closet."

"They're in love." She stepped down from the running board, landing in the soft, cold snow. "My gosh, you're old-fashioned, Cade."

"Don't tell me you hadn't noticed that before?" he asked as they walked toward the house through the driving snow. It tickled Abby's face, melting cold and wet over her delicate features.

"It's hard to miss," she agreed. She glanced up at him, walking so tall and straight beside her. He moved with easy grace, long strides that marked him an outdoorsman. It would take wide-open country like Montana to hold him. "But people in love are notoriously hard to separate."

"What would you know about love?" he asked, shooting a glance down at her. "Have you ever felt it?"

She laughed with brittle humor. "Most people have a crush or two in a lifetime."

"You had one on me once, as I remember," he said quietly. He was staring straight ahead, or he'd have seen the shock that widened Abby's pale brown eyes.

"I'm surprised you even noticed," she muttered. "In between raising cattle and fighting off girls at square dances."

"I noticed." The words didn't mean a lot, but the way he said them did. There was a world of meaning in the curt, harsh sound of them.

She drew in a slow breath and wrapped her arms around her chest, averting her gaze from him. Would she ever forget that night? Despite the recent experience that had soured physical relationships for her, she felt an explosion of pleasure at the memory of Cade's warm, rough mouth on her own, his hands touching her so gently....

They were at the back door. He opened it and let her into the warm, dry kitchen ahead of him. Calla had apparently stepped out for a minute, because it was deserted.

"Abby," he called.

She turned at the entrance to the dining room and looked back at him. He'd pulled off his hat, and his dark hair glittered damply black in the light.

His eyes slid down her body, taking in the ill-fitting clothing, and went back up to her flushed face and wide, soft eyes. The tension was suddenly between them, the old tension that she'd felt that night at the swimming pool when he'd seen her as no other man ever had. She could feel the shock of his gaze, the wild beat of her own heart in the silence that throbbed with unexpected promise.

"Are you happy in New York?" he asked.

She faltered, trying to get words past her tight throat. She had been—or she'd convinced herself that she had been—until the incident that had made her run home for shelter, for comfort. But always she'd missed Painted Ridge...and Cade.

"Of course I am," she lied. "Why?"

His tall frame shifted impatiently, as if he'd wanted an answer she hadn't given him. He made a strange gesture with one hand. "I just wondered, that's all. I saw your face on a magazine cover the other day," he added, studying her. "One of the better ones. That means something, I gather?"

"Yes," she agreed with a wan smile. "It's quite a coup to have a cover on that kind of magazine. My agency was thrilled about it."

His eyes wandered over her face, searching eyes that grew dark with some emotion she couldn't name. "You're beautiful, all right," he said quietly. "You always were. Not just physically, either. You reminded me of sunlight on a morning meadow. All silky and bright and sweet to look at. Whatever happened to that little girl?"

She felt an ache deep inside, a hunger that nothing had ever filled. Her eyes touched every hard line of his face, lines she would have loved to smooth away. She withered away from you, she wanted to tell him. Part of her died when she left Painted Ridge.

But of course she couldn't say that. "She grew up, Cade," she said instead.

He shook his head and smiled—a strange, soft smile that puzzled her. "No, not quite. I carry her around in my memory and every once in a while, I take her out and look at her."

"She was dreadfully naive," she murmured, trying not to let him see how his statement had touched her.

He moved slowly toward her, stopping just in front of her. He towered over her, powerful and big and faintly threatening, and she fought down the fear of his strength that had already surfaced once that night.

She looked up, intrigued by the smell of leather and wind that clung to him. "I'd forgotten how tall you are," she said involuntarily.

"I've forgotten nothing about you, Abby," he said curtly.

"Including the fact that once you couldn't get close enough to me. But now you back away the minute I come near you."

So he had noticed. She dropped her eyes to the front of his shepherd's coat. "Do I?"

"You shied away from me in the calving shed tonight. Do you think I didn't notice? Then in the truck…" He drew in a deep breath. "My God, I'd never hurt you. Don't you know that?"

Her eyes traced the stitching on the coat and she noticed a tiny smudge near one of the buttons, as if ashes from his cigarette had fallen on it. Silly things to be aware of when she could feel the heat of his big body, and she remembered as if it were yesterday how sweet it was to be held against him.

"I know," she said after a minute. She forced her eyes up to his. "I…have some problems I'm trying to work out."

"A man?" he asked curtly.

She nodded. "In a way."

His face hardened, and his hands came up as if he would have liked to grip her with them. But he abruptly jammed them into his pockets. "Want to tell me about it?"

Her head went slowly from side to side. "Not yet. I have to find myself, Cade. I have to work it out in my own way."

"Does it have something to do with your career?" he asked.

"Yes, it does. I have to decide whether or not I want to go on with it," she confessed.

He seemed to brighten. His face changed, relaxed, making him look strangely young. "Thinking of quitting?"

"Why not?" she asked, grinning. "Need an extra cowhand? I close gates good—you ask Hank if I don't."

He smiled back, his dark eyes sparkling with humor. "I'll do that."

She sighed. "You'll be ready to run me off by the time

that month's up," she said with a short laugh. "Anyway, I've got a lot of thinking to do."

He searched her quiet face. "Maybe I can help you make up your mind," he murmured. One hand caught her chin and turned it up, while his eyes searched hers curiously. "Melly said there was a man. A bad experience. What happened, honey, a love affair gone sour?"

She flinched, moving backward to release herself from the disturbing pressure of his fingers. She hadn't fled New York only to wind up back in Cade McLaren's hip pocket again; letting him get too close would be suicide in more ways than one. His strength unnerved her, but there was more to it than that. She reacted to him in ways that she'd never reacted to any other man. Every man she'd dated or been with socially had been for her a poor imitation of this one, and she was only now realizing how large he loomed in her memory. For years she'd pushed that night at the swimming pool to the back of her mind, afraid to take it out and look at it. And tonight, going back in time had stirred something deep inside her, had momentarily banished the bad memories to make way for remembered sensations and longings.

She stared up into Cade's dark eyes and saw her whole world. He was as big as this country, and nothing she ever found in New York was going to replace him. But there was no way she was going to let him know it. He'd pushed her away ever since that long-ago night. It was as if he couldn't bear having her close to him, in any way. Even now, when she backed away, he wasn't following. He could still let her go without flinching, without regret, even in this small way.

"A man," she agreed, and let it go at that, not looking at him. "What do you think I did in New York, stare out windows longing to be back here?" That was the truth, little did he know it. The glitter had long ago worn off her life, leaving it barren and lonely.

"Not me, honey," he said. "I know all too well how dull this place is to you. You've done everything but shout it from the roof." He glared at her. "Did the man come too close, Abby? Did he want to settle down, and you couldn't face the thought of that?"

She stared at him blankly. "Is that shocking?" she asked, adding fuel to the fire. "I told you, Cade, I like my life the way it is. I like having money to spend and things to see and places to go. I went to Jamaica to do a layout last month, and in September I'm going to Greece for another one. That's exciting. It's great fun."

He stared at her with cold eyes, believing the lie. "Yes, I can see that," he growled.

He pulled a cigarette from his pocket and lit it while his eyes ran quietly over every line of her face. "Then where does your boyfriend come in?"

She swallowed and turned away. "He wasn't…a boy-friend, and it's a long story."

"I'll find time to listen."

She shifted restlessly and turned. "Not tonight, if you don't mind. I'd like to say hello to Jerry."

He drew in an angry breath, and for just an instant she thought he was going to insist. But he reached past her and opened the door.

She went ahead of him, relieved that he'd swallowed her explanation. Boyfriend! Oh, God, what a horrible joke that was, but she'd rather have died than tell him the truth. Anyway, what would it matter? Let him think she was just getting over a love affair. What did it matter?

CHAPTER FIVE

MELLY WAS CURLED up on the sofa next to the tall, blond man who was going to be her husband. They both jumped when Cade deliberately slammed the door behind Abby and himself.

"Oh, hi, boss." Jerry Ridgely grinned, looking over the sofa back with dancing blue eyes. "Hi, Abby, welcome home!"

"Thanks, Jerry," she said, grinning back. She'd known him almost as long as Melly had. One of the advantages of growing up in country like this was that you knew most everybody from childhood onward. It gave people a sense of security to know that some things stayed constant.

"Staying for the wedding?" he asked, and Melly smiled at her sister.

"I wouldn't miss it for the world," she promised. "Which reminds me, Melly," she added, sticking her hands in her pockets, "I've roughed out some sketches for your wedding dress. They're in my suitcase."

"I'd love to see them," Melly said, enthusiastic. "You're sure you don't mind making it for me?"

"Don't be silly, of course I don't mind. Sometimes I wonder why I got into modeling when I love designing so much." Abby sighed. Modeling. The word reminded her of New York, which brought back other memories, and she turned away, her eyes clouding.

Melly got to her feet quickly. "Let's go see if Calla has the berry cobbler dished out," she said, catching Abby's arm. "Can you men live without us?"

"Cade can." Jerry laughed, glancing toward the taciturn rancher. "But I'll have trouble, sweetheart, so hurry, will you?"

"Sure," Melly agreed, in a tone that was meant for the foreman alone. She winked and tugged Abby along with her, closing the door behind them.

"Have you and Cade been at it again?" she asked Abby as soon as the door was closed behind them. "He looks like a thundercloud, and you're flushed."

"He's persistent as all get-out," Abby groaned. "He nearly backed me into a corner in the kitchen just now. He's not going to worm it out of me, Melly. I can't talk to him about it, I can't!"

Melly sighed and hugged her sister. "Oh, Abby, I hoped you might be able to, once the two of you were alone."

"Talk to Cade?" She laughed. "My God, all I have time to do is defend myself. He's even worse than I remembered. Why does he hate my career so much?"

"You really don't know, do you?" Melly murmured.

Abby ignored that, wrapping her arms tight around herself. "We got into it in the truck, and I tried to hit him, and when he grabbed my wrist…" She shivered. "He's so strong.…"

"He's also Cade," Melly reminded her. "He'd never hurt you, not the longest day he lived."

Abby tried to smile. "I want a miracle, I guess. I want Cade to touch me and make the fear all go away."

"That could still happen," Melly said softly. "But you have to give it time. And telling Cade the truth would be a heck of a start. For God's sake, Abby, it wasn't your fault…!"

"So everyone tells me." She sighed. "Let's go help Calla. I just want to get my mind on something else right now. It will all work out somehow, I suppose. Someday."

She carried that thought all through the long evening, watching Cade sit in his big chair and smoke cigarette after cigarette while he went over paperwork with Jerry and drank two neat whiskeys after the delicious dessert Calla put before them. Cade was so good to look at. He always had been, and the four years since he'd kissed her for the first time hadn't changed him very much on the surface. He was still overpoweringly masculine. Strong and capable and as tough as well-worn leather.

She watched the way his hands held the sheets of paper in their firm grip. They were tanned and sprinkled with dark hair. He didn't wear jewelry of any kind; the watch strapped around his wrist had a thick leather band and a dial that did everything except predict the future. He went in for utility, not style. But he managed to look like a fashion plate for all that, even in worn jeans and a faded shirt. He had a big, powerful body, and it was all steely muscle. Cade was just plain man, and he stood out anywhere.

He looked up once and caught her gaze, and she felt just a touch of the old magic. But she looked away and only the fear was left.

Later, Melly went into the bedroom with Abby. They sat on the old bed that had been Abby's from girlhood and went over the wedding dress pattern.

"It's just magnificent," Melly breathed. "But it will take forever for you to make it…."

"A week, in my spare time." Abby grinned. "Do you really like it?"

"I love it!" She traced the design with a caressing finger. "It's the best design I've ever seen. You ought to sell it."

"Sell your wedding gown?" Abby exclaimed. "Do I look like I have a cash register for a heart?"

"Don't be silly. You know very well what I mean. It's good, Abby. It's really good. You're wasted showing other people's designs."

"Thank you for thinking so," Abby said with a smile.

"I'm not the only one, either. Did Jessica Dane ever get in touch with you?" Melly asked. "She absolutely raved over that dress you made me last summer."

"The boutique owner?" Abby asked. "No. Actually, I was kind of hoping she might. I do love designing, Melly. I feel as if modeling is burning me up. I stay tired all the time, and I have no social life at all. The money's nice," she added quietly. "But money isn't worth much in the long run if you aren't happy. And I'm not."

"Will you mind if I tell you that I never thought you would be?" her sister asked softly. She smiled. "You pretended it was what you wanted, but I saw right through you."

Abby stared at her ringless hands. "I hope nobody else did," she said.

"He's thirty-six now," Melly reminded her. "Inevitably, he'll marry sooner or later."

Abby laughed bitterly. "Will he? He hasn't exactly been in a flaming hurry to commit himself to anybody. You know what he used to say about marriage? That it was a noose only a fool stuck his head into."

"He's a lonely man, Abby," came the surprising reply. "I know better than anybody—I work for him. I see him every day. He works himself into the ground, but there are still evenings when he sits on the porch by himself and just stares off into the horizon."

That hurt. Abby turned her face away to keep Melly from seeing how much. "He could have any woman he wanted," she said, forcing herself not to let her voice show the emotion she was feeling. "He used to stay out with some woman or other every day I was here."

"So he let you think," Melly murmured. "He runs three ranches—a corporation the size of a small city—and in his spare time he sleeps. When does he have the time to be a playboy? I'll grant you, he's got the money to be one, even if he weren't so good-looking. But he's a puritan in his outlook. It even makes him uncomfortable when Jerry kisses me in front of him."

"Just like Donavan," she agreed, remembering Cade's father. "Remember the night you were kissing Danny Johnson on our front porch and Donavan rode by with Cade? Whew! I didn't think Danny would ever come back again after that lecture."

"Neither did I. Donavan had an overdeveloped sense of propriety. No wonder Cade's got so many inhibitions. Of course, being brought up in a small place like Cheyenne Lodge…"

"Only you could call Montana a small place," Abby teased.

"This little teeny corner of it, I meant," came the irrepressible reply. "I'll bet you get culture shock every time you come here from New York," she added.

"No," Abby denied. Her eyes began to glow softly. "It's like homecoming every time. I never realize how much I miss it until I come back."

"And stand at the window, hoping for a glimpse of Cade," Melly said quietly, nodding when Abby flushed. "Oh, yes, I've caught you at it. You watch him with such love in your eyes, Abby. As if the sight of him would sustain you through any nightmare."

Abby turned away. "Stop that. I'll wear my heart out

on him, and you know it. No," she said firmly when Melly started to speak. "No more. Melly, you do love Jerry, don't you?" she added, concern replacing the brief flare-up of irritation.

"Unbearably," Melly confessed. "We fought like animals the first few weeks I worked here, when I came home from business college. But then, one day he threw me down in the hay and fell on me," she added with a grin. "And we kissed like two starving lovers. He asked me to marry him on the spot and I said yes without even thinking. We've had our disagreements, but there's no one I'll ever love as much."

Abby thought about being pushed down and fallen on, and she trembled with reaction. She felt herself stiffen, and Melly noticed.

"Sorry," she said quickly, touching Abby's arm. "I didn't think about how it might sound to you."

"It's just the thought of being helpless," she said in a suppressed tone. Her eyes came up. "Melly, men are so strong...you don't realize how strong until you try to get away and can't!"

"Don't think about it," Melly said softly. "Come on, we've got to decide on the trimmings for this dress. Calla has a bag full of material samples she got from the fabric shop. We'll look through them, and she'll go into town and get what you need tomorrow, okay?"

"Okay." Abby hugged her warmly. "I love you," she said in a rare outburst of emotion.

"I love you, too," Melly returned, smiling as she drew away. "Now, here, this is what I liked especially...." She pulled out a swatch of material and the girls drifted into a discussion of fabrics that lasted until bedtime.

Abby spent the next few days reacquainting herself with the ranch. She was careful to keep out of the way of the men—and Cade—but she trudged through the barns look-ing at calves and sat on the bales of hay in the loft and re-membered back to her childhood on her family's ranch. It was part of Painted Ridge now, having been bought by Cade at Jesse Shane's death. It would have gone on the auction block otherwise, because neither Melly nor Abby had any desire to try to run it. Ranching was a full-time headache, best left to experts.

When the snow melted and the weather turned spring-like again, Abby wandered through the gates up to a grassy hill where a small stand of pines stood guard, and settled herself under one of the towering giants. It was good to breathe clean air, to sit and soak in the cool, green peace and untouched beauty of this land.

Where else were there still places like this, where you could look and see nothing but rolling grassy hills that stretched to the horizon—with tall, ragged mountains on the other side and the river that cut like a wide ribbon through it all? Cade had liked to fish in that river in the old days, when Donavan was still alive to assume some of the bur-den of their business. Abby went with him occasionally, watching him land big bass and crappie, rainbow trout and channel catfish.

The nice thing about Cade, she thought dreamily, was that he had such a love for the land and its protection. He was constantly investigating new ways of improving his own range, working closely with the Soil Conservation Ser-vice to protect the natural resources of his state.

Her eyes turned toward the gate as she heard a horse's hooves, and she found Cade riding up the ridge toward her on his big black gelding. He sat a horse so beautifully, re-minding her of a Western movie hero. He was all muscle and grace, and she respected him more than any man she'd ever known.

He reined in when he reached her and swung one long leg around the pommel, a smoking cigarette in his lean, dark hands as he watched her from under the wide brim of his gray Stetson.

"Slumming, miss model?" he teased with a faint smile.

"This is the place for it," she said, leaning back against the tree to smile up at him. Her long, pale hair caught the breeze and curved around her flushed cheeks. "Isn't it peaceful here?" she asked. "No wonder the Indians fought so very hard to keep it."

His eyes darkened, narrowed. "A man does fight to keep the things he wants most," he said enigmatically, studying her. "Why do you wear those damned baggy things?" he demanded, nodding toward her bulky shirt and loose jeans.

She shrugged, avoiding that piercing gaze. "They're comfortable," she said inadequately.

"They look like hell. I'd rather see you in transparent blouses," he added coldly.

Her eyebrows arched. "You lecherous old thing," she accused.

He chuckled softly, deeply, a sound she hadn't heard in a long time. It made him seem younger. "Only with you, honey," he said softly. "I'm the soul of chivalry around most women."

Her eyes searched his. "You could have any woman you want these days," she murmured absently.

"Then isn't it a hell of a shame that I have such a fussy appetite?" he asked. He took a draw from the cigarette and studied her quietly. "I'm a busy man."

"You look it," she agreed, studying the dusty jeans that encased his hard, powerful legs, and his scuffed brown boots and sweat-stained denim shirt. There was a black mat of hair under that shirt, and a muscular chest that she remembered desperately wanting to touch.

"It's spring," he reminded her. "Cattle to doctor, calves to separate and brand and herds to move up to summer pasture as soon as we finish roundup. Hay to plant, machinery to repair and replace, temporary hands to hire for roundup, supplies to get in…if it isn't one damned thing, it's another."

"And you love every minute of it," she accused. "You'd die anywhere else."

"Amen." He finished the cigarette and tossed it down. "Crush that out for me, will you, honey?"

"It's not dry enough for it to cause a grass fire," she reminded him, but she got up and did it all the same.

"Back in the old days, Indians and white men would stop fighting to battle grass fires together," he told her with a grin. "They're still hard to stop, even today."

She looked up at him, tracing his shadowed face with eyes that ached for what might have been. "You look so at home in the saddle," she remarked.

"I grew up in it." He reached down an arm. "Step on my boot and come up here. I'll give you a ride home."

"It's a good thing you don't ride a horse the way you drive," she observed.

"That's not a good way to get reacquainted," he said shortly.

"It's only the truth. Donavan wouldn't even get in a truck with you," she reminded him. "Although I have to admit that you're a pretty good driver on the highway."

"Thanks for nothing. Are you coming or not?"

She wanted and dreaded the closeness. He was so very strong. What if she panicked again, what if he demanded an answer to her sudden nervousness?

"Abby," he said suddenly, his voice as full of authority as if he were tossing orders at his cowboys. "Come on."

She reacted to that automatically and took his hand, tingling as it slid up her arm to hold her. She stepped deftly onto the toe of his boot in the stirrup and swung up in front of him.

He drew her back against him with a steely arm, and she felt the powerful muscles of his chest at her shoulder blades.

"Comfortable?" he asked shortly.

"I'm fine," she replied in a voice that was unusually high-pitched.

He eased the horse into a canter. "You'll be more comfortable if you'll relax, little one," he murmured. "I'm no threat."

That was what he thought, she told herself, reacting wildly to the feel of his body against her back. He smelled of leather and cow and tobacco, and his breath sighed over her head, into her loosened hair.

If only she could relax instead of sitting like a fire poker in his light embrace. But he made her nervous, just as he always had; he made her feel vulnerable and soft and hungry. Despite the bad experience in New York, he appealed to her senses in ways that unnerved her.

He chuckled softly and she stiffened more. "What's so funny?" she muttered above the sound of the horse's hooves striking hard ground.

"You are. Should I be flattered that you're afraid to let me hold you on a horse? My God, I didn't realize I was so devastating at close range. Or," he added musingly, "is it that I smell like a man who's been working with cattle?"

Laughter bubbled up inside her. It had been years since she and Cade had spent any time alone, and she'd forgotten his dry sense of humor.

"Sorry." She sighed. "I've been away longer than I realized."

His big arm tightened for an instant and relaxed, and she
let him hold her without a struggle. His strength was less
intimidating now than it had been the last time, as if the
nightmare experience were truly fading away in the scope
and bigness of this country where she had grown up. She
felt safe. Safer than she'd felt in years.

"Four years," he murmured behind her head. "Except
for a few days here and there, when you could tear yourself
away from New York."

She went taut with indignation. "Are you going to start
that again?"

"I never stopped it. You just stopped listening." His arm
contracted impatiently for an instant, and his warm breath
was on her ear. "When are you going to grow up, Abby?
Glitter isn't enough for a lifetime. In the end, it's not going
to satisfy you as a woman!"

"What is?" she asked curtly. "Living with some man and
raising children?"

He seemed to freeze, as if she'd thrown cold water in his
face, and she was sorry she'd said that. She hadn't meant
it—she was just getting back at him.

"It's more than enough for women out here," he said
shortly.

She stared across at the horizon, loving the familiar contours of the land, the shape of the tall trees, the blueness of
the sky. "Your grandmother had ten children, didn't she,
Cade?" she asked, remembering the photos in the McLaren
family album.

"Yes." He laughed shortly. "There wasn't much choice
in those days, honey. Women didn't have a lot of control
over their bodies, like they do now."

"And it took big families to run ranches and farms," she
agreed. She leaned back against him, feeling his muscles
ripple with the motion of the horse. Her eyes closed as she
drank in the sensation of being close.

"It was more than that," he remarked as they approached
the house. "People in love want children."

She laughed aloud at that. "I can't imagine you in love,"
she said. "It's completely out of character. What was it you
always said about never letting a woman put a ring through
your nose?"

He didn't laugh. If anything, he seemed to grow cold.
"You don't know me at all, Abby. You never have."

"Who could get close enough?" she asked coolly. "You've
got a wall ten feet thick around yourself, just like Donavan
had. It must be a McLaren trait."

"When people come close, they can hurt," he said shortly.
"I've had my fill of being cut to the quick."

"I can't imagine anyone brave enough to try that," she
told him.

"Can't you?" He sounded goaded, and the arm that was
holding her tautened.

She got a glimpse of his face as he leaned down to open
the gate between them and the house, and its hardness un-
settled her. He looked hurt somehow, and she couldn't understand why.

"Cade?" she murmured before he straightened again.

His eyes looked straight into hers, and she trembled at
the intensity of the glare, its suppressed violence.

"One day, you'll push too hard," he said quietly. "I'm not
made of stone, despite the fact that you seem to believe I
am. I let you get away with murder when you were younger.
But you're not a child anymore, Abby, and the kid gloves
are off. Do you understand me?"

How could she help it? Her heart shuddered with mingled fear and excitement. Involuntarily, her eyes went to
his hard mouth and she remembered vividly the touch and
taste and expertness of it.

"Don't worry, Cade, I won't seduce you," she promised,
trying to sound as if she were teasing him in a sophisticated way.

He caught her chin and forced her eyes back up to his,
and she jumped at the ferocity in his dark gaze. "I could
have had you that night at the swimming pool, Abigail Jen-
nifer Shane," he reminded her with merciless bluntness.
"We're both four years older, but don't think you're immune
to me. If you start playing games, we might do something
we'd both regret."

She tried to breathe normally and failed miserably. She
forced her eyes down to the harsh rise and fall of his chest,
and then closed them.

"Just because I had a huge crush on you once, don't get
conceited and think I'm still stupid enough to moon over
you, Cade," she bit off.

As if the words set him off, his eyes flashed and all at
once he had her across the saddle, over his knees, with her
head imprisoned in the crook of his arm.

She struggled, frightened by his strength as she'd been
afraid from the beginning that she would be. "No," she
whispered, pushing frantically at his chest.

"Let's see how conceited I am, Abby," he ground out,
bending his head to hers.

One glance into those blazing eyes was enough to tell her
that he wasn't teasing. She groaned helplessly as his hard
mouth crushed down onto hers in cold, angry possession.

It might have been so different if he'd been careful, if he
hadn't given in to his temper. But she was too frightened to

think rationally. It was New York all over again, and a man's strength was holding her helpless while a merciless mouth ground against her own. Through the fear, she thought she felt Cade tremble, but she couldn't be sure. Her mind was focused only on the hard pressure of his mouth, the painful tightening of his arms. Suddenly she began to fight. She hit him with her fists, anywhere she could, and when the shock of it made him lift his head, she screamed.

An indescribable expression washed over his features, and he seemed to go pale.

Abby hung back against his arm, her pale brown eyes full of terror, her lips bloodless as she stared up at him, her breasts rising and falling with her strangled breaths.

"My God, what's happened to you?" he asked, in a shocked undertone.

She swallowed nervously, her lips trembling with re-action, her body frozen in its arch. "Please...don't handle me...roughly," she pleaded, her voice strange and high.

His eyes narrowed, glittering. His face went rock-hard as he searched her features. "What made you come here, Abby?" he demanded. "What drove you out of the city?"

Her eyes closed and she shuddered. "I told you, I was tired," she choked out. "Tired!"

He said something terrible under his breath and straight-ened, moving her away from him with a smooth motion. "It's all right," he said when her eyes flew open at the move-ment. "I'm only going to let you sit up."

She avoided his piercing scrutiny, sitting quickly erect with her back to him.

He spurred the horse toward the house. "If you can't bear to be touched, there has to be a reason," he said shortly. "You've been hurt some way, or frightened. I asked you if you'd been knocked around by a man, and you denied it. But you lied to me, didn't you, Abby?"

Her jaw set firmly. "All this fuss because you kissed me against my will and I fought you!" she burst out. "Are you so conceited that you think I can't wait to fall into your arms, Cade?"

He didn't say a word. He rode right up to the front steps and abruptly set her down on the ground.

She stood by the horse for a long moment before she looked up. "Thanks for the ride," she ventured.

He'd lit a cigarette and was smoking it quietly, his face grim as he looked down at her. "You're going to tell me what happened sooner or later."

"Nothing happened," she lied, raising her voice.

"I didn't wind up with three ranches and a corporation because I was an idiot," he informed her. "You didn't come rushing down here a month early just to help Melly get ready for her wedding. And it damned sure wasn't because you were dying for the sight of me."

He was hitting too close to the truth. She turned away. "Believe what you like, Great White Rancher."

"Abby!"

She whirled, eyes blazing, as gloriously beautiful in anger as a sunburst, with her pale hair making a frame for her delicate face and wide brown eyes. "What?"

His eyes went over her reverently, from toes to head, while the cigarette smoked away in his tanned fingers. "Don't fight me."

It was like having the breath knocked out of her. She looked up at him and felt the anger drain away. He was so gorgeously masculine, so handsome. Her eyes softened helplessly.

"Then don't hurt me," she said quietly.

He laughed mirthlessly. "That works both ways."

"Pull the other one," she muttered. "I'd have to use dynamite. You're hard, Cade."

"This is hard country. I don't have time for the limp-wristed courtesies you city women swear by in men."

"Sophistication doesn't make a man peculiar," she returned. "I like a polished man."

His dark eyes glittered. "Not always," he replied. "There was a time when I could look at you and make you blush."

"That old crush?" she said. "I thought the sun rose and set on you, all right. But you made a career of pushing me away, didn't you?"

"You were eighteen, damn it!" he shot at her. "Eighteen, to my thirty-two! I felt like a damned fool when I left you that night. I should never have touched you!"

The one beautiful memory in her life, and he was sorry it had happened. If she'd ever wondered how he really felt inside his shell, she knew now.

She lowered her eyes and turned away. She walked to the house without another word, without a backward glance. As she went up the steps, she imagined she heard him swear, but when she looked back, he was riding away.

ABBY BROODED ABOUT the confrontation for the rest of the day, and at the supper table it was patently obvious to Melly and Jerry that something was wrong. Even Calla, walking back and forth to serve up the delicious beef the ranch was famous for with the accompanying dishes, commented that the weather sure had gotten cold quick.

Cade finished his meal before the rest of them and lit a cigarette over his second cup of coffee.

"I've got those reports printed out whenever you want them, Cade," Melly ventured.

He nodded. "I'll look them over now. Jerry, come on in when you finish," he added, rising. "We'll have to make a decision pretty quick about those cows we're going to sell off. Jake White wants a few dozen head for embryo transplants."

"Wants them cheap, too." Jerry laughed. "I reckon he thinks our culls will be the very thing to carry his purebred Angus."

Melly grinned at them, aware of Abby sitting rigidly at her side. "Oh, the advances in cattle breeding. Herefords throwing Angus calves, without even the joys of natural conception."

Cade gave her a hard glare and walked out of the room.

"Shame on you," Jerry muttered as he started to join the boss. "Embarrassing him that way."

"I'm just helping him lose some of his inhibitions, darling," Melly whispered back, blowing him a kiss before he winked and left the room.

"He'll get even," Abby said solemnly, picking at her food. "He always does."

"You could help him with those inhibitions, too," her sister said, tongue in cheek.

"Not me, sis," came the instant reply. She glared toward the doorway. "He can keep his hang-ups for all I care."

Melly stared at her hard. "Why don't you and Cade start kissing and stop fighting?"

"Ask him," she grumbled, getting up. "It's one and the same thing with Cade, if you want to know. I've got a frightful headache, Melly. Say good-night to the others for me, will you?" And she rushed upstairs without another word before Melly could ask the questions that were forming on her lips.

Abby hadn't had a nightmare since she arrived at the

ranch, but after the confrontation with Cade, it was almost inevitable that it would recur. And sure enough, it did.

She woke up in the early hours of the morning, screaming. Even as the sounds were dying away, her door burst open and Cade came storming into her room, flashing on the overhead light, with Melly at his heels.

CHAPTER SIX

ABBY SAT THERE in the plain cotton gown that concealed every inch of her body, her hair wild, her eyes raining tears down her pale cheeks, and gaped at them on the tail of terror.

Cade was in his pajama trousers and nothing else. They rode low on his lean hips, and the sheer masculinity of his big body with its generous black, curling hair and bronzed muscle was enough to frighten her even more.

"How about making some coffee?" Cade asked Melly, although his tone made it an order, not a request.

"But…" Melly began, nervously looking from her sister to her employer.

"You heard me."

Melly hesitated for just an instant before she left them alone, her footsteps dying away down the hall.

Cade put his hands on his hips and stared down at Abby. With his hair tousled and his face hard, he looked as threatening as any storm.

"Get up and put on a robe," he said after a minute, turning away, "while I get dressed."

"You don't have to," she managed weakly.

He half turned, his eyes glittering. "Don't I?" he growled. "You're looking at me as if I were a rapist."

Her face blanched and he nodded. "That's how you feel, too, isn't it, baby? Put on a robe and come into the living room. And stop looking at me like that. I'm not going to touch you. But you're going to tell me the truth, one way or the other."

He left her sitting there, his back as stiff as a poker.

Melly brought the coffee in just as Abby came out of her room, wrapped to the throat in a heavy navy terry-cloth robe.

Cade was dressed, barely, in jeans and an open-throated blue shirt that he hadn't tucked in. He was barefoot, sitting forward in an armchair, worrying his hair with his hands. He looked up as Abby came in.

"Sit down," he said quietly. "Melly, thank you for the coffee. Good night."

"Cade..." Melly began.

"Good night," he repeated.

The younger woman sighed as she looked over at Abby, her whole expression one of regret and apology.

"It's all right," Abby said gently. "You and I both know that Cade would never hurt me."

Cade looked faintly shocked by the words, but he busied himself with lighting a cigarette while Melly said good-night and left them alone.

"Fix me a cup, will you, honey?" he asked.

Abby automatically poured cream in it and handed it to him.

He took it, cup and saucer balanced on his big palm, and smiled at her. "You remembered, didn't you?"

She flushed. Yes, she had, just the way he liked it. She remembered almost everything she'd learned over the years— that he didn't take sugar, that he hated rhubarb, that he loved a thick steak and cottage potatoes to go with it, that he could go for forty-eight hours without sleep but not one hour without a cigarette...

"Tit for tat?" he murmured, and reached out to put two sugars and cream in the second cup and hand it to her, smiling when she raised astonished eyes to his.

She took it, sitting back on the sofa to study the creamy liquid, turning the cup nervously back and forth in its saucer.

"Little things," she murmured, finally lifting her eyes to his. "Isn't it amazing how we remember them after so many years?"

"I remember a lot about you," he said quietly, studying her. "Especially," he added on a rueful sigh, "how you look without clothes."

She flushed, dropping her eyes. "It was a long time ago."

"Four years," he agreed. "But it doesn't seem that long to me." He took a gulp of his coffee, ignoring the fact that it was hot enough to blister a normal throat, stubbed out his cigarette and leaned back in his chair. "Tell me what happened, Abby."

She felt the cup tremble in her hand and only just righted it in time. "I can't, Cade."

He took another sip of coffee and leaned forward suddenly, resting his hands on his knees. "Look up. That's right, look at me. Do you remember when you ran over your father's dog with my old Jeep?"

She swallowed and nodded.

"You couldn't face him, but you came running to me bawling your heart out, and I held you while you cried." He shifted his hands, studying her drawn face. "When Vennie Walden called you a tomboy and said you looked like a stick with bumps, you came crying to me then."

She nodded again, managing a smile for him. "I always cried on you, didn't I?"

"Always. Why not now?" He reached out a big hand and

waited, patiently, until she could put her own, hesitantly, into it and feel its warmth and strength. "From now on, it's going to be just like this. I won't touch you unless you want me to. Now tell me what happened. Did you find out he was married?"

"He?" she asked, studying him blankly.

"The man you had an affair with," he said quietly. "The one you wake up screaming over in the middle of the night."

She swallowed down the urge to get up and run. How in the world was she going to be able to tell him the truth. How?

"Come on, Abby, tell me," he coaxed with a faint smile. "I'm not going to sit in judgment on you."

"You've got it wrong, Cade," she said after a minute. "It...wasn't an affair."

His heavy brows came together. He searched her face. "No? I understood Melly to say there was a man...."

"There was." Her eyes opened and closed, and the pain of admission was in them suddenly. She tried to speak, and her mouth trembled on the words.

He was beginning to sense something. His face seemed to darken, his eyes glittered. His hand, on hers, tightened promptingly. "Abby, tell me!" he ground out, his patience exhausted.

Her eyes closed, because she couldn't bear to see what would be in his when she told him. "I was assaulted, Cade."

The silence seemed to go on forever. Forever! The hand around her own stilled, and withdrew. Somewhere a clock was ticking with comical loudness; she could hear it above the tortured pounding of her own heart....

At first, she wondered if he'd heard her. Until she looked up and saw his lean hands, tough from years of ranch work, contract slowly around the cup until it shattered and coffee went in a half-dozen directions onto the deep gray pile carpet.

Her eyes shot up to his face, reading the aching compassion and murderous rage that passed across it in wild succession.

"Who?" he asked, the word dangerously soft.

"I don't know," she said quietly.

"Surely to God there was a suspect!" he burst out, oblivious to the shards of pottery and the coffee that was staining his jeans, the carpet.

"Not yet," she told him. "Cade, the carpet...look, you've cut your hand!" she exclaimed, seeing blood.

"Oh, to hell with that," he growled. He glanced at his hand and tugged a handkerchief from his jeans pocket to wind haphazardly around it. "What do you mean, not yet?"

"Just what I said. It's a big city." She got up, kneeling beside him. "Let me see. Come on, let me see!" she grumbled, forcing him to give her the big, warm hand. She unwrapped the handkerchief gently; there was a shallow cut on the ball of his thumb. "We'd better put something on it."

"Is that why you backed away from me earlier?" he asked, his eyes on her bent head. "Why you were afraid when I was rough with you earlier, outside?"

Her eyes clouded. "Yes."

He started to touch her hair and froze, withdrawing his hand before it could make contact. He laid it back on the arm of the chair with a wistful sigh. "What can I say, Abby?" he asked gently. "What in hell can I say?"

Her fingers let go of his hand and she got to her feet. "There's some antiseptic in the guest bathroom, isn't there?" she asked.

"I suppose so." He got up and followed her down the hall, sitting uncomfortably on the little vanity bench, which swayed precariously while she rifled through the medicine cabinet for antiseptic and a bandage.

He sat quietly while she dressed the cut, but his eyes watched her intently.

"Please don't watch me like that," she asked tightly.

His eyes fell to his hand. "It's an old habit." His chiseled mouth made a half smile when she looked down at him, startled. "You didn't know that, I suppose." The smile faded. "Can you talk about it?"

She studied him quietly and lowered her eyes. "I was coming home from an assignment, at night. It was a nice night, just a little nippy, and I had a coat on over my dress. I only lived a few blocks away, so I walked." She laughed bitterly. "The streets were deserted, and before I realized it, a man started following me. I ran, and he caught up with me and dragged me into an alley." She shuddered at the memory. "I tried so hard to get away, but he was big and terribly strong…." Her eyes closed. "He pushed me down and started kissing me, touching me… I screamed then, just as loud as I could, and there were three men coming out of a nearby bar who heard me. They came running and he took off." She drew in a steadying breath, oblivious to Cade's white, strained face. "Thank God, they heard me. People talk about cities being cold and heartless places, but it didn't happen that way for me. The people at the emergency room told me I'd been damned lucky."

"Was there someone to take care of you?" he asked as if it mattered, really mattered.

"Yes. There was a Rape Crisis Center. All women," she said with a faint smile, recalling the gentle treatment, the care she'd received. "They sent me over there, despite the fact that I hadn't been raped. It's still a mentally scarring thing, to be handled that way, mauled. Thinking about the way it might have been…but I felt dirty, you know. Soiled. I still think about it constantly…."

His face hardened as he watched her quietly. "If I'd made love to you that night, kept you here with me, none of this would ever have happened."

"Did you want to, really?" she wondered softly.

He drew in a long, steady breath. "I wanted to," he admitted after a minute, and his eyes darkened. He got to his feet, towering over her. "But it would have been a slap in the face to your father. He trusted me to look after you. And God knows, it would have been a mistake, a bad one." He studied her intently. "I'd never touched a virgin until that night."

She felt a surge of pride at that confession, and it showed in her eyes.

"I've never touched one since, either," he added with a quiet smile.

"Learned your lesson, huh?" she murmured with a feeble attempt at humor.

He nodded. "Can you sleep now?"

The thought of the dark room was disquieting, but she erased the nervousness from her eyes. "Yes. I think so."

"You can sleep with me if you want to," he said quietly, and she knew exactly what he meant—that he'd die before he'd touch her, unless she wanted it.

Hesitantly, her hand went out to touch his arm, a light touch that was quickly removed. "Thank you," she said softly. "But I'll be all right now."

His eyes searched hers for a long moment. "You trust me, don't you?" he asked gently.

"Yes," she said simply. "More than anyone else in the world, Cade, if it means anything."

"Yes," he bit off, "it means something."

"The carpet!" she exclaimed suddenly. "Oh, Cade, I'll bet the carpet's ruined...."

"I'll buy a new one. Go to bed."

"Thank you," she said as he turned to go out into the hall. "I...I... Melly said I should have told you about it, but I didn't... I wasn't sure...."

"You didn't think that I'd blame you?" he asked softly.

She stared down at the carpeted floor, embarrassed now that he knew.

"Stop it, for God's sake," he said bluntly. "So you got mauled. You've had a terrible experience, and I'm sorry as hell, but it doesn't change who you are!"

Her lips trembled. "I feel unclean," she whispered, shaken. "As if I'd been robbed of something I had the right to give to a man I chose. He touched me in ways no man ever did, not even you..."

He drew in a ragged breath. "Yes, you were robbed, but not of your chastity. Even if he'd raped you, you'd still have that."

She stared up at him numbly. "What?"

He lit a cigarette with unsteady fingers. "Oh, hell, I'm putting this badly." He blew out a cloud of smoke and stared down at her with narrowed eyes. "Abby, how long ago did it happen?"

"Week before last," she confessed.

"Okay, and you're still raw, that makes sense. But you'll get over it. And it will be different, with a man you care about."

Her lips pouted. "It wasn't any different this afternoon. You scared me to death."

His face paled, but he didn't look away. "My fault. I've been without a woman for a while, and the feel of you went to my head. I was rougher than I ever meant to be. But you've got to help yourself a little by not dwelling on what happened to you."

"How can I help it? It makes me sick just remembering…!" she burst out.

"Put it in perspective, honey," he said curtly, jamming his bandaged hand in his pocket as if he were afraid he might try to touch her with it. "Has it occurred to you that by letting the experience warp your mind, you're giving that piece of scum who attacked you more rights over you than you'd give a husband?"

She stared at him, stunned.

He took another long draw from the cigarette. "You're giving him the right to dominate your life, by dwelling on what happened, by blowing up what he did to you and letting it lock you up emotionally and physically."

"I…hadn't thought of it like that."

"Suppose you start."

She wrapped her arms around her trembling body. "You can't know how it is for a woman," she murmured. "Against a man's strength…"

"I can remember a time in your life when you very much liked being helpless against mine," he said under his breath.

"That was different. I knew you'd never hurt me."

"You knew that this afternoon, but you fought me like a wildcat."

She flushed. "You hurt me!"

His jaw tightened. "Do you think because I have to be hard with my men that I'm that hard inside? You get under my skin like no other woman ever has. You deliberately needle me and then take offense when I defend myself. It's always been that way."

"I never thought you could be hurt," she murmured, avoiding his piercing gaze. "Least of all by me."

"Why talk about it?" he asked wearily. "It's all water under the bridge now."

"Thanks for the therapy session," she said softly and smiled, because she meant it.

He smiled back. "Did it help?"

She nodded. Her eyes searched his. "Cade, I'm sorry I screamed this afternoon."

He reached down and smoothed a lock of hair from her face. "I didn't know. Now I do. Give it time—you'll be fine. I'll help."

"Thanks for letting me come."

He looked strange for a minute. "When Melly said you wanted to get here early for the wedding, so you could spend some time on the ranch, I didn't know the real reason. I thought…" He dropped his hand with a gruff laugh. "You can still sleep with me, if you want. I wouldn't touch you."

Her soft eyes searched his, and he looked back as if it were beyond his power to remove his eyes from hers. "Calla and Melly would be shocked to the back teeth," she whispered, trying to joke about it and failing. It would have been heaven to lie in his arms all night. "But thank you for the offer."

He shrugged. "It wasn't for purely selfless reasons," he said, winking at her. "Bed's damned cold in early spring," he chuckled.

She hit him softly. "Beast!"

"Think you can sleep now?"

She nodded. "I feel a little different about it. Maybe I just need time to put things into perspective after all."

"If you'd like something to occupy your mind, I'll take you out to see the rest of the calves in the morning."

"Oh, boy," she said enthusiastically. "But what if it snows

again?" she asked. "It was awfully cloudy this afternoon and cold as blazes and the radio says—"

"When has snow ever stopped me?" he asked, chuckling. "Night, honey." He turned and strode off toward the stairs.

When has anything ever stopped you? she asked herself silently.

Except once...she'd never realized until now that he'd really wanted her that night. He'd been so cool and calm on the surface that she'd halfway convinced herself he had only been satisfying her curiosity to keep her from experimenting with younger, more hot-blooded males. But now she began to wonder. She was still wondering when she fell into a deep, satisfying sleep.

CHAPTER SEVEN

CADE HAD OFFERED to take Abby back to see the calves, but by morning the snow had covered Painted Ridge and he was out with his men trying to bring in the half-frozen calves and their new mothers. According to Hank, Cade was cursing a blue streak from one end of the ranch to the other.

"Wants his other gloves," Hank growled at Calla when he paused in the hall, the familiar wad of tobacco tucked into his cheek. "Ruined a pair trying to unhook one of them damned cows from the barbed wire."

"He goes through gloves like some men go through food," Calla grumbled, shooting an irritated glance at Hank for interrupting her in the middle of lunch preparation. "Only got one pair left as it is. You best remember to tell him that!"

"Can't tell him a damned thing," Hank muttered, waiting uncomfortably in the hall. His wide-brimmed hat was spotted with melted snow, and his heavy cloth coat was equally damp. "He hit the ground cussing this morning and he ain't stopped yet. I just follow orders, I don't give 'em!" he shouted after Calla.

"Is it bad out there?" Melly called from the den, where she was busily operating Cade's computer.

"Bad enough," Hank replied. "Hope your fingers are rested, Miss Melly, 'cause you're sure going to do some typing when we get a tally on these new calves!"

"As usual." Melly laughed. "Don't worry about it, Hank, I get paid good."

"If we got paid what we was worth, Cade would go in the hole, I guess," the thin cowboy said to no one in particular. He glanced at Abby, who was standing there quietly in her jeans and a blue turtleneck sweater. "I hear you're going to stay with us till Miss Melly's wedding. How're you settling in?"

She smiled. "Just fine. It feels like old times."

"Far cry from the city," he observed.

She nodded. "Less traffic," she said with a hint of her old humor.

Hank looked disgusted. "Give me a horse any day," he muttered, "and open country to ride him in. If God wanted the world covered in concrete, he'd have made human beings with tires!"

It was the cowboy's favorite theme, and Abby was looking for a way to escape before he had time to get started when Calla came thumping back down the hall with a worn pair of gloves in her hand.

"Here," she said shortly, slapping them into Hank's outstretched hand. "And make sure he doesn't get holes in them. That's all there is."

"What am I, a nursemaid?" he spat out. "My gosh, Calla, all I do is babysit cows these days. If Cade gave a hang about my feelings, he'd give me some decent work."

"Maybe he'll set you to digging post holes," the older woman suggested with malicious glee. "I'll tell him what you said."

"You do," he threatened, "and I'll tell him what you did with that cherry cake he had his heart set on the other night."

She sucked in a furious breath. "You wouldn't dare!"

He grinned, something rare for Hank. "You tell him I like

digging post holes, and I'll do it or bust. Bye, Abby, Melly," he called over his shoulder as he stomped out the door.

"What did you do with Cade's cherry cake?" Abby asked with a sideways stare.

Calla cleared her throat and walked back toward the kitchen. "I gave it to Jeb. Cade's not the only one who's partial to my cherry cake."

Abby smothered a chuckle as she wandered into the den. With its bare wood floors, Indian rugs and wood furniture, it was a far cry from the luxury of the living room.

Melly looked up as Abby came toward the desk where the computer and printer were set up. "I didn't want to desert you last night," she said apologetically. "Did you tell him?"

"I had to," Abby admitted, perching herself on the edge of the chair beside Melly's. "You know Cade when he sets his mind on something. But it wasn't as bad as I thought it would be. He didn't even say 'I told you so.'"

"I didn't expect him to. You underestimate him sometimes, I think." Melly looked smug. "There's a brown spot on the carpet in the living room."

Abby looked guilty. "I was afraid of that, but he wouldn't hear of my cleaning it up." She sighed. "He was holding the coffee cup when I told him. He...crushed it."

Melly closed her eyes for an instant. "I noticed his hand was bandaged this morning," she murmured. "I wondered why..."

"He said some things that made me think," Abby recalled, smiling faintly. "He may not be a psychologist, but he's got a lot of common sense about things. He said I was giving the man who attacked me a hold over me, by dwelling on it. I'd never considered it in that light, but I think he has a point."

Melly smiled at her gently. "Maybe he ought to open an office," she said impishly.

Abby grinned back. "Maybe he ought." She studied her sister closely for a minute as her head bent over the computer keyboard while she typed in a code and glanced up at the screen. The abbreviations were Greek to Abby, but they seemed to make sense to Melly.

"What are you doing?"

"Herd records. We're getting ready to cull cattle, you know. Any cows that don't come up to par are going to be sold off, especially if they aren't producing enough calves or if the ones they're producing aren't good enough or if they're old...."

"Slavery," Abby burst out. "Horrible!"

Melly laughed merrily. "Yes, Cade was telling me what you thought about veal smothered in onions."

"That's really horrible," she muttered. "Poor little thing, all cold and half-frozen and its mama turned her back on it, and Cade talks about eating it...."

"Life goes on, darling," Melly reminded her, "and a cattle ranch is no place for sentiment. I can't just see you owning one—you'd make pets of all the cattle and become a vegetarian."

"Hmm," Abby said, frowning thoughtfully, "I wonder if Cade's ever thought of that?"

"I don't know," came the amused reply, "but if I were you, I'd wait until way after roundup to ask him!"

Abby laughed. "You may have a point."

Melly murmured something, but her mind went quickly back to the computer and her work. Abby, curious, asked questions and Melly told her about the computer network between Cade's ranches, and the capacity of the computer for storing information about the cattle. There was even a

videocassette setup so that Cade could sell cattle to people who had never been to the ranch to see them—they
could buy from the tape. He could buy the same way, by
watching film of a bull he was interested in, for example.
It was a far cry from the old days of ranching when ranchers kept written records and went crazy trying to keep up
with thousands of head of cattle. Abby was fascinated by
the computer and the rapidity of its operation. But after a
few minutes the phone started ringing and didn't stop, and
Abby wandered off to watch the snow.

"Isn't Cade going to come in and eat?" Melly asked as
Calla set a platter of ham and bread and condiments on the
table, along with a plate of homemade French fries.

"Nope." The older woman sighed. "Said to pack him a
sandwich and a thermos of coffee and he'd run up to the
house to get it." She nodded toward a sack and a thermos
on the buffet.

"Is he coming right up?" Abby asked.

"Any minute."

"I'll carry it out," Abby volunteered, and grabbed it
up, hurrying toward the front door. She only paused long
enough to tug on galoshes and her thick cloth coat, and
rushed out onto the porch as she heard a pickup skid up to
the house and stop.

Cade was sitting in the cab when she crunched her way
through the blowing snow to the truck. He threw open the
passenger door.

"Thanks, honey," he said, taking the sack and thermos
from her and placing them on the seat beside him. "Get in
out of the snow."

She started to close the truck door, but he shook his head.
"In here," he corrected. "With me."

Something about the way he said it made her pulse

pound, and she shook herself mentally. She was reading things into his deep voice, that was all.

"Hank said you were turning the air blue. Is this new snow your fault?" Abby asked him with humor in her pale brown eyes.

He returned the smile and there was a light in his eyes she hadn't noticed before. "I reckon," he murmured, watching the color come and go in her flushed face. "Feel better this morning?"

"Yes, thank you," she said softly.

He reached out a big hand and held it, palm up.

She hesitated for an instant before she reached out her own cold, slender hand and put it gingerly into his. The hard fingers closed softly around it and squeezed.

"This is how it's going to be from now on," he said, his voice deep and quiet, the two of them isolated in the cold cab while feathery snow fell onto the windshield, the hood, the landscape. "I'll ask, I won't take."

She looked into his eyes and felt, for a second, the old magic of electricity between them. "That goes against the grain, I'll bet," she said.

"I'm used to taking," he replied. "But I can get used to asking, I suppose. How about you?"

She looked down at his big hand swallowing hers, liking the warmth and strength of it even while something in the back of her mind rebelled at that strength. "I don't know," she said honestly.

"What frightens you most?" he asked.

"Your strength," she said, without taking time to think, and her eyes came up to his.

He nodded, and not by a flicker of an eyelash did he betray any emotion beyond curiosity. "And if I let you make all the moves?" he asked quietly. "If I let you come close or touch or hold, instead of moving in on you?"

The thought fascinated her. That showed in her unblinking gaze, in the slight tilt of her head.

"Therapy, Cade?" she asked in a soft, steady tone.

"Whatever name you want to call it." He opened his hand so that she could leave hers there or remove it, as she wished. It was more than a gesture—it was a statement.

She smiled slowly. "Such power might go to my head," she said with a tentative laugh. "Suppose I decided to have my way with you?" she added, finding that she could treat the matter lightly for the moment.

He cocked an eyebrow and looked stern. "Don't start getting any ideas about me. I'm not easy. None of you wild city girls are going to come out here and lure me into any haystacks."

She let her fingers curl into his and hold them. "It's a long shot," she said after a minute.

"My grandfather won this ranch in a poker game in Cheyenne," he remarked. "I guess it's in my blood to take long shots."

"Won't it interfere with your private life?" she added, hoping her question wouldn't sound as if she were fishing.

He studied her closely for a minute before he replied. "I thought you knew that I don't have affairs."

She almost jumped at the quiet intensity of his eyes. "I... never really thought about it," she lied.

"I've had women," he said, "but nothing permanent, nothing lasting. There's no private life for you to interfere with."

She was suddenly fiercely glad of that, although she didn't know how to tell him. "It's not going to be very easy," she confessed shyly. "I've never been forward, even before this happened."

"I know," he murmured, smiling down at her. "I could sit here and look at you all day," he said after a minute, "but it wouldn't get the work done," he added ruefully.

"I could come and help you," she volunteered, wondering at her sudden reluctance to leave him.

"It's too cold, honey," he said. His eyes wandered over her soft, flushed face. "Feel like kissing me?"

Her heart jumped. She felt a new kind of excitement at the thought of it. "I thought you weren't easy," she challenged as she slid hesitantly toward him.

Surprise registered in his eyes, but only for a second. "Well, only with some girls," he corrected, smiling wickedly. "Come on, hurry up, I've got calves to deliver."

"Young Dr. McLaren," she murmured, looking up at him from close range, seeing new lines in his face, fatigue in his dark eyes. There were a few silver hairs over his temples and she touched them with unsteady fingers. "You're going gray, Cade."

"I got those because of you, when you were in your early teens," he reminded her. "Hanging off saddles trying to do trick riding, falling into the rapids out of a rickety canoe, flying over fences trying to ride Donavan's broncs...my God, you were a handful!"

"Well, Melly and I didn't have a mama," she reminded him, "and Dad was in poor health from the time we got in grammar school on. If it hadn't been for you and Calla and the cowboys, I guess Melly and I wouldn't have made it."

"Stop that," he growled. "And don't make me out to be an old man. I'm just fourteen years older than you, and I never did feel like a relative."

She put her fingers against his warm lips and felt their

involuntary pursing with a tingle of satisfaction. "I didn't mean it that way." She looked into his dark eyes with a thrill of pure pleasure. "Can I really kiss you?"

His chest seemed to rise and fall with unusual rapidity; his nostrils flared under heavy breaths. "Do you want to?"

"I...I want to." She reached around his neck to pull his dark head down to hers, letting her fingers savor the thick coolness of his hair. Her eyes fell to his hard lips and she noticed that they didn't part when hers touched them, as if he were keeping himself on a tight rein to prevent the kiss from becoming intimate.

She liked the warmth of his mouth under hers, and she liked the faint rasp of his cheek where her nose rubbed against it as she pressed harder against his lips. His breath was even harder now but he wasn't moving a muscle. With a quiet, trusting sigh she eased away from him and looked up.

His face was rigid, his eyes blazing back at her. "Okay?" she asked uncertainly, needing reassurance.

A faint smile softened his expression. "Okay."

She frowned slightly, studying his set lips. "You kept your mouth closed, though," she said absently.

"I don't think we need to go that far that fast, baby," he said quietly.

He moved away from her, his hand going to the ignition to start the truck and let it idle. "It's like learning to walk. You have to do it one step at a time."

"That was a nice step," she told him with a smile.

"I thought so myself." He raised his chin and his eyes were all arrogance. "Are you going to need an engraved invitation every time from now on?"

"I guess I could sneak up on your blind side," she confessed with a grin. "Or drag you off into dark corners.

Maybe if I watch Melly and Jerry I'll get some new ideas. She said he pushed her into a hay stall and fell on her."

He burst out laughing, and she found that she could laugh, too—a far cry from her first reaction when Melly had confessed it.

"That sounds like Jerry," he said after a minute. His eyes searched hers. "It's what I'd have done, once."

The smile faded, and she felt a deep sadness for what might have been if she hadn't been so crazy to go to New York and break into modeling.

"In a hay stall?" she teased halfheartedly.

"Anywhere. As long as it was with you, and I could feel you...all of you...under my body."

She turned away from the hunger in his eyes with a tiny little sound, and he hit the steering wheel with his hand and stared blindly out the windshield, cursing under his breath.

"I'm sorry," he ground out. "That was a damned stupid thing to say...!"

"Don't handle me with kid gloves," she said, looking back at him. "Melly was right, and so were you. I can't run away from the memory of the attack, and I can't run away from life. I'm going to have to learn to deal with... relationships, physical relationships." Her eyes met his bravely. "Help me."

"I've already told you that I will."

She studied the worn mat on the floorboard. "And don't get angry when I react...predictably."

"Like just now?" he asked, and managed a smile.

She nodded, smiling back. "Like just now." Her eyes searched his, looking for reassurance. "It frightens me, still, the...the weight of a man's body," she whispered shakily, and only realized much later that she'd confessed that to no one else.

"In that case," he said gently, "I'll have to let you push me down in the hay, won't I?"

Tears misted in her eyes. "Oh, Cade..."

"Will you get out of my truck?" he asked pleasantly, preventing her, probably intentionally, from showing any gratitude. "I think I did mention about a half hour ago that I was in a flaming hurry."

"Some hurry," she scoffed. "If you were really in a hurry," she added, nodding toward the snow, "you'd walk."

"That's an idea. But I left my snowshoes in the attic. Out! Go let Melly show you how to work the computer. You do realize that somebody's going to have to do her job while she's on her honeymoon?"

"Me? But, Cade, I don't know anything about computers...."

"What a great time for you to learn," he advised. He searched her flushed face, seeing a new purpose in it, a slackening of the fear, and he nodded. "Don't rush off to New York after the wedding. Stay with me."

"I'd like to stay with you," she said in a soft, gentle tone as she looked into his dark eyes.

He held her gaze for a long, warm moment before he averted his eyes to the gearshift. "Now I'm going," he said firmly. "Either you skedaddle or you come with me."

"I'd like to come with you," she said with a sigh, "but I'd just get in the way, wouldn't I?"

"Sure," he said with a flash of white teeth. Then his eyes narrowed. "Do you want to come, really? Because I'm going to let you, and to hell with getting in the way, if you say yes."

She took a deep, slow breath, and shrugged. "Better not, I suppose," she said regretfully. "Melly's wedding dress... I have to get started."

"Okay. How about fabric?"

"Calla bought it for me. It's just a matter of deciding what to use," she told him. "Don't get sick, okay?"

He lifted an eyebrow. "Why? Afraid you'd have to nurse me?"

"I'd stay up all night for weeks if you needed me. Don't be silly," she chided, reaching for the door handle.

"Tell Calla not to keep supper, honey, it's going to be another long night."

She nodded as she held the door ajar. "Want me to bring your supper down to you?"

He smiled. "On your snowshoes? Better not, it's damned cold out here. I'll have a bite later. See you."

"See you."

She closed the door and watched him drive away with wistful eyes. She already regretted not going with him, but she didn't wait around to wonder why.

That night, she and Melly chose the fabric from the yards and yards of it that Calla had tucked away in the cedar chest.

"Isn't it strange that I'm getting married first?" Melly asked as they studied the pattern. "I always thought it would be you."

"Me and who?" Abby laughed.

"Cade, of course."

Abby caught her breath. "He never felt that way."

"Oh, you poor blind thing," Melly said softly. "He used to watch you like a man watching a rainbow. Sometimes his hands would tremble when he was helping you onto a horse or opening a door for you, and you never even noticed, did you?"

Abby's pale brown eyes widened helplessly. "Cade?"

"Cade." Melly sat back in her chair and sighed. "He was head over heels about you when you left here. He roared around for two weeks after you were gone, making the men nervous, driving the rest of us up walls. He'd sit by the fire at night and just stare straight ahead. I've never seen a man grieve like that over a woman. And you didn't even know."

Abby's eyes closed in pain. If she'd known that, career or no career, she would have come running back to Montana on her bare feet if she'd had to. "I didn't have any idea. If I'd known that, I never would have left here. Never!" she burst out.

Melly caught her breath at the passion that flared up in her sister's eyes. "You loved him?"

"Deathlessly." Her eyes closed, then opened again, misty with tears. "I'll die loving him."

"Abby!"

She took a steadying breath and slumped. "Four years. Four long years, and a nightmare at the end of it. And if I'd stayed here...why didn't he tell me?"

"I suppose he thought he was doing the best thing for you," Melly said gently. "You were so excited about a career in modeling."

"I thought at the time that it would be better to moon over Cade at a distance instead of going to seed while I waited in vain for him to notice me again," Abby said miserably.

"Again?"

Darn Melly's quick mind. "Just never you mind. Let's go over this pattern."

"He still cares about you," Melly murmured.

"In a different way, though."

"That could change," came the soft reply, "if you want it to."

"If only Cade didn't have such a soft spot for stray things," Abby said, her eyes wistful. "I never know what he really feels—I never have. He was sorry for me when I was a kid and, in a way, he still is. I don't want a man who pities me, Melly."

"How do you know that Cade does? You're a lovely woman."

"A woman with a very big problem," Abby reminded her, "and Cade goes out of his way to help people, you know that. We go back a long way and he's fond of me. How can I be sure that what he feels isn't just compassion, Melly?"

"Give it time and find out."

"That," she said with a sigh, "is sage advice. By the way, you're going to have to teach me how to do your job, because he's already maneuvered me into replacing you while you're on your honeymoon."

"Oh, he has, has he?" Melly pursed her lips and her eyes laughed. "That isn't something he'd do if he really felt sorry for you!" she assured her sister.

"Now cut that out! Here, tell me if you like the dress better with a long train or a short one...."

And for the rest of the night, they concentrated on the wedding gown.

CHAPTER EIGHT

IN THE DAYS that followed, Abby learned more about the logistics of roundup on Painted Ridge than she wanted to. The whole ranch suddenly revolved around preparations for it. There were supplies to get in, men to hire and add to the weekly payroll. And at the head of it all was Cade, mapping out strategy, tossing out orders as he organized everything from the butane for the torches they used to heat the branding irons to ear tags. At the same time, he was involved with roundup on the other two ranches he had interests in, and in between were cattle auctions, board meetings and a rushed trip to New York to discuss his corporation's plans to buy a feedlot in Oklahoma.

Abby couldn't help thinking how sexy Cade looked in his pale gray suit with matching boots and Stetson when he came downstairs with his suitcase in his hand.

"Well, I guess I'm ready," he grumbled, heading toward the front door. Hank was waiting impatiently outside in the truck.

"You really need something snazzier than a pickup truck to ride to the airport in," Abby remarked with a smile. "You look very sophisticated."

He glanced at her, his eyes clearly approving her jeans and pale T-shirt. "I'd rather be wearing what you've got on."

"You'd sure look funny in it," she murmured wickedly.

He chuckled softly. "I guess I would. Oh, damn, I hate

these dress-up things, and I hate to ride around the country on airplanes with other people at the controls."

"If you fly like you drive—" she began.

"Cut that out," he said darkly. He checked his watch. "Stay off the horses until I get back, too. I told Hank to make sure you do."

Her eyes flashed, and she drew herself up to her full height, lifting her shoulders proudly. "I'm not a child."

His gaze went pointedly to the high, firm thrust of her breasts and he smiled faintly. "No, ma'am, you sure aren't."

"Cade Alexander McLaren!" she gasped.

He chuckled at her red face. "Well, you can't blame a man for noticing things, honey."

"Hank's leaning on the horn," she murmured, glancing nervously toward the door.

"Let him lean on it. Or stand on it. Hank was born in a hurry." He studied her for a long moment. "I'll let you kiss me goodbye if you ask me nice."

She colored even more. "Why do I always have to do all the kissing?" she asked.

"Because you might not like the way I do it," he said.

"Are you sure?" Her heart pounded wildly and she felt her breath coming hard and fast when she saw the expression that washed over his dark face. He dropped the suitcase with a hard thud and strode right for her.

Before she even had time to decide whether to run or duck, he had her by the waist. He lifted her completely off the floor so that she was on a level with his glittering dark eyes, and she noticed that he was breathing as raggedly as she was.

"Let's see, Abby," he said quietly, and tilted his head.

His mouth bit softly at hers in brief, rough kisses that made her blood run hot. Her hands tangled in his dark hair as she tried to hold his mouth over hers, hungry to feel the full pressure of it. Her body felt taut as a cord and she opened her lips to the coaxing play of his. It seemed to be just what he was waiting for, because he took possession then, and she felt his tongue go into her mouth in an intimacy they'd shared only once before.

She caught a sharp breath, but she didn't protest. Not even when he eased her sensuously down and held her close against his taut body. He eased her mouth open further, tasting it with growing hunger, increasing the pressure until she moaned with sudden pleasure.

One big hand released her and slid up her side to her breast. It hesitated for an instant, and then it engulfed her, his thumb coaxing a helpless response even through two layers of fabric. She moaned again.

He lifted his mouth, breathing roughly, and studied her rapt face. "Look, Abby," he whispered, glancing down to the darkness of his hand where her body was frankly showing its response to his touch. "See how you react to me...."

"Don't," she whispered achingly, pushing his hand away even as she leaned her head against his vest while she caught her breath. Her heartbeat was still rapid, and she felt flushed with embarrassment.

His forehead nuzzled against her soft blond hair. "Don't be shy with me," he said quietly. "I know you wouldn't let another man touch you like this. I don't think less of you for it."

Tears welled in her eyes. He was the most tender man she'd ever known; he had a way of making the most traumatic things seem easy, uncomplicated.

"It shocked me a little," she whispered unsteadily.

"I like the way you kiss me when you're shocked," he mused with a faint smile when he lifted his head.

Her eyes darkened as she looked up at him, unafraid. "I tasted you," she whispered shakily.

His hands tautened like steel around her upper arms and his face seemed to harden even as she watched. "Don't say things like that to me," he said unsteadily. "You don't realize the effect it has, and I'm already late for the airport."

She looked down at his broad chest. "Sorry. Will you be gone long?"

His hands contracted and then released her. "A couple days. I can't spare them, but I don't want the man to change his mind about that feedlot. The corporation needs it."

She nodded, glancing up at his set features. "I'll do my best not to foul up your bookkeeping while you're gone."

"Melly won't let you," he replied. He took a long breath and moved back to the suitcase, swinging it up easily. "Besides, all the bookkeeping we do here is payroll, and you'll be doing cattle records, not that. Take care, honey."

"You, too," she said softly, missing him already. He would take the color away when he left. It had been that way all her adult life.

Hank was blowing the horn again, and Cade shook his head. "He's afraid the plane will leave me behind," he said amusedly. "I chewed him out this morning for forgetting to put in a supply order. He feels safer when I'm a state or two away."

"Don't they all," she murmured with a wicked grin.

He tilted the Stetson low over his eyes. "Bye. Don't kiss any other boys while I'm gone, okay?"

"What's the matter, afraid I might make comparisons?" She laughed.

"How did you know?" He winked at her and walked down the steps without looking back, yelling at Hank to stop wearing out his best horn.

ABBY SPENT HER time with Melly, learning how to use the computer. It gave the sisters time to talk and get reacquainted, and it gave Abby something to occupy her mind.

Even when Cade returned, she hardly saw him. He was up with the dawn and out past dark, getting everything ready for the roundup and the massive task of moving the cattle up to summer pasture. By the end of the week, Abby could pick out a single registered bull from the herd records, print out the information required and do it without losing a single punctuation mark.

Meanwhile, Cade, in his spare time, dictated one letter after another to Melly and answered the flood of phone calls that never seemed to stop. The next week, Cade was called out from signing letters at his desk by one of the men when his prize-winning bull keeled over in the barn. He went stalking out the door with Abby at his heels. Melly and Jerry had gone out just after breakfast, and Abby was trying to keep up with Cade's machine-gun dictation and quick temper all alone.

Abby followed him outside with a typed letter in her hand as he took the reins of his black gelding from one of the men and started to swing into the saddle.

"Cade, could you sign this letter before you go?" she called. "It's about that new hay baler."

"Oh, hell, I forgot," he muttered. "Hand it here, honey."

He propped it against the saddle and slashed his name in a bold scrawl across the bottom of it. "I'll see if—"

"Mr. McLaren," one of the new cowboys interrupted, reining up beside them. "Hank said to find you and tell you that the new tractor we just bought is busted. Axle broke clean in half on us while we were planting over in the bottoms. Hank says you want we should call that feller who sold it to us and see if it's still under warranty? The other tractor's still down, you know. Billy's trying to fix it, and we loaned three out to Mr. Hastings and let Jones have one…."

"Oh, good God," Cade muttered angrily. "All right, tell Hank to check with the salesman and see how long it will take to get a replacement."

"Yes, sir," the cowboy agreed politely. "And the hardware wants to know if you'll want any more butane."

Cade looked positively hunted. "They can wait until I get through looking at my sick bull, can't they?" he asked the man. "Damn it, son, that bull cost me a quarter of a million dollars, and the insurance won't heal my heart if he dies!" He glowered at the cowboy. "Tell Jerry to take care of it."

"Uh, he's kind of busy," the young cowboy muttered, avoiding Cade's eyes.

"Doing what?" came the terse reply.

"Uh, he and Miss Melly are down at their house, her house, checking paint swatches…"

Cade's cheeks colored darkly with temper. "You get down there and tell Jerry I said he can stop that kind of thing. I pay him to run this damned ranch, not to go around checking paint swatches on my time!"

"Yes, sir, Mr. McLaren!" He saluted and rode quickly away.

Abby was watching Cade with twinkling eyes. It was something else to watch him delegate. He did it well, and his temper mostly amused the men because it was never malicious.

He turned, catching that gleam in her eyes, and cocked an eyebrow at her from under the wide-brimmed hat. "Something tickle your fancy, Miss Shane?"

"You," she admitted quietly. "I just stand in awe of you, Mr. McLaren."

He chuckled softly. "And you thought a rancher's life was all petting cattle, I suppose?"

"I grew up here," she reminded him. "But I never realized just how much work it was until I started helping Melly. How do you stand it, Cade?"

"I'm used to it." He was holding the reins in one hand, but he reached out and drew his fingers down her cheek. "I love it. The way you love the glitter of your own work, I imagine, miss model."

"I wish you wouldn't make fun of what I do," she said sadly, searching his dark eyes. "I've worked very hard to get where I am. And modeling is much more than painting on a pretty face and smiling."

He withdrew his hand and lit a cigarette. "It must seem pretty tame to you out here."

"Tame?" Her eyes widened. "Are you kidding?"

He frowned thoughtfully, and his searching eyes caught hers. They stared at each other quietly, while the silence grew tense and electric around them, and her lips parted under a wild rush of breath.

His breath was coming hard, too. He dropped the reins as if he couldn't help himself and moved close, so that she could feel the heat of his body and the smell of the spicy cologne that clung to him. Her eyes went to his mouth and she wanted it so much that she ached with the wanting.

His steely fingers bit into her waist. "Want to kiss me, Abby Shane?" he asked roughly.

"Very much," she whispered, unembarrassed and unintimidated as she looked into his darkening eyes. "Lift me up, please..."

She felt his hands contract, and she seemed to float within reach of that chiseled mouth. Her hands slid around his neck to the back of his head and she eased her mouth onto his, letting her lips part softly as they touched him.

His head tilted and his mouth opened under hers with a heavy sigh. He didn't insist, but she could sense his own growing hunger, and she fed it. Her lips nibbled softly at his, her tongue eased out to trace the firm line of his upper lip. And the reaction she got was startling.

All at once, she was swept against the long, hard line of his body and he was kissing her, violently. His mouth demanded in a kiss so sensuous she moaned at the sensations it aroused. She felt his tongue in her mouth, against her lips. A shudder worked its way down her body and fires blazed up in her blood.

"No," she protested when he tried to lift his dark head. She trembled in his arms as she clung. "Cade, please, just once more…."

She heard the ragged breath he took before his mouth crushed back against hers, warm and rough and forceful for an instant. Then she was back on her feet again and leaning heavily against him, his lips brushing her forehead.

"What do you want from me, Abby?" he ground out.

Your love, she thought miserably. I want you to love me as fiercely as I love you. "I'm sorry," she muttered against his shirt front. "I like kissing you."

He was trying to get his breath back, or at least it sounded that way. "I like kissing you, too. But I'm a man, not a boy. Kissing isn't enough for me anymore."

Her fingers curled against his shirt, and she could feel the thick hair on his chest through it. She wanted to open his shirt and touch him there. Involuntarily, her fingers moved across his chest and he shuddered.

"No, baby," he said softly. He stilled her hands, and she wondered dizzily what had happened to the cigarette he'd been holding. Her eyes found it, smoking away in the dirt, where he must have flung it.

She sighed wearily, loving the comforting feel of his hands at her back. She didn't want to move away from him, but it was obvious that he wasn't going to let her get any closer.

"I forgot," she murmured.

"What?"

She drew away and grinned, although her heart was aching. "That you're wary of us wild city girls," she said, her light brown eyes sparkling in the pale frame of her hair. "You needn't worry, Cade, I'm not quite strong enough to wrestle you down in a haystack."

Her quip should have made him smile, but it didn't. He searched her face for a long time, touching every curve and line of it with his eyes. "I think we both need to remember that you're here to recuperate, Abby," he said after a minute. "This is temporary. You've got a successful career waiting for you in New York, but this is my world." He nodded toward the distant hills, dotted with red-coated, white-faced Herefords. "I don't have time for casual flings, even if I believed in them."

She drew away from him as if she'd been burned. "Excuse me for throwing myself at you...."

"Stop it." His fingers caught her upper arms and held her in front of him when she would have moved away. "A few kisses aren't going to hurt either of us. I just want you to understand the limits. You're very vulnerable right now, Abby. You could easily make a decision that you'd regret for the rest of your life."

He was speaking in riddles, and she stared up at him with wounded eyes, because it sounded as if he were gently rejecting her. Well, she should be used to it, shouldn't she?

And if he could be adult about it, so could she. Damn her breaking heart, she'd never let him see it!

Keep it light, girl, she told herself, keep your pride, at least. She managed a bright smile. "Sensible Cade," she murmured. "Don't worry, I promise not to rip your clothes off."

He tried to smother a chuckle and failed. "That would be one for the books, in several ways." He touched her lips with a lazy finger. "Abby, I've never undressed in front of a woman."

She could feel her own surprise coloring her cheeks. "Never?" she burst out.

"Look who's shocked," he mused. "Have you ever stripped for a man?"

"For you, once," she reminded him, avoiding his suddenly explosive gaze. "It was an accident, of course, I had no idea you were anywhere near the ranch that night."

"I know that." A rough sound broke from his throat, as if an unwanted memory was plaguing him. "I'd better go see about that bull. We'll be moving cattle into the pens today. If that call I'm expecting from California comes, take the number and call Hank on the radio. He'll find me."

"Yes, boss," she said smartly.

He looked down at her with narrowed eyes. "How did you get so short?"

"I'm wearing flat-heeled shoes," she said. "And you tower over everybody."

He grinned. "Keeps the men intimidated."

"Your temper's enough to do that." She laughed. "Don't work yourself into a stupor."

"Work keeps my mind off other things," he returned, letting his eyes run boldly up and down her body. "If it's pretty tomorrow, I'll take you on a picnic."

Her whole face brightened and she smiled so sweetly that his eyes froze on her and she couldn't seem to move away.

"Down by the river?" she asked hopefully.

"You love those damned cottonwoods and pines, don't you?" he asked.

"It's spring," she reminded him. "I love the color of the cottonwoods when they're just budding out. The softest kind of green, and the grass is just beginning to get lush...."

"Well, I need to check the fences down there," he mused.

"You work all the time," she grumbled. "You can't even go on a picnic without combining it with business!"

"The ranch isn't my business, Abby. It's my life," he said quietly.

She sighed angrily. "Don't I know it? You're married to it!"

His dark eyes narrowed. "What else have I got?" he demanded.

The question startled her. She watched him swing gracefully into the saddle. The rich leather creaked under his formidable weight as he settled himself and gripped the reins.

"Don't forget about that California call," he said. "And keep close to the house. I don't know some of these new men except by reputation."

"Cowboys are mostly polite and courteous," she reminded him.

"And some of them aren't." He stared down at her hard. "I'd kill a man who tried to hurt you while you were on my land. You keep that in mind."

He wheeled the big horse and went cantering away, leaving Abby standing in the shade of the trees, staring after him. She hadn't needed to ask if he meant that threat. She knew him too well. In the old days, when he was younger and much more hot-tempered, she'd seen him give "object lessons" to cowboys who thought they could push him. He was quick on his feet, and he knew how to handle himself in a fight. The men might grin when he blustered around in a temper over ranch problems, but they knew just the same that there was a line nobody crossed with him.

She wrapped her arms around herself and walked back into the house. It was only then that she realized how vague the memory of the attack was becoming. Being here, away from the city, had given her new perspective, healed the mental wounds. She'd be more careful in the future, but she wouldn't let that one bad experience ruin her life. Her mind kept going back to what Cade had said, about giving the would-be rapist rights over her. Trust him to know the right thing to say.

She wandered back into the den and sat down at the computer. She was glad Cade didn't have a ranch office as such, like many cattlemen did. The den was comfortable and informal, and she liked its homey atmosphere.

The sudden jangling of the phone made her jump, but she recovered quickly and reached for it.

"McLaren Ranch office," she said automatically.

"Abby Shane, please," came a pleasant female voice in reply.

"This is she."

There was a tinkling laugh. "Well, I've run you down at last. This is Jessica Dane, Abby. Has Melly mentioned me to you?"

The boutique owner! Abby's pale brown eyes glittered with excitement. "Heavens, yes!" she returned, bubbling over. "I was afraid she'd got it wrong and you weren't really interested."

"I was, I am, but I couldn't catch you in your apartment." Jessica laughed. "Now I've got you trapped. Listen, I own a little boutique over the border from you in Sheridan, Wyoming. I'm never going to be able to compete with Saks, you understand, but I have a good mail-order business in addition to a thriving shop."

"Yes, I've heard all about your success from Melly," Abby said. "She thinks you carry the prettiest leisure clothes short of New York."

"And that's why I'm bothering you," the other woman replied. "Those dresses you designed for Melly are just what I'm looking for to add to my spring and summer line. They're simple and elegant, they wouldn't cost a fortune to make and my customers would eat them up."

"Do you mean it?" Abby burst out.

"Of course I mean it. We could work something out, if you're interested. I know you make a lot modeling—I broke out of that rat race ten years ago and risked everything to open this shop. Now I'm making just as much as I did in New York, but my feet don't hurt so much anymore," she added with laughter in her voice.

"You were a model? Then you know how it is, don't you?" she asked.

Jessica laughed. "Oh, yes, I know very well. I spent half my time trying to stay out of trouble, and I imagine it's even worse now."

"I don't just go to the parties," Abby confessed, "and I keep to myself. But then, too, I'm not in that top ten percent. Frankly, I'm sick of it all. I can't think of anything I love more than designing…."

"Then why not do some work for me?" Jessica pleaded. "At least think about it. I know we could come to an arrangement. You could come down here and look over my business, and I could show you what I have in mind."

"I'd like that," Abby said. "I have commitments lined

up for the next few months, but come late September, I'm a free agent. Could I let you know then?"

"Fine! Meanwhile, give me your address in New York and I'll send you some of my catalogs." There was a smile in the woman's voice. "Maybe they'll tempt you."

"I'm already tempted." Abby sighed.

"Good. You'll be easy to convince." She laughed. "Here, take down my number and call me the minute you make up your mind." She dictated the digits while Abby jotted them on her calendar. "By the way, Abby, are you going to be at Melly's wedding?"

"Yes. I designed her wedding dress."

"Fantastic! I'm invited, too, so we'll get a chance to meet then. We'll go off in a corner and I'll describe some of the new designs I'm looking for. How about that?"

"I can hardly wait," Abby said genuinely. "Jessica, I can't tell you how much I appreciate the offer."

"I'm the one who ought to do the thanking. You've got great potential, honey. And believe me, in the long run, you'll make as much designing for the boutique as you will trudging all over New York. And you can do it at your own pace, too."

"I hope I'm not dreaming all this. Thanks again, Jessica. I'll look forward to seeing you at the wedding."

"Me, too, honey. Have a nice day. Enjoyed it!"

"So did I!" Abby laughed. She hung up and stared at the receiver in astonishment. It was like the answer to a prayer. She could give up the long hours and the stress and do what she loved best. She could even come home to Montana!

For one insane moment, she thought about going out to find Cade, to tell him. Maybe it would show him that she wanted to give up all the glitter he thought she couldn't do without. But as soon as the thought came, she shut it out.

He'd just blow up if she interrupted him. And why should he care if she came home? He was letting her stay on his ranch to be near Melly and get herself back together. He might want her—why not?—she was an attractive woman. But wanting wasn't loving, and he was the world's most determined bachelor. Marriage wasn't in his vocabulary—he'd said as much. The ranch was his woman.

Abby sighed and pulled out the herd records she was working on. Anyway, it was nice to have a choice. She could look forward to talking to Jessica about her boutique, and it would pass the time.

The day was a long one, even after Melly came back to help her catch up with the work.

"I'm just tickled pink about Jessica's offer," Melly confided as she watched Abby seal a letter. "Are you going to do it?"

"I don't know," Abby said honestly. "I'd love to come home. But I don't know if I could bear it."

"The loneliness, you mean?"

"Being so close to Cade and so far away from him, all at once," Abby replied. Her eyes showed the wound of loving hopelessly. "I'd rather be hundreds of miles away than practically next door, Melly. If I can't have him, I'd just as soon not have to see him at all. It hurts too much."

"For someone who doesn't care, he sure kisses you a lot lately."

"He said it wouldn't hurt either one of us," she said bitterly. "But he reminded me all the same that I'm here to get over the attack, and I've got a career to go back to. You'd think he couldn't wait to get me off the place."

"Has it ever occurred to you that he might want you gone for the same reason you're going?" Melly asked quietly. "I get the idea that he doesn't think you could give up modeling."

"It's not that at all," Abby protested. "This ranch is his whole life. He's always talking about how stupid people are to get married, and that he never will. And almost in the same breath, he'll swear that he doesn't believe in affairs. I don't know what to make of him."

Melly threw up her hands. "I give up. You're as dense as he is. Okay, show me these records and I'll help you catch up. When are you supposed to get back to Jessica, by the way?"

"She's coming to the wedding, and we're going to talk. What does she look like?"

Melly grinned. "Wait and see. It'll be a revelation to you. Now, this is where we need to start taking off cattle...."

They worked steadily until supper. Melly went out with Jerry to a friend's house. Abby had just finished changing her clothes and was telling a persistent caller for the fourth time in as many hours that Cade was still out when he came slamming angrily in the door. His face was rigid, his lips compressed. He was still wearing his chaps and the brim of his wide hat was crushed in one hand.

"Well, don't just stand there, for God's sake, hang that thing up and get the liniment," he muttered, hobbling up the stairs to his room.

"What happened?" she called after him, absently hanging up on the caller before she thought.

"Cow fell on me," he growled. "Hurry up, damn it!" He went into his bedroom and slammed the door.

Abby rushed into the kitchen to get the liniment. Calla got it out of the cabinet for her.

"Bull again, huh?" old Jeb asked from the doorway as he entered the kitchen.

"He said it was a cow," Abby volunteered.

"Told him he ought to let the younger boys wrestle them things." Jeb nodded. "Yep, I told him, but he wouldn't listen. He's got more broke bones and scars than any man I ever knowed. Lot of them were from his rodeo days, but he's got more being bullheaded and doing jobs he's too brittle for."

"He never listens," Calla agreed, nodding her head. "Why I remember one time…"

She was still going strong when Abby left the two of them recalling other incidents of Cade's intentional deafness.

He had his shirt off when she went into the bedroom. She closed the door behind her, hesitating. The last time she'd been in this particular room was that night when he'd carried her in from the swimming pool in nothing but her damp jeans. It brought back bittersweet memories.

"Open the door if you're nervous being alone with me," he growled, rubbing his shoulder.

"Sorry," she murmured, trying not to appear too interested in his naked chest. Without his shirt, he was the sexiest thing she'd ever seen, bronzed and muscular, with a thick wedge of dark, curling hair narrowing down to his flat stomach.

She uncapped the bottle of liniment and wrinkled her nose. "My gosh, you'd better make your men sign affidavits that they won't quit if I put this stuff on you."

"Shut up and rub," he grumbled, indicating the smooth flesh of his shoulder.

She poured liniment in her palm and began to apply it. Her fingers tingled at the feel of his flesh under them. "How did a cow manage to fall on you?"

"It's a long story." He lit a cigarette while she massaged the aching limb, wincing as she went over a tender spot.

"Should you smoke?" she murmured. "We might both blow up if a spark ignites the fumes…."

He glared at her. His hair was tousled over his broad forehead, over his dark, glittering eyes and heavy brows, and he looked impossibly masculine.

"Funny girl," he mocked.

"Laughing beats crying, my papa always used to say," she reminded him.

He turned his eyes away and sighed. "I can't imagine you crying over me."

Abby blinked, wondering at how stupid God had made some men. "That works both ways. I'll bet you're just counting the days until I'm on my way back to New York."

He didn't answer her. He took a long draw from the cigarette and exhaled through pursed lips. "Nightmares fading away, honey?" he asked.

She managed a faint smile. "All but gone, in fact." She shrugged, applying more liniment. "It was so hellish at the time. But looking back, I was lucky. Really lucky. All he did was push me around a little before the bystanders chased him off. It was the idea of what could have happened that was so scary. Gosh, men are strong, Cade."

"Some men," he agreed. He glanced at her.

She looked down as he looked up, and her eyes drowned in his dark, intense stare. Her hands stilled on his arm, and time seemed to go into a standstill around them. She was remembering another night, another time, when she'd lain on this very bed in his arms and experienced her first intimacy with a man. But Cade had changed since then. The easygoing, humorous man she'd once known had been replaced by a far more mature man, a harder man. He'd never been easy to read, but now nothing showed in his expression.

He reached out without warning and caught her around the waist, pulling her down on the bed beside him.

"Cade!" she gasped, too shocked to struggle.

He rolled over on his side and one bare arm arched across her body to hold her there while he leaned on an elbow and watched the expressions cross her face. Her eyes dropped to his chest, and she wanted to touch him so desperately that she closed them to resist the impulse.

"Afraid?" he asked softly.

Her fingers touched his hard face, sensitive to the rough texture of it where he needed a shave, to the feel of his cool, thick hair against them. "I'm with you now. I'm safe."

"Not so safe," he said with a faint smile. "But protected, for what it's worth. Suppose I kiss you half to death and then I can grab a bite to eat and go back out."

"Suppose you just kiss me half to death and forget about going back out?" she asked, tingling all over as she waited to feel that hard, warm mouth over hers.

"Because," he breathed, fitting his lips slowly, sensitively to hers, "as sure as God made little green apples, Calla's going to be knocking at that door any minute to make sure you're safe. And once I'm fed, she'll want to make sure that I'm too tired to find my way to you."

"Calla wouldn't…"

He kissed her slowly, softly. "Calla would. She's not blind. She sees the way I look at you."

Her heart was racing. "How do you look at me?" she asked.

His mouth smiled mockingly against hers. "Haven't you noticed? Hush. I seem to have waited half my life to get you in bed with me like this…."

She felt his lips nibbling at hers, nudging at them with

exquisite slowness, and she relaxed, letting her fingers curl into the hair at his nape.

His tongue teased its way into her mouth and she gasped sharply at the sudden intimacy, even as she felt his body moving sensuously against hers. His mouth softened and became coaxing with expert sureness as his chest scraped abrasively, teasingly across her breasts until the tips hardened. She moaned softly and he lifted his dark head to look into her eyes, searching them quickly. "Was that fear or pleasure?" he whispered.

Her lips parted involuntarily. One slender hand moved from the back of his head down over his chest and stroked him, smoothing the curling dark hair over the warm muscles. "I'm not afraid of you," she said in a breathless whisper, searching his dark eyes.

"I could make you afraid, though, couldn't I, Abby?" he asked, as if it mattered. "You're still very vulnerable."

"You make me sound like a terrified virgin," she replied.

His warm fingers stroked the long, pale hair back from her flushed face. "I'm doing my damndest to remember that you are one," he said softly. "It's hard for a man to make love like this, Abby. To remember not to kiss too hard, not to touch too intimately…."

Her eyes betrayed the surprise she felt at what he was confessing. "Have you been deliberately holding back all this time?" she asked, searching his eyes. "Because you thought you might frighten me?"

He drew in a deep breath, and she felt his chest expand against her breasts. "I couldn't bear to hurt you," he said. His voice was like velvet, deep and dark and softly textured. "I've treated you like porcelain since you've been here. I've damned near worked myself into an early grave to keep away…and tonight, I caved in. I kept remembering how

you were this morning, how you begged for my mouth...."
His eyes closed, his face tautened. "Oh, God, Abby, what am I going to do about you?" he groaned.

She couldn't even speak. He looked so incredibly vulnerable, as if he were at the end of some imaginary rope. Her fingers stroked his broad shoulders, loving the very texture of his skin. She loved everything about him, every line and curve of him.

"You said this morning," she reminded him softly, "that a few kisses wouldn't hurt either one of us. Didn't you?"

His eyes opened, and they were like black fires. "And that's the whole problem, little one. I want more than a few kisses."

Her eyes fell to his chiseled mouth and she felt her body begin to tremble. "Cade... I don't mind if you touch me," she whispered.

His face moved against hers, his breath sighing out heavily at her ear. "That could be dangerous."

With a surge of fearlessness, she caught one of the hands beside her on the bed and lifted it in hers. Before her courage gave out completely, she took it to her T-shirt and eased it hesitantly over the soft curve of her breast.

She wasn't prepared for the sensations it caused. She drew in a sharp breath and bit her lip to keep from crying out.

Cade lifted his dark head and looked at her, holding her eyes while his hand pressed softly against her. His thumb moved onto the taut peak and teased it. His heart slammed wildly against her with the action, and she could see the desire that was smoldering in his eyes.

"Four years," he said in a hunted tone. "And I haven't forgotten a second of it. I remember the way you looked, the way you cried out when I touched you like this."

"Do you think I don't remember, too?" she asked under her breath. "I lived on it for years, Cade—" Her voice broke, her mouth trembled as she looked up at him.

"So did I," he breathed out shakily. He bent again and let his mouth brush warmly against her parted lips. "You were so young. You still are. Years too young, and a world away from me. Abby, are you wearing anything under this?"

She wished she were more sophisticated. She blushed, feeling her body stiffen as he slid his hand under the hem of the shirt and up to find the answer himself. He caught his breath when he touched her, really touched her, and felt the helpless response of her soft, bare flesh.

Her own hands reached up to stroke the tangled mat of hair on his chest. "I used to dream about touching you like this," she confessed, watching him. "Feeling you…"

"Oh, God!" he ground out, trembling. His free hand cupped her head and held it still while his mouth devoured hers in the static stillness of the room. She felt his other hand moving over her bareness in a long, aching caress that made her arch up and moan with exquisite pleasure.

She protested once, gently, drawing away to breathe.

"Come back here," he murmured, "I'm not through."

"I have to breathe," she whispered as he turned her mouth back to his.

"Breathe me," he murmured against her soft, eager mouth. His hands smoothed over her back, pushing up the shirt as they swept with warm abrasiveness across her soft skin.

"You told me once that you'd never let another man touch you this way. Did you mean it?" he asked roughly.

"I meant it," she whispered, her voice trembling. Her fingers were clinging at the nape of his neck, her body arching to give him freer access to it. "I've never, ever wanted a man...after you."

Breathing like a distance runner, he lifted his head and looked down at her where the shirt was pulled up. His eyes darkened with a hunger she could actually see. Against her pale golden flesh, his hands were as dark as leather.

"You can't imagine how it feels," she breathed, her eyes loving him.

"Being touched?" he asked, lifting his eyes to watch her rapt face.

She shook her head slowly. "Being with you...like this. Oh, Cade, I'd be embarrassed with my own sister, but I love it when you look at me...this way."

His breathing, already ragged, seemed to freeze inside him. His thumbs edged up, dragging softly against the rigid peaks, and she moaned sharply, looking straight into his eyes.

All at once he removed his hands and sat up, his big body shuddering with the force of his heartbeat, his eyes reckless and faintly dangerous.

"That's enough," he said roughly.

But it wasn't for Abby, and without even thinking, she followed him, kneeling just in front of him. She placed her trembling hands on his shoulders and swayed close, brushing her body softly, slowly against his hair-roughened chest, watching her own paleness disappearing into the curling hair with awe.

"Abby," he whispered shakily. His hands moved to her bare back and brought her slowly against him, prolonging the contact, easing her closer with a rhythm that made her tremble all the way to her toes.

His hands caught her hips and ground them against his, and she cried out as she felt the force of his hunger. Trembling, her arms locked around his neck as they fell sideways on the bed. He was beside her, then they shifted, and she felt his full weight evenly distributed along the length of her aching body. She could feel the abrasiveness of his wiry hair against her bareness where they touched, the scent of the liniment becoming as potent as perfume as they kissed wildly, and she wondered at the depth of her own love for him.

Feeling unusually reckless, she began to move. Her hands slid down his back to the base of his spine, and the mouth crushing hers groaned harshly. Against her body, he was warm and hard and she could feel every steely muscle in him. Even all those years ago, it had never been like this between them. The feel of him drowned her in sensation, in need and half-awakened hunger. She wanted to be closer than this, she wanted all the fabric out of the way, she wanted his eyes and his hands to touch her. She shifted restlessly, hungry as she never had been in her life, needing him…!

She touched him with hands that trembled, delighting in the feel of his smooth back muscles. Her fingers moved around to caress the thick mat of hair over his chest, and hesitantly, softly, traced the arrow of hair that ran below his belt. I love you, she thought silently. I love you….

Cade's big body contracted as if he'd been shot, and all at once he seemed to come to his senses. He muttered a harsh curse and jerked himself away from Abby, rolling over to lie on his back. His body shuddered with frustrated need; his eyes closed, his jaw tautened. His breath came wildly. Watching him, she felt guilty that she'd let it go so far, because they'd both known all the time that Cade wasn't going over his own limits. Only she'd forgotten, and he hadn't.

Fumbling, she pulled down her shirt with shaking hands

and sat up. She took a deep breath and threw her legs over the side of the bed. "Excuse me," she said in a barely audible voice, "I didn't know where the limits were."

"Well, you found out, didn't you?" he shot at her.

She got off the bed and glanced toward him. He was pale, and his face was drawn as he sat up and reached for his shirt.

"I'm sorry," she said unsteadily. "I...I know it's unpleasant for men to...well..."

"Don't turn the knife," he said. His voice was cutting. He dragged a cigarette from his pocket and lit it with unsteady hands. "Damn it, Abby, you knock me right off balance."

She tried to smile. "And after I promised not to try and have my way with you, too."

But he didn't smile. His face grew harder. "You're tearing me inside out," he said, standing. "If I'd thought I could stand Calla's infernal sarcasm, I would have let her put the liniment on!"

"Next time, I'll remember that," she shot back. She whirled, her eyes simmering with anger. "You started it!" she accused childishly.

His nostrils flared. "Yes, I started it," he said under his breath. "Nothing's changed. Nothing! I touch you, and we both start trembling. It was that way when you were only eighteen, and I carried you in here, wanting you until I was just about out of my mind!" He ran an angry hand through his thick hair and glared up at her. "But I didn't take you then, and I won't take you now. There's no future in it. There never was."

"What an ego," she threw back. "My God, you're full of yourself!"

"That's what you think," he said harshly. "I went through the motions of work all day, but all I could think about was how it felt when we kissed this morning. I remembered your mouth the way a man dying of thirst remembers ice water, soft and sweet. Just how much do you think I can take?"

"Well, don't strain yourself," she said, turning away with a hot ache all the way to her toes. "I'll be gone soon enough."

"I know that," he said. His voice sounded hollow. The mattress creaked as he got to his feet. "Sex is a lousy foundation for a relationship, Abby. We're not going to build on it."

She flushed in spite of herself, but she wouldn't turn and let him see it. "Amen," she agreed. "If you want to call off the picnic tomorrow—"

"No," he said unexpectedly. "No, I don't want to call it off. It will be the last time we have together."

He said that as if it meant forever—that they'd never spend another minute alone—and she wanted to scream and cry and beg him to try and love her just a little. But she clenched her jaw and drew in a steadying breath. "Calla's going to scream about fixing a picnic with those new hands to feed."

"We'll risk it," he said shortly. "Right now, I've got to get back to the barn. That damned bull's improving a little, but I want to see what the vet has to say when he checks him for the night."

"I could pack you a sandwich and some coffee," she offered.

"I don't want anything."

She opened the door and paused. "Especially me?" She laughed shakily and ran down the stairs with tears shimmering in her eyes.

CHAPTER NINE

CALLA WAS CURSING a blue streak when Abby walked into the kitchen the next morning at six, wearing a yellow sundress with an elasticized bodice and tiny straps that tied over each shoulder.

"Having to fry bacon and chicken all at once," the housekeeper muttered darkly as she stood over the stove. "Picnics, with all I got to do!" She glared over her shoulder at Abby. "Well, don't just stand there, girl, go set the table!"

"Yes, ma'am," Abby said smartly and curtsied. The dress was one she'd designed herself, and with her loosened blond hair, she looked like something out of a fashion magazine. Calla stopped muttering long enough to give her an approving stare. "Nice," she said after a minute. "You make that yourself?"

"Sure did." She whirled around for Calla's benefit, her skirt flying against her long, smooth legs. "It's cool and comfortable and it doesn't bind. I'll make you one, if you like."

"I can just see me in something like that." The older woman sighed, indicating the dowdy housedress that covered her ample figure. Then her watery blue eyes narrowed. "You watch Cade while you're out there alone with him, you hear me? I ain't blind. I saw how you looked when you came out of his room last night. You make him keep his distance."

Abby felt her cheeks go hot. "Now, Calla…"

"Don't you 'now, Calla' me! I know Cade. He hasn't been the same since you walked through the front door, and it ain't because of the cattle." Her chin lifted. "You and I both know how he feels about weddings, Abigail," she added gently, using the younger woman's full name, as she rarely did except when she was serious. "You're my lamb, and I love him, too, but I don't want you hurt. Melly told me what happened. Don't you jump out of the frying pan into the fire. All you'll find here is heartache."

Abby smothered an urge to hug the concerned old woman, knowing it wouldn't be welcome. "You're sure about that?" she asked softly.

"He looks at you like a starving man looks at a steak smothered with onions," Calla replied. "But once he's fed, young lady, he's just as likely to find he's lost his taste for steak. You get my meaning? Wanting ain't loving."

"I know that," she said on a wistful sigh.

"Then act accordingly. He's been sticking close to the ranch for quite a while now," Calla added gently. "A hungry man is dangerous."

"I'm a big girl," Abby reminded her. "I can look out for myself—most of the time, anyway."

"And what time you can't, I will," came the fervent promise. "Now go set the table."

"Yes, ma'am," Abby said, grinning.

She carried two place settings of everyday china into the dining room and helped put the food on the table. Cade was uncharacteristically late getting downstairs, and she was almost ready to go up and call him when he walked into the room.

He looked as if he hadn't slept a wink. His dark hair was damp from a shower, and he was wearing a tan patterned Western shirt over rust-colored denims, and polished tan boots. He looked rugged and formidable, and so solemn that he intimidated her.

"I thought you were going to fix fences," Abby remarked.

"I am," he muttered. He sat down at the head of the table and stared at her for a long moment, taking in every line of her face and body. "When you finish your breakfast, go back upstairs and get dressed. I'm not taking you on a picnic half-naked."

The sudden attack left her dumb. She gaped at him with wide, hurt eyes before she put down her napkin and got up from the table in tears. She'd worn the sundress especially for him, to please him.

"Where are you going?" Calla demanded, elbowing in with a platter of scrambled eggs.

"To put on some clothes," Abby said in a subdued tone, and didn't look back.

"Now what have you done?" Calla was demanding, but Abby didn't wait around to hear the answer. She rushed up to her room and slammed the door with tears boiling down her flushed cheeks.

She cried for what seemed hours before she dragged herself up and put on her blue jeans and a short-sleeved blue blouse. She put on a vest over that, a fringed leather one, and put her hair up in a bun. Before she went back downstairs, she scrubbed off every trace of makeup, as well.

When she walked back into the room, pale and silent, Cade barely glanced at her.

"If you'd like to call the picnic off, I can finish Melly's wedding dress instead," she said as she sipped her coffee, ignoring the eggs and sausage and fresh, hot biscuits.

"I'd like to call everything off, if you want to know," he said shortly.

"That's fine with me. I have plenty to keep me busy." She

finished her coffee and, trying not to let him see how hurt she really was, smiled in his general direction and got up.

"Abby."

She stopped, keeping her back to him. "What?"

He drew in a slow breath. "Let's talk."

"I can't think what we have to talk about," she said with a careless laugh, turning to face him with fearless eyes. "I'll be leaving as soon as Melly comes back after her honeymoon, you know. But I can go right now, if you like. I've had an interesting offer from a boutique owner—"

His eyes flashed fire, and he cut her off sharply before she could tell him the rest. "And you'll be off to another landmark in your career, I suppose?" he asked with a mocking smile. "It's just as well, honey—I plan to do some traveling on my own in the next few months. There's only one job here, and Melly's got it."

"Don't worry, I don't particularly enjoy keeping records on cattle," she replied with a cool smile.

He stood up and lit a cigarette, leaving his second cup of coffee untouched on the table. "Calla's got the picnic basket packed. We might as well spend today together. It'll sure as hell be the last time we have, because starting tomorrow I'll be out with the boys constantly."

"Why don't you take Calla on a picnic?" she asked coldly. "You like her."

His nostrils flared as he stared down at her from his superior height. "I used to like you pretty well," he reminded her.

"Sure, as long as I stayed away." She moved about restlessly. "I should have stayed in New York. I didn't think I'd be welcomed here with open arms...."

"You might have been, once," he said enigmatically, "if

you hadn't decided that the world of fashion meant more to you than a home and family."

She glanced up at him narrowly. "Pull the other one." She laughed. "If I'd stayed here, I would have withered away and become just another old maid dotting the landscape, and you know it. Or are you going to try and tell me that you were dying for love of me?" she added mockingly.

His dark eyes went quietly over her face. "Why would I waste time telling you something you wouldn't believe in the first place?" he asked. "If we're going, let's go. I don't have time to stand around talking."

"Oh, by all means, the ranch might fall apart!" she replied, and walked into the kitchen.

Calla glanced at her and scowled, a scowl that grew even fiercer when she saw Cade. "There's the basket," she grumbled at him.

"Thanks a hell of a lot," Cade snapped back, grabbing the picnic basket. "If you need extra help here, hire it. Or quit. But don't bother me with it. I'm slam out of patience, Calla."

And he slammed his hat over his brow and stormed out the back door ahead of Abby.

"Watch out," the housekeeper said sympathetically. "Something's eating him today."

"If he keeps that up, I'll find something that really will eat him!" Abby promised. "A wandering cannibal..." she muttered as she followed him out the door.

Cade drove them through pastures where there were little more than ruts for the truck to follow, and Abby held on to the seat for dear life, afraid to say a word. His face was grim, eyes doggedly on the ruts, and he looked as if the slightest sound would set him off.

But later, after he'd stripped off his shirt and rewired

two or three strands of barbed wire in a pasture near the river, he seemed to have worked off some of his irritation.

Abby, who'd already spread out the picnic lunch under the cottonwoods near the river, wandered through the towering break of pines and spruce to find him.

He was leaning back against the truck smoking a cigarette, his eyes on the distant mountains across the rolling grasslands. His hat was off, his gloves were still in place and he looked as much a part of the land as the tall grasses that grew there. With his shirt gone, his chest was revealed, the thick wedge of hair damp with sweat, his tanned shoulders gleaming with moisture. Abby almost closed her eyes at the sight of all that provocative masculinity so close and tempting. She wanted desperately to touch him, to run her hands over those broad shoulders and feel the texture of the thick hair that covered the bronzed muscles of his chest. But she didn't dare.

"Lunch is ready, when you are," she said quietly.

He glanced at her solemnly. "I've patched the fence," he said. His eyes went back to the mountains. "God, I love this country," he added in a tone deep and soft with reverence. "I could stand and look over it for hours and never tire of the sight."

"It wouldn't have been much different in the old days, when trappers and fur traders and explorers like William Clark came here," she remarked, going to stand beside him. The wind was tearing at the tight bun of her hair, but she pinned it back relentlessly.

"It's different," Cade said shortly, his eyes straight ahead. "It's damned hard balancing between environmental protection and progress, Abby."

"Between mining and ranching, agriculture and industry?" she asked gently, because it was a subject that could set him off like a time bomb.

"Exactly." He glanced toward one of the grassy ridges that faced away from the mountains. There was mining a few miles beyond that ridge, on land Cade had leased for the purpose. It had been a struggle, that decision, but in the end he'd bowed to the nation's struggle for fuel independence.

"I wanted to keep the ranch exactly as it was, for my sons to inherit," he said, his voice strangely intense. His eyes searched hers for a long moment. "Do you want children, Abby?"

The question knocked her sideways. She hadn't thought much about children, except when she was around Cade. Now she looked at him and pictured him with a child on his knee, and something inside her burst into wild bloom.

"Yes," she murmured involuntarily.

His gaze dropped lower, to her slender body. "Aren't you afraid of losing your figure?" he asked carelessly, and averted his head while he finished the cigarette.

She didn't dare answer, afraid that her longing for his children would be evident in her voice. Instead, she changed the subject. "Where do you plan to get those sons to leave Painted Ridge to? Are you adopting?"

His dark eyebrows shot up. "I'll get them in the usual way. You do know how people make babies?" he added, a mocking smile shadowing his hard face.

She flushed and turned away. "You always say marriage isn't in your book, Cade. I just wondered, that's all."

"Maybe I'll be forced to change my mind eventually," he remarked, tossing his gloves in the open window of the truck as he followed her back through the trees to the river.

She knelt on one side of the red-checked tablecloth,

where she'd laid out foil-covered plates of food and the jug of coffee Calla had packed in the basket.

"Are you going to taste it first?" he asked, moving to the river to slosh water over his face and chest while she dished up the food.

"I think I'll let you, after what you said to her," Abby replied. "She might have put arsenic in it."

"She didn't have time." He came back to the cloth, grabbing up one of several linen towels in the basket. He dabbed at his face and chest, and Abby watched him helplessly, hungrily, as his hands drew the cloth over the warm muscles with their furry covering.

He happened to look up, and his eyes flashed violently at her intense scrutiny.

She couldn't remember a time when she'd felt so intimidated by him or so attracted to him, all at once. She dropped her eyes back to the cloth and dished up the fried chicken, potato salad and rolls, with hands she could barely keep steady.

"Nervous of me, Abby?" he asked quietly, easing his formidable bulk down beside her, far too close, to take the plate she handed him.

"Should I be?" she countered. She poured him a cup of black coffee and automatically added cream before she handed him the foam cup. "After all, you're the one who should be worrying. I seem to make a habit of throwing myself at you," she added with bitter humor.

"And if you don't get off my ranch pretty quick, Abigail Shane, you may do it once too often," he said flatly. His eyes were dark and full of secrets as he nibbled at a piece of chicken.

"I have utter trust in your remarkable self-control, Mr.

McLaren," she muttered, picking at her own food while he put his away like a last meal.

He made a strange sound, a laugh that died away too quickly, and finished his food before he spoke again. He swallowed his coffee and stretched out lazily on the ground while Abby gathered up the remnants of the picnic and put everything except the red-checkered cloth back in the hamper and set it aside.

"You'll be busy with roundup from now on, I guess," she commented after a long silence. Her eyes went to the distant grassy ridges, green and lonely, with pale blue mountains beyond them. The only trees in sight were the ones they were under, and the small thicket of pines nearby. It was like paradise, all clean air and open land and fluffy clouds drifting overhead.

"It's spring," he remarked. "Calves won't brand themselves."

"How's your shoulder?"

"I reckon I won't die," he muttered. He was smoking another cigarette, something he seemed to be doing constantly these days. He had once said it was something he did a lot when he was nervous. That almost made her laugh. He would never be nervous around her.

She drew up her jean-clad legs and rested her chin on her updrawn knees, sighing as she watched the river flow lazily by. "Remember when we came fishing up here the summer I graduated from high school?" she said. "You and me and Melly and a couple of the hands? You caught the biggest crappie I'd ever seen, and Melly got her hook caught in one of the cowboy's jeans…." She laughed, remembering the incident as if it were yesterday.

She stared at the river, lost in memory. It had been a day much like this one. Green and full of sun and laughter.

Hank had been along; so had a cowboy whose name she couldn't remember—one Melly had a crush on. But Abby had somehow wandered close to Cade and stayed there while they fished in the river.

It was just a few weeks after he'd taken her to his room, and she'd been much too shy to approach him, but she'd eased as close as she could get.

"Cold?" he'd teased, glancing down at her.

And she'd blushed, looking away. "Oh, maybe a little," she'd lied. But they both knew the truth, although it didn't seem to bother him a bit.

"Jesse said you'd been thinking about going to New York," he'd mentioned.

"One of my teachers said I had the right carriage and figure and face for it," Abby had said enthusiastically, dreaming how it would be to have Cade and a career all at once.

"New York is a long way from Painted Ridge," he'd murmured, scowling at his fishing rod. "And full of disappointment."

That had pricked her temper, as if he didn't think she were pretty enough or poised enough for such a career in a big city.

"You don't think I can do it?" she'd asked with deceptive softness.

He'd laughed. "You're just a kid, Abby."

"I was eighteen last month. I'm a woman," she'd argued.

His head had turned. His dark eyes had gone over every inch of the shorts and tank top she wore, darkening at the sight of her slender, well-proportioned body.

"You're a woman, all right," he'd said, and looked up.

Her eyes had met his at point-blank range. Even now, she could remember the wild feelings that look had stirred, the hot pleasure of his eyes holding hers. Oblivious to everything around them, she'd actually moved toward him.

And Melly had said something to break the delicate spell. For the rest of the afternoon, they'd fished, and Cade's manner had relaxed a little. She'd tossed a worm at him out of pique when he caught the fish she'd been trying to land for several hours. And he'd picked her up bodily and thrown her in the river....

"You threw me in the river," she remarked suddenly, glaring at him.

His eyebrows arched. "I what?"

"That day we went fishing, the month before I left for New York," she reminded him. "You threw me in the river."

He chuckled softly. "So I did. But you started it, honey. That damned worm hit me right between the eyes."

"It was my fish you caught," she muttered. "My big crappie. I'd half hooked him and he'd gotten away three times. And you just sat there and hauled him out of circulation forever."

"I let you have half of him when Calla cooked him," he reminded her. "That should have made up for it a little."

Her full lips pouted. "I don't know about your half, but mine tasted bitter."

"Sour grapes," he said, grinning. "If you'd caught him, your half would have been twice as good as mine, wouldn't it?"

She shrugged. "Well, I guess so." Her eyes gazed over the river dreamily. "I used to love fishing. Now I don't have time for anything except work. Or didn't have, until I came back here. Funny how time seems to stop in a place like this," she added quietly. "Not another soul in sight, and you can drive for miles without seeing a ranch house or a store.

It must have looked like this when the first settlers came and put down roots. The winter killed a lot of them didn't it?"

He nodded. "Montana winters are rough. I know. I lose cattle every year, and once we lost a man in a line cabin. He froze to death sitting up."

She shivered. "I remember. That was when I was just out of grammar school. When Melly and I went riding, we wouldn't go near that cabin, thinking it was haunted."

He shook his head. "Well, I've got a couple of old hands now who feel the same way. Hank's one."

"I didn't think Hank was afraid of anything."

He lifted an amused eyebrow. "Do you ever miss this, in New York?"

She searched his face, thinking how she missed him every waking moment. She looked away. "I miss it a lot. There's so much history here. So much privacy and peace." She remembered the role she had to play, almost too late. "But, of course, New York has its good points, as well. There's always a new play to see. Sometimes I go to the opera or the ballet. And there are nightclubs and little coffeehouses, and museums...."

"None of which you find around here," he said harshly. "There's not much place for sophistication in the middle of a cattle spread, is there?"

He was watching her with narrowed, calculating eyes, and a dark kind of pain washed over his face before she saw it. Deliberately he crushed out the cigarette on the ground beside him.

She turned, glancing down at him. He was lying on his back with his hands under his head, and his eyes were closed. His powerful legs were crossed, stretching the denim sensuously over their muscular contours. Her eyes took in every detail, from head to broad chest to quiet face, and she felt suddenly reckless.

She picked up a long blade of grass and moved close enough to draw it lightly over his chest.

He grabbed it. "Courting trouble, Abby?" he asked curtly.

There was a wildness in her that sprang from looking at his impassive face. He wouldn't let her close—he spent his life pushing her away. Today would be the last day she'd ever have with him to remember, and today she was going to make him feel something. Even if it was only rage.

"Oh, I just live for it, Cade," she murmured, edging closer. She bent over him before he could stop her, and pressed her lips down on his broad, warm chest.

"God!" he burst out, catching the back of her head. But his hands hesitated, as if he couldn't decide whether to push or pull.

Her nostrils tickled where the thick, curling hair brushed them and she smelled the faint traces of soap and cologne that clung to him. His chest rose and fell with ragged irregularity and she felt the powerful muscles stiffen as she drew her mouth across them, acting on pure instinct alone.

"You sweet little fool," he rasped. "Oh, God, I'm only human, and I want you until I can hardly stand up straight…!"

He jerked her alongside him and bent over her with hands that trembled as his mouth homed in on hers.

Hungry as she'd never imagined she could be, she turned in his big arms and pressed close, half shocked to find his body blatantly aroused as it touched hers. For an instant she tried to draw away, but one lean, steely hand slid quickly to the base of her spine and gathered her hips back against his.

"You wanted it," he ground out against her mouth. "Don't start fighting me now."

Her hands were tangled in the hair over his chest, but she was still rational enough to realize just how involved he already was. "Cade, I only wanted—" she began, only to have the words crushed under his devouring mouth.

"This is what I've been trying to tell you all along," he whispered shakily, moving his lips to her throat. "I want you, Abby. I'd die to have you! And you can feel how much now, can't you? This is how it is between lovers. This is what happens to a man when he's pushed beyond his limits."

Even as he spoke, his hands were sliding under her blouse, finding bare skin at her back and a clasp that snapped apart with devastating ease.

"I haven't been with a woman for so damned long, I'd forgotten how soft..." he murmured, sliding his fingers under her breasts to cup their tender weight. His thumbs found suddenly hard peaks, making her shudder with new pleasure.

Abby's legs moved restlessly as Cade's eased between them. He turned, and she felt the ground under her and the full weight of his big body over her. She moaned at the intimacy, unfamiliar and arousing.

Her sharp nails dug into his back and raked down to his waist, feeling the warmth and moistness of his flesh as his hands touched her in ways that should have shocked her. His mouth was hungrier than she would ever have believed possible. She opened her own mouth helplessly, eagerly, tasting him, experiencing him.

She felt his hands on the buttons of her blouse, and seconds later his chest crushed the softness of her breasts in a joining that made her cry out again.

He lifted his head and his eyes glittered frighteningly. He was trembling all over with desire, and his face was hard with it.

"Is this what you wanted to know?" he demanded unsteadily. "If you could drive me out of my mind with wanting? To see how it would be if you pushed too hard? I want you, all right. I wanted you when you were eighteen, I'd have killed for you. But when I'd made up my mind to ask you to stay with me, you got on that damned bus and you never looked at me!"

Her eyes widened with shock. "What?"

He searched her face with eyes that barely saw. "Every vacation, all I heard about was how great New York was, how well you were doing in your damned career. Until finally I made sure I was out of the house when you came to visit, because it hurt so much to hear how happy you were away from me."

"But, I wasn't..." she began.

He wasn't listening. His hands slid under her hips and forced her up against his. "Feel it, damn you," he whispered harshly. "You've done this to me since you were fifteen. But it's something I hate, Abby, and I hate you, too, for doing it to me, for teasing me. Because I know you don't give a damn for anything except your career and your city men. And nothing you say is going to convince me otherwise!"

She swallowed nervously, her mouth trembling as she realized how set his mind really was. He'd cared, and she hadn't known. Even when Melly told her, she had refused to believe. What had she done?

"Cade," she whispered, reaching a hand up to his face.

"What do you want, baby, to see how I make love? To get a taste of what you missed when you stepped onto that bus four years ago?" He jerked her closer and bent his head. "I don't mind showing you. It will be something to tell your sophisticated friends about when you get back to your own world!" He kissed her again, hurting her, as if it didn't matter anymore whether he hurt her.

She could hardly believe what she'd just heard. He'd cared, he'd really cared enough to ask her not to leave Painted Ridge. And because she'd put on a brave front and gone away laughing, he'd believed it was because she was glad to be leaving him. Of all the horrible ironies...

She went limp in his arms, tears washing her face while he treated her like something he'd bought for the night, his hands insulting, his mouth probing mercilessly into hers. It didn't matter that she loved him more than life, because if she told him now, he wouldn't believe her. He'd just said so, and he thought she was only teasing, playing games with him until she went home. Home. If only he knew that Painted Ridge would always be home—because it was where he was.

She felt cold to the bone, as though there were not a trace of warmth anywhere inside her trembling body. She felt the restless motion of his body against hers, and wondered through a fog of misery if he really meant to take her completely.

But seconds later, he lifted his head as if he'd just tasted the tears, and looked down at her. His face was haunted-looking, his eyes blazing with frustrated passion. His powerful body shuddered.

"And this is as far as it goes, honey," he said with a cold, mocking smile. "You wouldn't want to risk going back to New York with my child growing inside you, would you, Abby? That would be taking the game too far."

Her face felt tight with hurt. She could feel her body trembling under the hard pressure of his, but he'd never know it was with helpless desire, not fear. Despite everything—even his harsh treatment—she still wanted him, would always want him. Nor did the thought of a child bring any terror to her. It was the very door of heaven.

He took a deep breath and rolled away from her, lying with his eyes closed and his bare chest lifting and falling unevenly while she fumbled with catches and buttons.

She got jerkily to her feet and smoothed down her wild blond hair, trying to find the hairpins his insistent fingers had removed. She leaned against one of the sturdy trees by the riverbank until she could get her breath back and stop crying. Finally, she dragged the hem of her blouse over her red eyes to remove the hot, salty tears from her cheeks.

She heard a sound behind her, over the noise of the river washing lazily between the banks, and she knew Cade was standing behind her. But she didn't turn.

"Are you all right?" he asked after a minute, and the words sounded torn from him.

She looked over her shoulder at him, and her ravaged face caused something violent to flash in his eyes.

"Don't look so worried, Cade," she said with enormous dignity. "You made your point. I'm through throwing myself at you. You've cured me for good this time." She managed a soft little laugh, although her swollen lips trembled and spoiled the effect.

He rammed his hands into his pockets and stared at her stiff back. "I'll keep out of your way until Melly gets back from the honeymoon," he said curtly. "I'll expect the same courtesy from you. What happened...almost happened here isn't going to be allowed to happen again."

She bit her lower lip to keep from crying. "Cade...what you said...were you really going to ask me to stay, when I was eighteen?" she asked in a ghost of a whisper.

He laughed bitterly. "Sure," he said. "I was going to offer you the job I finally gave Melly." He looked away so that she wouldn't see the lie in his dark eyes, or the deep pain that accompanied it.

She straightened, a surge of disappointment and hurt raging through her body. She had hoped that he'd wanted to marry her.

"Can we go back now?" she asked in a subdued tone.

"Might as well. I've got cattle to work."

"And I've got a wedding dress to finish." The sound of her words made her want to scream with anguish. There would never be a wedding for her. She walked quietly to the truck without looking at him and got in.

He loaded the basket and the cloth in the back of the truck with quick, furious motions and paused to shrug into his shirt and slam his ranch hat on his head before he got in beside her.

She felt his eyes on her, but she was staring out at the landscape.

"Abby," he said quietly, "it's better this way. You'll hate me for a while, but you'll get over it."

"I don't hate you," she said in a whisper. "You don't want commitment any more than I do, Cade, so there's nothing to regret."

His hands gripped the steering wheel until his fingers went white. "Don't make it any harder than it already is," he said under his breath. "Let's forget today ever happened, Abby."

"That suits me," she said. She stared out the window as he started the truck and gunned it back onto the road. She wasn't going to cry, she wasn't. She'd thrown her pride at his feet once too often already. He couldn't wait to be rid of her, and she was just as anxious to get away from him. The torment of loving him was too much. As far as he was concerned, she was just a city girl amusing herself by playing up to him, and nothing was going to convince him otherwise. What a horrible opinion he had of her. Only a man who thought her utterly contemptible could have treated her as he had.

She drew in a shaky breath. It had been so beautiful at first, feeling the hunger raging in him, knowing that he wanted her that much. Until he told her what he really thought, and she realized that it was only physical desire with him after all. Why hadn't she remembered what he'd said the night before about sex being a lousy foundation for a relationship? Well, she remembered now, and she wouldn't forget again. She'd harden her heart and grit her teeth and pray that the three weeks left would go by in a rush. Cade would never get close enough to hurt her again. She was going to make sure of that.

CHAPTER TEN

MELLY'S WEDDING DAY was a flurry of last-minute preparation, with caterers all over the house and wedding guests arriving in droves even as Abby was helping her sister get into the wedding gown she'd designed.

"It's just heaven." Melly sighed, looking at herself in the mirror. The dress had a keyhole neckline, and it was lavishly trimmed with appliquéd Venice lace. The veil of illusion net that went with it fell from a Juliet cap down to drape over an elegant train. The sleeves were pure lace, the skirt a fantasy of satin and chiffon and more lace, and the Empire waistline featured a row of the most intricate tiny roses in contrasting oyster white. With Melly's blond hair and fair skin, it was sheer magic.

"I can't believe I actually finished it on time," Abby murmured as she made a last tuck in the hem.

"I can't believe you actually designed it," her sister replied. "Abby, it's the most gorgeous thing! Jessica will just die."

"I hope not," came the amused reply. Abby sighed, thinking about what might have been. She'd have to refuse that attractive offer now. It would only have worked if she had stayed in Montana. And, of course, that was impossible. Cade had done everything but move away to keep the distance between them. He wasn't ever at home now, finding excuse after excuse to be up with the dawn and out until bedtime. Sometimes he even camped out with the men in the line cabins, shocking Calla, who gave up on keeping his supper for him and started sending his meals up with Jeb and the boys.

"Melly, be happy," she said suddenly, breaking out of her reverie.

Melly turned, her eyes sparkling and full of love and excitement, her hands trembling with anticipation. "How could I help but be, when I'm marrying Jerry?" she asked. Her joy faded slightly though, when she looked at Abby. "Darling, what's gone wrong between you and Cade?"

"Nothing that hasn't always been wrong," she replied with a cool smile. "Don't you worry about me on your wedding day! Let's get you married, okay?"

"Are you sure you can cope with the computer and all the extra work?"

"I can cope," Abby said quietly. Impulsively, she hugged Melly. "I want years and years of happiness for you. I only wish our parents could be here, to see what a beautiful bride you make!"

"Maybe they're watching," came the soft reply. "Did you see the flowers, Abby? Wasn't it grand of Cade to let us have the wedding here? All those guests…"

"…will probably have the opportunity to take a look at the bulls he's selling while they're on the place," Abby finished with a bitter smile.

"Shame on you," Melly said gently. "You know how generous Cade is."

Abby flushed and turned away. "We see him in different ways, though. I wonder if he'll show up for the ceremony?"

"He's best man—he'll have to." Melly laughed. "Think you can walk down the aisle on his arm without tripping him?"

"I'll fight the temptation, just for you. You'll listen for the music?"

"I'll listen. See you downstairs."

Abby smiled. "See you downstairs."

She walked out into the hall, checking her own long, V-necked lavender gown for spots or wrinkles. It was sleeveless, and her hair was pinned elegantly atop her head. She carried a bouquet of cymbidium orchids, and she was shaking with nerves. This would be her first wedding, and while she was honored to be her sister's maid of honor, she would rather have been an observer. The hardest thing of all was going to be standing beside Cade at that altar.

She went down the stairs and stopped dead when she caught sight of a redheaded Amazon standing in the doorway. Ignoring the ranch wives, some of whom she knew, she made a beeline for the newcomer, knowing instinctively who she was. Cade, watching from the cleared-out living room where the ceremony would take place, scowled darkly when he saw her bypass the country women to rush to the elegantly dressed newcomer.

"You've got to be Jessica Dane," Abby said immediately.

The towering redhead grinned. "How'd you guess? It was my beaming smile, right?" She laughed, towering over Abby in her three-inch heels. Barefoot, Jessica would have been almost six feet tall. With her red hair and pale skin and big black eyes, she would have drawn eyes anywhere, even without the mink stole and vivid green silk dress she was wearing with matching shoes and bag.

"You must be Abby, then," Jessica said, extending her hand in a firm, warm handshake. "Come on out to my car for a minute, and let me show you what I brought! Have we got time?"

"A few minutes, anyway." Abby laughed. She went out

with Jessica without a backward glance, unaware of the
dark scowling face watching her.

"These were just some of my lines," Jessica said when
they were seated in the Lincoln Continental's comfortable
interior, and Abby thumbed through several catalogs, ad-
miring the fashions.

"They're very good," she said finally.

"They could be better, if I had a house designer," Jessica
said. "I'm prepared to offer you a percentage of my gross,
Abby. I think you could make us both rich. Richer," she
corrected, laughing. "You've got some unique designs, if
Melly's wardrobe is anything to go by. I'd love to have you
do a few sketches, at least, and send them to me."

Despite her haste to get back to New York, Abby was
willing to do that. In fact, she and Jessica got so caught up
in a discussion of the particulars, they almost missed the
opening chords of the organ. It wasn't until Cade shouted
from the front porch that Abby clambered out of Jessica's
car and rushed up the steps, with the Amazon at her heels.

"If you can spare the time, everyone else is ready to
start," Cade said under his breath as she passed him.

"And the sooner this is over, the sooner she'll be back
from her honeymoon, which means I can leave," she shot
back, glaring up at him.

"Lady, it won't be quick enough to suit me," he returned
hotly.

She brushed past him, oblivious to Jessica's puzzled
stare, and went right to the doorway of the living room,
arriving just as the prelude finished.

Cade joined Jerry at the altar, the two of them such a
contrast in their suits—Cade dark and elegant, Jerry blond
and obviously uncomfortable. Then the wedding march
sounded and Abby gripped her orchids, shooting a glance

at the staircase to find Melly waiting there. As she walked between the folding chairs, she discovered that down the aisle Cade was watching every step she made, an expression in his eyes that she couldn't begin to understand.

For one wild instant, Abby pretended that this was her own wedding, that she was giving herself to Cade for all time. It was so delicious a fantasy that she stared at him the whole length of the aisle. He stared back at her, his face momentarily softening, his eyes black and glittering as she went to stand at her place beside the flowered arch of the altar. His eyes held hers for a long, blazing moment, and her lips parted on a rush of breath as she felt the force of the look all the way to her toes.

Then the organ sounded again, and the spell was broken as Melly came down the aisle in the gorgeous gown, carrying orchids and wildflowers in a unique bouquet.

Melly walked to the altar and stood nervously beside Jerry. The minister, a delightful man with thick glasses and a contagiously happy expression, read the marriage service. Jerry and Melly each read the special wording that they'd prepared for themselves, and they lit one candle together from two separate candles to signify the joining of two people into one. The final words were read. Jerry kissed the bride for so long that some members of the wedding party began to giggle. And all at once it was over and they were running down the aisle together.

Abby kept out of Cade's way at the reception, sitting aside with Jessica while they discussed modeling and clothes and the future of Jessica's boutique.

Then, all too soon, Melly was dressed in her street clothes and the happy couple rushed out the door to start on their honeymoon. Abby kissed them both and wished them well, and stood by while Melly stopped at the car to

toss her wedding bouquet. Calla, dressed in gray and looking unusually sedate, caught it and blushed a flaming red—
especially when thin old Jeb, suited up in a rare concession
to civilization, looked at her and grinned.

Abby was grateful that she hadn't caught it. That would
have been the final thrust of the knife, to feel Cade's sharp
eyes on her, seeing the aching hunger she couldn't have
hidden from him.

Hours passed before the guests drifted away, and Abby
saw Jessica off with a promise to put some sketches in the
mail at her earliest opportunity. She liked Jessica very much.
And perhaps there was a way for her to accept the job. If
she moved to Wyoming, she'd be far enough away that she
wouldn't ever have to see Cade again.

Abby changed into a cotton dress with gold patterning
that complemented her pinned-up blond hair and sat down
at the supper table expecting to eat alone. It was a surprise
when Cade walked into the dining room, wearing a white
shirt and blue blazer with dark slacks. He looked impossibly handsome, and as elegant as anything New York might
produce.

"Ain't we pretty, though?" Calla murmured, eyeing him
as she began to serve the food.

"We shore is," he returned, pursing his lips at her gray
dress, which she hadn't changed. "I noticed the way Jeb was
looking at you." His eyes narrowed. "Did you bake me another cherry cake and give it to him again?"

The older woman flushed and scowled all at once. "You
hush, or I'll burn your supper. You know I gave him the
cake on account of he bailed me out when I burned the supper I was cooking for those ranchers you invited here! And
what are you doing back here with roundup in full swing? I

thought you'd be heading for the hills the minute the words were spoke."

"I live here," he reminded her.

"Could have fooled me," she muttered, waddling out of the room.

Abby fixed her coffee and kept her eyes on her plate. She was still smarting from the ugly remark Cade had made earlier.

"Since we're not speaking, shall I ask Calla to ask you to pass me the salt?" Cade asked coolly.

She handed it over, setting it down before he could take it from her.

"Who was the redheaded Amazon you couldn't part company with?" he asked.

She didn't like the bite in his tone, but it was none of his business who Jessica was. "Another model," she lied, staring at him.

His face hardened. "A successful one, judging by that mink and the Lincoln," he remarked. He smiled bitterly. "Or is she being kept by some man?"

Abby slammed her napkin down by her plate and got up. "Eat by yourself. I can't stand any more of your self-righteousness!"

"You can't stand ordinary people, either, can you?" he challenged. "You walked right past Essie Johnson, and you grew up with her. She wasn't good enough for your exalted company, no doubt, being a simple rancher's wife and all."

That cut to the quick. How could he think her so heartless when in fact she'd gone out of her way to find Essie at the reception and had apologized for what might have appeared to be a snub?

"Think what you like—you will anyway," she said and walked out of the room.

During the week that followed, Cade made himself scarce. Abby spent her lonely days answering correspondence, putting records into the computer, ordering supplies and answering the phone. If she'd had any hopes that Cade might decide to ask her to stay, they were destroyed by his very indifference. He didn't seem to care whether she spoke to him or not, and while he was courteous, he wasn't the friendly, teasing man of happier times.

The Thursday night before Melly and Jerry were due back on Friday, Abby wandered out by the swimming pool, lost in memory.

Her eyes narrowed on the bare concrete—it was still too early in the year to fill the pool, so it was empty. It seemed a hundred years ago that she'd defiantly stripped off her clothes and gone swimming in it, a lifetime since Cade had found her here half-nude. She'd been hopeful then. She'd had dreams of sharing more than a bed with him. But he'd gently pushed her away. And he hadn't let her come close again, except briefly and physically.

"Remembering, Abby?" Cade asked quietly, coming up behind her from the house.

He was wearing slacks and a burgundy knit shirt that made him look darker and more formidable than ever. His hair was damp, as if he'd showered, and he made Abby's heart race.

She glanced away from his probing gaze. "I was just getting some air, Cade," she murmured.

"The kids come home tomorrow," he remarked carelessly, although the look in his eyes was anything but careless. "I suppose you'll be leaving shortly?"

That hurt. It was as though he couldn't wait to be rid of her, and she felt the hot threat of tears. She shrugged. "I have commitments. I told you that when I first got here."

He nodded. He held a smoking cigarette in his hand, but he gave it a hard glare and tossed it to the ground and crushed it under his boot.

"You smoke too much," she observed.

He laughed shortly. "I know. I hate the damned things, but it's a habit of long standing."

Like pushing me away, she thought, but didn't speak. Her eyes scanned the starry sky and she wrapped her arms tight around the little blue dress she was wearing.

"Cold, honey?" he asked gently.

She shook her head. "Not very. Calla and Jeb have gone to a movie," she said for no reason.

"And that means that we're alone in the house, doesn't it?" he said. His eyes narrowed. "What do you want me to do about it, Abby, carry you up those stairs to my bedroom, the way I did once before?" He laughed bitterly. "Sorry, honey, I stopped giving lessons that day by the river. Maybe you can find somebody in New York to take over where I left off."

It was like being cut to pieces. "Maybe I can," she said in a taut voice. She turned. "It's late. I'd better go in."

He caught her arm hesitantly, and that puzzled her. He didn't pull her closer, but held her just at his side. "Were you hoping I might come out here?"

She had been, but she would have died rather than admit it now. "I told you before, I'm through throwing myself at your feet, Cade," she replied calmly. "Don't worry, you're perfectly safe. You can always lock your bedroom door, can't you?"

"Stop that. It's nothing to joke about."

"I wasn't joking." She tugged her arm free. "Good night, Cade."

"Talk to me, damn it!" he burst out.

"About what?" she shot back. "About my bad manners,

my sickening career or my loose morals, all of which you seem to think I enjoy!"

He stiffened. "I've never accused you of having loose morals."

"Except when I come anywhere near you," she said with a bitter laugh.

"You won't try to see my side of it," he ground out. "You're just playing games, but I'm not. I'm too old for it."

"Excuse me, grandpa, I'll try not to unsettle you... Cade!"

He jerked her against him and his hands hurt where they gripped her arms. "I want you," he said under his breath. "Don't tempt me. I'm very nearly at the end of my patience as it is. I want you away from Painted Ridge before I do something I don't want to do."

Her lips trembled. "You think I'd let you?" she whispered.

His eyes met hers. "I know you would, and so do you. We go off like dynamite when we start touching each other." His hands dropped. "But it isn't enough. I want more than a feverish night of physical satisfaction. You'd give me that, and I'd give it back. But it's nothing I couldn't have from any of a dozen women," he added coldly. "And it's not going to happen—if you get out of here in time."

It was a warning that she was willing to heed. A night with Cade would make it impossible for her to live without him, and she was wise enough to realize it. She dropped her eyes.

"I'll arrange to go Saturday morning," she said.

His face hardened at her subdued tone, but he only nodded. "It's for the best. You came to me hurt, and I hope I've helped you to heal. But your world isn't mine. The longer you stay, the harder it gets...."

He didn't finish it. Instead he lit another cigarette. "You'd better go in. It is getting cold out here."

"Arctic," she mused, glancing up at him. She gathered her poise and her pride and smiled grimly as she brushed past him and went back inside. She moved quickly, grateful that he couldn't see the tears that slid down her cheeks as she went up the stairs. They made her oblivious to the dark eyes that followed her almost worshipfully until she was out of sight.

MELLY AND JERRY came home looking tanned and rested from their Florida vacation and blissfully happy with each other. Abby could hardly bear their happiness, since it reminded her so graphically that she'd lost every chance of having any of her own with Cade.

"How's everything going here?" Melly asked when they were alone, Jerry having ridden up into the hills to help with roundup.

"Just fine," Abby lied, "but I've had a call from my agency and there's a possibility of a long-term contract for a bottling company. I'm terribly excited about it."

Melly's face fell. "You're going back to New York? But I thought…?"

"Now that you're home, I can leave it all in your capable hands," Abby said with a forced smile. "I've missed New York, and it will be great to get back to work."

"But the attack, the reason you came here…"

"Cade helped me over it," Abby said quietly. "I'll always be grateful to him for that. But he wants no part of me—he's made that quite clear. I'm going to do him a favor and go away."

"He loves you, you stupid idiot!" Melly burst out.

Abby flinched and tears welled up in her eyes. "No!"

she said huskily. "If he feels anything, it's anger because I preferred modeling to ranch life."

"Have you talked to him, at least?"

"Sure," Abby agreed, not adding that they'd argued every second they were together. "We've both agreed that I have no place in his life, or he in mine." She turned around and walked toward the stairs. "I'm going to pack. Want to help me? I've made reservations on a plane in the morning."

"Oh, Abby, don't do it!" Melly pleaded.

But all her pleading and all her reasoning didn't sway her stubborn sister. The next morning Cade drove the two women out to the airport.

It had been a shock to find him at the wheel of the big sedan when it pulled up at the front door. He was wearing the same navy blazer and dark slacks he'd worn the other night at supper, but he had a striped blue tie over his white silk shirt. The only Western thing about him was his dressy cream Stetson and leather boots.

Her flight was being called as they walked into the terminal, and Abby hugged Melly quickly, suitcase in hand, before she boarded the plane. Tears welled up in her eyes.

"Write to me," she pleaded.

"I will," Melly promised. Her eyes narrowed. "I wish you wouldn't go."

"I have to. I have commitments." She told the lie with panache and a faint smile.

Cade didn't say a word. He stood looking down at her with eyes so dark they seemed black, a smoking cigarette in one hand, his face like flint.

Abby forced herself to look up at him. She was wearing shoes with only tiny heels, and he was taller than ever. Bigger. The most impossibly handsome man she'd ever known, and her heart ached just at the sight of him.

"Bye, Cade," she said quietly. "Thanks for letting me stay so long."

He only nodded. His chest rose and fell heavily, quickly, and his lips were set in a thin line.

"Well… I'd better go," Abby said in a high-pitched tone.

Cade threw the cigarette into one of the sand-filled ashtrays and abruptly reached for Abby, crushing her against the length of his body. The suitcase fell and she struggled helplessly for a moment, until he subdued her with nothing more than his firm hold.

She stared into his fierce eyes and stopped fighting, and they looked at each other in a tense, painful exchange that made Abby's knees feel as though they would fold under her. Her lips parted on a sobbing breath, and he bent his head.

It was like no kiss they'd ever shared. His mouth eased down over hers so softly she hardly felt it, and then it moved harder and deeper and slower and rougher until she moaned and reached up, clinging to his neck. He lifted her against him, still increasing the pressure of his arms, his mouth, until she felt as if they were burning into each other, fusing a bond nothing would ever sever. She wanted him. She wanted him! Her mouth, her body, her aching moan told him so, and she could feel the tremor of his own body as the kiss went on and on.

Finally, slowly, he eased her back down onto the floor and breath by breath took his mouth away. His arms slackened and withdrew, although his steely hands held her until she was steady again.

His eyes searched hers. "Goodbye, Abby," he said in a voice like steel.

"Goodbye, Cade," she whispered brokenly.

He brushed his fingers against her cheek, unsteady fin-

gers that touched her as if she'd already become a beautiful illusion. "My God, how I could have loved you!" he
breathed. And then, before she could believe her own ears,
he turned and strode quietly away, without once looking
back.

Abby stared after him, uncomprehending. "Did...did I
just hear what I thought I heard?" she murmured.

"What, honey?" Melly asked gently, coming back within
earshot. "I was being discreet. Gosh, what a kiss that was!
And you're leaving?"

Abby sighed bitterly. Surely she'd dreamed it, or mis-
understood...or had she? She took a steadying breath. "I
have to go. I'll miss my flight. Melly, take care of him?"

"You could have done that yourself, if you'd told him the
truth," Melly said softly. "It's still not too late. You could
catch him."

"He wouldn't listen," she said wearily. "You know how
Cade is when he makes up his mind, and I've gone mad and
started hearing things again. Back to the salt mines, Melly.
I'm fine now, I'm just fine. Take care. I love you."

"I love you, too." She searched her sister's eyes. "He
couldn't have kissed you that way without caring one hell
of a lot. Think about that. Hurry now!"

Abby waved and ran for the plane. And all the way back
to New York she thought and thought about that long, hard
kiss and what she imagined Cade had said until she all but
went crazy. Finally, in desperation, she tucked the memory
in the back of her mind and closed her eyes. It was over now;
he'd sent her away. Looking back was no good at all. She'd
had time to recuperate and get herself back together. Now
she had to put Montana and Cade behind her and start over.
She could do it. After all, her career was all she had left.

CHAPTER ELEVEN

IT TOOK SEVERAL days for Abby to adjust to city life again after the wide-open country of Montana. Accustomed to staying up late at the ranch, she now had to go to bed early, watch her diet, be concerned with shadows and lines of weariness, add to her wardrobe and pack her huge handbag with the dozens of items she might need for an assignment. And every night she soaked her aching feet and smothered herself in cold cream and longed for Cade McLaren with every cell in her body.

She did Jessica's sketches in the weeks that followed and mailed them to Wyoming. Jessica phoned her shortly afterward and invited her out to see the boutique, but Abby had to put her off. She was working feverishly, and the lie she'd told Melly about the bottling company commercials had been amazingly prophetic. She was offered a television commercial for a soft drink company, which she immediately accepted. Her career was skyrocketing. And it was as empty as her life.

She didn't even bother dating other men. What was the use, when all she could do was compare them to Cade. So she worked and grieved for him, and before very long the toll of loneliness began to show on her.

All the years before, she'd had that sweet memory of him to sustain her, and the hope that someday things might change. But now there was no hope left. There was nothing to cling to, only a future that was empty and lonely. Even if she accepted Jessica's offer and went to live in Wyoming, she might be near Cade but she'd still be alone. She didn't know how she was going to bear it.

Late on Friday night, she was halfheartedly watching television when the phone rang. She couldn't imagine who it could be at that hour, and she was frowning when she picked up the receiver.

"Hello?" she murmured.

"Hello, honey," came a deep, painfully familiar voice. She sat down, paling. It had been almost four months since she'd last heard that particular voice, but she would have known it on her deathbed.

"Cade?" she whispered shakily.

"Yes." There was a pause. "How are you, Abby?"

She drew in a slow breath. Don't panic, she told herself, don't give yourself away. "I'm just fine, Cade," she said brightly.

"No date on a Friday night?" he murmured.

She drew her gold caftan closer around her, as if he could see her all the way from Montana. "I was tired," she replied. "Is everything all right? Melly…?"

"Melly's fine. She and Jerry are down at Yellowstone for the weekend."

"Oh." She gripped the receiver tightly. "Then nothing's wrong?"

"Everything's wrong," he said after a minute. "Hank's quitting."

"Hank!" She sat straight up. "Why?"

He laughed mirthlessly. "He says I'm too damned mean to stay around."

"Are you?" she asked softly. There was something

strange about his voice, different. "Cade, are you all right?" she asked, and the concern seeped through.

"I'm...fine." He laughed again. "I'll be finer when I get through this bottle."

"You're drinking!" It was the only thing that could explain the way he sounded.

"Are you shocked? I'm human, Abby, although you sure as hell never thought I was, did you?" There was a thud and a muffled curse. "Damn, why does furniture have to sprout legs when you try to go around it?"

She wrapped the telephone cord around her fingers. "Cade, is someone there with you? Calla?"

"Calla's gone to a movie with Jeb. Any day now I expect to be asked to the wedding." He sighed. "Abby, before long you and I are going to be the only two single people on earth."

"Why are you drinking?" she asked, worried. "You haven't gotten hurt, have you?"

"You're a hell of a person to ask me that," he growled. "You cut the heart out of me when you got on that damned plane. Just the way you cut it out when you got on the bus four years ago. Oh, God, Abby, I miss you!" he ground out, his voice throbbing with emotion. "I miss you!"

Tears burst from her eyes and rolled down her cheeks. "I miss you, too," she whispered. Her eyes closed and she bit her lip. "Every hour of every day."

There was a long, deep sigh from the other end of the line. "We should have made love that day by the river," he said achingly. "Maybe we would have gotten each other out of our systems. I've got a picture of you by my bed, Abby. I sit here and look at it and ache all over."

Her fingers clenched until the blood went out of them. She had one of him, too, that she'd carried to New York with her four years before. It was wrinkled from being hugged against her heart.

"You're the one who told me sex was a bad foundation to build on," she reminded him wearily.

"It wasn't just sex," he said. "It's never been that. Four years ago, I couldn't risk getting you pregnant, don't you see? I couldn't take the choice away from you. To hell with how I felt, I couldn't force you to stay here, Abby."

Her breath caught in her throat. She caught the receiver with both hands and sat as still as a poker. Did he even realize what he was admitting?

"You…you thought that given the choice between you and modeling…"

"You showed me which was more important, didn't you, honey?" he asked with a bitter laugh. He sighed heavily. "You got on that bus, laughing like a freed prisoner, and you never even looked at me. I told your father I'd marry you, if you'd have me, and we fought it out half the night. He said you were too young and you wanted a chance to get away from the ranch, to be somebody. I argued with him then, but when it came down to it, I couldn't make you stay with me." His voice was faintly slurred, but just as beautiful as ever, and Abby was hurting in ways she'd never dreamed she could. "You see, I'd already realized how vulnerable you were with me. And I was just as vulnerable with you. I had to be careful not to come too close, Abby, because we could have gotten in over our heads. I figured you'd go to New York and get tired of the city and come back to me. But you didn't."

There was a world of emotion in those words. Bitterness. Hopelessness. Hurt.

"You never asked me to stay," she whispered. "You said

you didn't want a commitment to any woman, a...a leash on your freedom."

He laughed. "I haven't been free since you were fifteen years old. I've never wanted anyone else. I never will."

"You let me go!" she burst out, suddenly hating him. "Damn you, you let me go! I was only eighteen, but there was nothing New York had to offer that could have torn me away from you if you'd just told me to stay! One lousy word, just one word—stay. And you let me go, Cade!"

There was a shocked pause on the other end of the line, a silence like darkness in a graveyard.

But she didn't notice. The words were tumbling out of her, while tears burned down her cheeks. "I loved the glamour, you said, I couldn't live without the city! And all I've done for four years is stare at this picture of you and cry my eyes out! You put me on a bus four years ago, and you put me on a plane four months ago...damn you, what do you care? You push me away, you accuse me of teasing you, you... Cade? Cade!"

But the line was dead. She slammed the receiver down and burst into tears. If he called back, she wasn't even going to answer. Let him sit and drown in his whiskey. She didn't care! She turned off the lights and went to bed in a fit of furious temper.

Several hours later, she sat straight up in bed as the doorbell rang and rang and rang. Maybe she was dreaming it. It had taken her forever to get to sleep, and she was still drowsy. She laid her head back on the pillow, but there it came again, even more insistently.

Frowning sleepily, she padded to the front door of her apartment with her gold caftan swirling around her.

"Who is it?" she grumbled.

"Who the hell do you think? Open the door, or do I have to break it down?"

"Cade?" Her heart jumped wildly and she fumbled the catch and the safety latch off and opened the door. And it was no dream.

He came into the apartment with a scowl as black as thunder on his dark face, looking sleepy and tired and worn-out. He was wearing jeans and a half-open denim shirt, and old boots and the battered brown ranch hat he wore to work cattle. His boots were dusty, his face needed a shave and he was altogether the most beautiful sight Abby had seen in her life.

"Cade!" she breathed, blinking up at him out of sleepy eyes, her tangled hair glorious in its disarray, the caftan clinging lovingly and quite revealingly to every line of her body.

"I've had half a bottle of whiskey," he said, towering over her with the locked door behind him. "And I'm not quite sober yet, despite the three cups of black coffee I had on the plane. But you said something to me that I'm sure I really heard and didn't dream, and I flew up here to let you say it again. Just to make sure."

She stared at him unblinkingly, loving every unshaven plane of his face.

"You hung up the phone and got on a plane in the middle of the night...?" she began nervously.

His eyes roamed down her body and one dark eyebrow arched curiously. "You've lost weight, Abigail," he murmured, studying her. "A lot of it, and you look like pure hell."

"Have you seen yourself in a mirror?" she countered, noticing new lines, new shadows under his dark eyes.

He shook his head. "Couldn't stand the sight of myself," he admitted. "Come on, Abby, let's hear it."

She swallowed. "It was easier when you were still in Montana," she began nervously.

"I guess it was." He took off his hat and tossed it onto a chair. His big hands framed her face and he looked down at it like a starving man. "Suppose I take you to bed, Abby?" he asked softly. "And after we've made love for three or four hours, I'll ask you again."

CHAPTER TWELVE

SHE COULD BARELY breathe when she saw what was in his eyes. It was hardly possible that she was dreaming, but it was so much like a dream come true that she felt faint.

"Look at me, Abby," he whispered.

She raised her eyes and his gaze fell to the transparent material over her firm, high breasts. He reached out and drew his knuckles down from her collarbone over one perfect breast, and he smiled at her body's helpless reaction to his touch, at the hunger he could see and feel.

"Same damned thing happens to me every time I think about you," he murmured with a soft, deep laugh. "Four months, Abby. Four long months, and I've walked around aching every minute of every day, wanting you until I was like a wounded bear with everyone around me. Tonight I'd had all I could take, I couldn't even get properly drunk… damn you, come here!"

He lifted her in his hard arms, taking her mouth with a hungry, aching thoroughness, ignoring her sweet moan of pleasure and her clinging arms as he walked back into her bedroom and slammed the door behind them.

"I'm going to make love to you all night long," he said as he carried her straight toward the bed. "In the morning, you'll be damned lucky if you can walk at all. Then we'll talk."

"Cade, I could get pregnant!" she said in a high-pitched tone, afraid that it was only the liquor talking.

"Yes, you could," he said quietly, staring into her eyes. "And that would mean total commitment. To me. For life. Say yes or no. But if it's no, I'm going straight back to Montana, and I'll never come near you again."

She felt her body trembling in his strong embrace, and her heart yielded totally as she searched his face with a loving, possessive gaze.

"I don't know if I can survive an affair with you," she said softly. "But if that's what you want, I...I can try. I just don't understand what we'd do about a child...."

He breathed slowly, deliberately, and his eyes softened. "Melly said you were blind about me. I suppose she knew better than I did," he murmured. He laid her gently down on the bed and unbuttoned his shirt with slow, easy motions, tossing it aside. His hands went to his belt and unfastened it. His trousers followed, while Abby watched him, shocked to the bone.

"If you think it's rough on you," he muttered, glancing at her as he turned to divest himself of everything else, "remember what I told you before, Abby. I've never undressed in front of a woman."

"That's the loss of women everywhere," she whispered, awed as he turned around again. "Oh, Cade...!"

His face softened, and the red stain on his cheeks faded away. He sat down beside her, coaxing her to sit up so that he could remove the caftan. And then he just looked and looked, until she felt her heart trembling wildly, her body helplessly arching in invitation, moving restlessly under the pure sensuality of the appraisal.

"Before this goes any further," he said quietly, sliding a big, warm hand over her smooth belly, up to rest maddeningly below one taut breast, "you'd better tell me if you meant what you said on the phone."

She swallowed. "About being lonely and lost in the city?" she whispered.

He nodded. "Are you happy?"

"When I'm with you," she managed through trembling lips. "Only when I'm with you. Oh, God, you don't know... you'll never know how it was to leave you!"

His fingers trembled and he searched for his voice. "I know how it was to be left, Abby," he said slowly. "I've been walking around like half a man for four years. And until tonight, I had no idea, no idea at all what you felt."

"How could I tell you, when you kept going on about not wanting a commitment, not wanting marriage?" she asked unsteadily. "You pushed me away...."

"I had to," he ground out. "I can't control what I feel for you, I never could. You'll never know how close I came to taking you the night I found you by the pool. When I left you I was shaking like a boy. I had to drink myself to sleep—the only other time I've been at the bottle like I have tonight." His fingers moved up to her breasts, touching them like a man touching a treasure trove. "So beautiful," he whispered. "You were then, you are now. My Abby. My own."

Abby's hands reached up and stroked his chest, tickling as they pressed into the tangle of dark hair. "I never knew," she whispered.

"Neither did I." He shuddered as her hands caressed him. "Don't do that, not yet. I go crazy when you touch me that way."

"You said we were going to make love," she reminded him softly.

"We are. When you agree to marry me," he said quietly.

"I couldn't handle an affair with you, either. If I take you, you take me for life."

It was important to know the truth, not just guess at it. There had been too much misunderstanding already. "Because you need sons to inherit Painted Ridge?" she asked in a whisper.

"Because I love you, Abigail Shane," he corrected breathlessly. "Because I've loved you for so many years that loving you is a way of life for me. Because if you don't come home with me, I'll pack my bags and move in with you and make love to you until you'll marry me in self-defense, just to get some rest."

Tears welled up in her wide brown eyes as they searched his. "You love me, Cade?" she burst out.

"What a mild word for so much feeling," he managed in a voice that shook. His hands framed her face, and his eyes worshipped it. "I want to be with you all the time. I want to sit and watch you when we're together. I want to stay by your bed when you're sick and you need me. I want to hold you in my arms in bed at night, even when we don't make love. I want to give you children. Most of all, I want to live with you until I die. All the good days and bad. All the way to the grave."

She was crying helplessly at his admission, at having all her wildest dreams come true. Her fingers moved up to his hard face and lovingly traced every warm inch of it. "I couldn't look at you when I got on the bus four years ago," she said brokenly, "because if I had, I would have thrown myself at your feet and begged you to let me stay. I started loving you when I was barely fifteen, and I've loved you every day since. Hopelessly, with all my heart. Oh, God, Cade, it was never New York and modeling. It was you! I love you until I hurt all over! I'll love you all my life, all the days I live…!"

He stopped the frantic words with his mouth and eased down beside her. They kissed slowly, sweetly, rocking in each other's warm arms, savoring the newness of belonging to each other, of shared loving. Until his tongue gently penetrated her mouth. Until her lips opened to its deep searching. Until they moved, together, slowly, into a new and shattering kind of intimacy with each other.

"Teach me how, Cade," she whispered with love splintering her voice as she felt his hands touching her in new ways. "Teach me how…to show love…this way."

His mouth gentled hers. "We'll learn it together, honey," he whispered back. "Because this is like my first time, too. Tell me if I hurt you. I'd rather die than hurt you now."

But even as he spoke, his mouth was moving against her body, and she forgot that it was the first time, she forgot everything but the glory of being kissed and touched so tenderly by the only man she'd ever loved. She relaxed and moved deliberately, touched deliberately, delighting in his reactions to her fingers, her mouth. She whispered her love; her body shouted it.

Sensation piled on sensation, while she turned and arched and whispered wildly into his ear as he moved against her so slowly, with such staggering control. She could barely believe that the level of pleasure she was experiencing was bearable as it mounted and mounted and began to possess her.

Her eyes opened on a surge of mingled need and fear, and his were open, too, staring back at her.

"Don't be afraid of me," he whispered shakenly, urgently. "I love you. Trust me."

It was all she needed to push her over the edge. Her eyes

closed again, and she felt his mouth gentling hers, preparing her for what was coming.

Her hands tangled in his thick, dark hair as his body slowly, tenderly, overwhelmed hers. His mouth was gentle, despite the need she could feel in him, a need he was deliberately denying for her sake. The very tenderness of his movements, his slow, soft kisses, made it so beautiful that she forgot her fear and gave herself up to the incredible intimacy of belonging to him.

If there was pain, she hardly noticed it, so involved was she in trying to get closer to him, trying to please him as he was pleasing her. She wanted nothing more than the joy of giving everything she had to give.

He cherished her as she'd never dreamed a man could cherish a woman, every second fueling the hunger and the sweetness of sharing love. She clung to him, loving him, loving him! And it was so easy. So perfect. So beautiful. Her eyes burned with tears that rolled helplessly down her cheeks into their joined mouths. A moment later she heard his voice in her ear, whispering words that only vaguely registered, whispering her name like a litany.

And from tenderness came passion—suddenly, like a summer storm billowing over them, lifting and tossing them in a vortex of urgency that blazed brighter than the lights around them.

She heard her voice break, and felt his hands controlling her wild movements firmly, guiding, teaching. Her teeth bit into his hard shoulder in an agony of pleasure, so exquisite that she cried out. And then there was no more time for the gentle beginnings, only for the wild, furious stretch toward fulfillment that sent them crashing together in frantic torment, trembling wildly, whispering urgently until there was oneness. And then peace.

Later, she curled up against him, trembling, while he lit a cigarette and smoked it. She laughed softly, triumphantly, delightedly.

His arm drew her closer, and he chuckled softly, too. "My God, in all my wildest dreams I never imagined feeling like that."

"Neither did I," she returned. "I thought I'd died."

His chest rose and fell heavily. "I'm going to have that book framed and hung over our bed after we're married."

She blinked. "Book?"

He chuckled wickedly. "There's this book about making love that I bought a few weeks ago," he murmured. He lifted his brows at her stunned expression and laughed uproariously. "Well, hell, Abby, I told you I spent half my life working with the damned cattle? Where did you expect me to learn about sex? You women, always expecting men to know all the answers and hating us for the way we get them...."

Her face brightened with wonder. "Why, you old devil," she said. "And I thought you had a string of women a mile long!"

He kissed her nose. "You're my woman. The only one I ever wanted. I haven't been a monk, but there was never any joy for me in sleeping with women I didn't even like."

She stared up at him curiously. "You mean, you learned everything you just did to me out of a book?"

His eyebrows arched. "It was a good book," he said defensively, "kind of a primer...well, damn it, I thought that after I gave you a while to think about me and the ranch, and maybe miss me, I might come up here and try to change your mind. I was going to wait until Christmas...." He shrugged his powerful shoulders. "Then tonight, after Calla went out with Jeb, I got lonely and started drinking." He sighed. "First time I've put away that much whiskey in years." He looked down at her radiant face. "When you started ranting and raving at me, it was the sweetest music I'd ever heard. I didn't even take time to shave, I just got Hank out of bed to drive me to the airport."

"You said he was quitting!"

"When he found out I was on my way to you, he took back his resignation," Cade said, grinning. "Told me he had wondered if I planned to stay stupid all my life."

"I think we were both a little dense," she replied. Her eyes devoured him. "I love you," she whispered intensely.

"I love you," he replied, bending to kiss her softly, slowly, with tender promise. "Can you live with me on Painted Ridge and give up all you've accomplished? If not, I'll compromise, now that I know you love me."

"I could give up breathing if you'll make love to me every night," she murmured, pressing close. "I hate it here. After the first few months, all the glamour and adventure wore off. I worked like a zombie all day and dreamed all night about how it would be to sleep in your arms and carry your child in my body…."

He drew in a sharp breath. "Don't say things like that to me, I'll go crazy."

"Take me with you," she said, brushing her hand over his chest and smiling when he trembled. "Let's go together."

"In a minute." He put out the cigarette and leaned over her, his eyes solemn. "I can't expect you to sacrifice four years of hard work just to raise children. I don't want you to give up being a person just because you're my wife. We all need to feel fulfillment, a sense of purpose."

"Oh, my gosh, I didn't ever tell you about Jessica Dane!" she burst out, and explained it all, even her behavior at the reception.

He sighed angrily. "Well, I was a damned fool over that, wasn't I?" he ground out. He kissed her gently. "I'm sorry, honey."

"It's all right. You didn't know." She touched his mouth. "So you see, I could work for Jessica and never leave the house except to supervise some seamstresses once in a while. And I've always preferred designing to modeling, anyway."

"Lucky me," he said. He grinned. "If we have little girls, you can make party dresses for them, too."

She laughed. "Not for the little boys, though. I don't want my sons parading around in petticoats." She leaned forward and kissed him lazily. "My throat's sore from talking. Teach me some more things you learned in that book of yours."

He chuckled. "There's just one more little thing to talk about. I had Hank promise to make a few phone calls for me after daylight."

"Did you?" she murmured, nibbling at his lips.

"I had him invite the minister over for next Saturday."

"That's nice," she whispered. Her hands smoothed over his long, tanned body.

"Plus about fifty other people."

"Um," she murmured. Her hands moved to his hair-roughened chest and she pressed against him. "That's nice, too."

"For the wedding."

She drew away. "Next Saturday?"

"Why wait?" he asked, biting at her mouth. "I sure was hoping you'd say yes, Abby. All the way here I had nightmares about trying to line up a bride and groom at such short notice if you refused me...."

"Cade Alexander McLaren, what am I going to do with you?" she asked sharply.

"Lie down here and I'll show you," he murmured with a laugh, easing her onto her back. "This is the best chapter of all...."

Abby smiled as she met his hungry mouth. When they got home to Painted Ridge, she had some heavy reading to do.

* * * * *

DARLING ENEMY

CHAPTER ONE

IT WAS THE most glorious kind of morning, and Teddi White-hall leaned dreamily on the windowsill of the dormitory room overlooking the courtyard below, watching the pigeons waddle like old men over the cobblestones.

The buildings on college campus were romantically Gothic, like something out of another century. But its green and flowering grounds were what Teddi liked most. They were a welcome change from the sophisticated New York apartment where she had to spend her holidays.

She leaned her face on her crossed arms with a sigh and drank in the smells and sounds of the early morning. She dreaded the time when she'd have to board the plane back to New York, away from the exclusive Connecticut college and her friend and roommate Jenna. There was a chill in the June air, and the beige gown that complemented Teddi's short dark hair and huge brown eyes was hardly proof against it. It was a good thing that Jenna had already gone downstairs, she thought, and couldn't chide her about her impulsiveness in throwing open the window.

Jenna wasn't impulsive. In that, she was like her older brother. Teddi shivered delicately. Just the thought of Kingston Devereaux was enough to cause that reaction. They'd clashed from the very beginning. The big rancher with his Australian drawl and cutting smile might have sent the other girls in the dormitory into swoons, but he only made

Teddi want to turn away. He'd made his contempt for her
more than evident during the years she'd been friends with
his sister. And it was all because of a false impression he
had, which nothing she said could change. His snap judgments were as unfair as his treatment of Teddi, and she
dreaded visits to the Canadian ranch with Jenna. Teddi had
an uncomfortable feeling that Jenna was getting ready to
spring another invitation on her, since they were both free
until fall quarter began. Kingston Devereaux would fly his
plane over from Calgary to get Jenna, and Teddi would find
excuses to avoid him...as usual.

She shook her head miserably. At least Jenna had a
mother and brother to go home to. Teddi had no one. Her
aunt, who was her only living relative, was somewhere on
the Riviera with her latest lover. The New York apartment
Teddi shared with her on holidays was going to be particularly empty now. At least there would be plenty of modeling offers forthcoming, she was assured of that. She'd been
modeling since her fifteenth birthday. She was blessed with
good bone structure and eyes so large and poignant that one
of her boyfriends had likened them to a doe's. The modeling agency that handled her was proud of its star client—if
they had a complaint, it was that she was being wasted in
the halls of academia.

She felt suddenly chilled to the bone and drew back
into the room, closing the window with nervous hands.
Modeling was the sore spot with Kingston, who had the
immutable opinion that models and virtue didn't mix. It
hadn't helped that Teddi's aunt was notorious for her affairs.
Kingston was an old-fashioned man with narrow-minded
views on modern permissiveness. He might have an affair
himself, but he had nothing but contempt for women who
indulged. And he was certain Teddi did.

She'd never forgotten her introduction to him. She'd met Jenna at boarding school when she was just fifteen, and the two girls had become fast friends. She'd expected Jenna's family to be equally friendly and caring, and had received the shock of her young life when Kingston Devereaux had shown up at Christmas to fly Jenna home to the ranch outside Calgary for the holidays.

His first reaction to Teddi had been strangely hostile, a long, lingering appraisal that had touched Teddi like a cold finger against her bare skin. Jenna's gay announcement that she'd invited Teddi for the holidays had been met with a cold, gray glare and a reluctant acceptance that had spoiled the trip for her. She'd done everything but move outside to keep out of the big man's way. Then, and since.

She shook off the memories along with her gown, and slipped into a silky beige pantsuit that her aunt had mailed to her for Easter—one of a number of presents that were supposed to take the place of love and affection. Teddi ran a comb through her short, thick hair and decided against makeup. Her complexion was naturally olive, her lips had a color all their own, and her long-lashed eyes never needed enhancing. She slipped into a pair of low-heeled shoes and went downstairs to find Jenna, idly wondering why her roommate had rushed out in the first place.

She started into the dormitory lounge and stopped, frozen, in the doorway. Jenna was sitting stiffly on the couch, facing a big, elegantly dressed man with gold-streaked blond hair.

"…And I said no," Kingston Devereaux stated flatly, his back to the doorway, his Australian accent thick. "She's not going to turn my damned cattle station upside down again the way she did at Easter. Can you see the men getting any work done? Hell, they do nothing but stare at her."

"She won't cause any trouble," Jenna retorted in defense of her friend, venom in her normally sweet tone. Her gray eyes, so much like Kingston's, were flashing with anger. "King, she's nothing like her aunt, she's not what you think…!"

"Too right, baby, she isn't rich, and she's never going to be, unless she can get her claws into some poor, trusting male." He rammed his big hands into the pockets of his slacks, stretching the expensive gray fabric across his flat stomach, his powerful, broad thighs. "Well, she isn't going to spend the summer making cow's eyes at my men—or at me," he added with a bitter laugh.

Teddi, listening, blushed. That Easter vacation had haunted her.

"King!" Jenna gasped. "You must know that Teddi's frightened of you, you've made sure of it. She'd never…"

"Wouldn't she?" he growled. "Surely you noticed the way she stared at me during Easter? An Easter I'd have preferred spending alone with my family," he added with a cruel smile. "Mother should have had another daughter to keep you company, then maybe you wouldn't spend your life picking up strays!"

Teddi's face went white. She stood there like a wounded little animal, her huge eyes misty with the hurt, and Kingston turned at that moment and saw her. The expression on his broad, hard face was almost comical.

"Oh, Teddi," Jenna wailed, grimacing as she, too, caught sight of her and realized that her friend had heard every harsh word of the conversation.

Teddi straightened proudly. "Hello, Jenna," she said softly. "I—I just wondered if you wanted to have breakfast with me. I'll be at the dining hall."

"King came early," Jenna said helplessly, with a shrug. "We were talking about vacation."

"You'll enjoy yours, I'm sure," Teddi said, forcing a smile to her full, faintly pouting lips. "I'll go ahead…"

"I want you to come to the ranch for the summer," Jenna said with a defiant glance at Kingston.

"No, thanks," Teddi said quietly.

"King won't even be there part of the time," the smaller girl said sharply, tossing her long, pale blond hair.

Teddi glanced at the taciturn rancher, whose jaw was clenched taut. "I've spent quite enough of my holidays being treated like an invading disease," she said deliberately. "I'd rather spend this one alone, and I'm sure your brother will be delighted to have his family to himself," she added venomously.

"Teddi—" Jenna began.

"I've got modeling assignments lined up, anyway," Teddi added truthfully with a last, killing glare at Kingston as she turned. "Why spend my vacation on a ranch when I can seduce half the men in New York while I make my fortune?" Her lower lip was trembling, but no one could see it now. "Thanks anyway, Jenna, thanks a lot. You can't help it that you've got an insufferable snob for a brother!"

And on that defiant note, she stormed out of the dormitory into the sunshine, her back rigid, the tears welling up in her smoldering eyes.

She walked over the cobblestones numbly, the tears coming in hot abundance, trickling down into her mouth. How could he be so cruel, how could he? The conceited ass! As if any woman would be stupid enough to get herself emotionally involved with that arrogant Australian…the gall of him to accuse her of making cow's eyes at him! She flushed at the memory. He'd never let her live down her foolish behavior at Easter; if only she'd realized that he was teasing....

She fished in her pocket for a tissue. As usual, there wasn't one. She brushed the back of her hand angrily across her cheeks, hating her own weakness. She'd write to Jenna, he couldn't stop her from doing that, and they'd be together when the fall quarter started. Kingston couldn't keep them from being friends, after all. He'd never had a chance once they'd enrolled at the same college.

She passed a couple of her classmates and tried to smile a greeting just as a lean, commanding hand caught her arm and jerked her around, marching her to the shade of a nearby oak.

"Running again?" Kingston Devereaux asked curtly, his glittering eyes biting into hers. "You've done a lot of that."

"Self-preservation, Mr. Devereaux," she replied coldly, brushing wildly at one stray tear. "You make me forget that I'm a lady."

"A lady?" he drawled. "You?" His eyes ran down her slender body, over the high young breasts and down the tiny waist and sweetly curving hips to her long, graceful legs in their clinging cover.

"Oh, excuse me—in your exalted opinion, that's a title I don't deserve," she replied coolly.

"Too right," he ground out. He lifted his broad shoulders restlessly. "Jenna's back at the dormitory crying her damned eyes out," he added roughly. "I didn't come all this way to upset her."

"Upsetting people is one of your greatest talents," Teddi told him, glaring back.

One eyebrow went up as he studied her face. "Careful, tiger," he drawled. "I bite back."

Teddi wrapped her arms around herself, turning her attention to passing students. "You've done nothing but attack me for the past five years," she reminded him. "And for your information, Mr. Devereaux," she added hotly, "if I stared, it was out of apprehension, wondering what minute you were going to start something!"

"You started it the last time, darling," he reminded her, smiling coldly at the blush she couldn't prevent. "Didn't you?"

She didn't like being reminded of that fiasco, and her eyes told him so. She turned away.

"How long did it take you to perfect that pose of innocence?" he asked.

"Oh, years," she assured him. "I started while a baby."

He looked down his arrogant nose at her. The sunlight made gold streaks in his dark blond hair. "You didn't get to your particular rung on the modeling ladder without giving out a little, honey. You'll never convince me otherwise."

"Why bother to try?" she countered. "You're so fond of the playgirl image you've foisted on me. And you're never wrong, are you?"

"Not often," he agreed. "And never about women," he added, with just a trace of sensuality in his deep drawl.

She supposed that he'd had his share of women. Her own small experience of him had been devastating. He had an eye-catching physique and when he liked, he could be charming. Teddi, having seen him stripped to the waist more than once, couldn't find a fault in him. A picture of his bronzed, hair-roughened muscles danced in front of her eyes, and she shook her head to get that disturbing memory out of her mind. Kingston disturbed her physically, he always had, and she disliked the sensations as much as she disliked him. He was the enemy, she mustn't ever lose sight of that fact.

"You know very little about the type of modeling I do," she said numbly.

"More than you think," he corrected. "We have a mutual acquaintance."

She let that enigmatic remark fly right over her head as she started walking.

"Going somewhere?" he challenged.

"To inflict myself on someone else over breakfast," she agreed cheerfully. "Strangely enough, there are people who don't think of me as a walking, talking 8 x 10 glossy photograph."

"Fair dinkum?" he murmured, falling into step beside her.

She glared at him. "Believe what you like about me, I don't care." But of course she cared, she always had. She'd gone out of her way to try to make Kingston like her, to earn even the smallest word of praise from him. But she'd never accomplished that, and she never would.

"You can have breakfast with Jenna and me," he said after a minute, as if the words choked him. They probably had, she thought miserably.

"No, thanks," she said politely. "I can't eat wondering if you've had time to sprinkle arsenic over my bacon and eggs."

A chuckle came out of his throat, a surprising sound. "You never stop fighting me, do you?"

She shifted her shoulders lightly. "I've spent most of my life fighting."

"Poor little orphan," he murmured coldly.

She glared at him. "I loved my parents," she said curtly. "Shame on you for that."

He had the grace to look uncomfortable, but only for

an instant. "Hitting below the belt?" he asked with a lifted eyebrow.

"Just exactly that."

"I'll pull my punches next time," he assured her.

"You make it sound like a game," she grumbled.

"Oh, no, it's stopped being that," he replied, his eyes on the dining hall ahead. "It stopped being that at Easter."

She colored delicately, her eyes closing for an instant to try to blot out the memory. She hated him for reminding her of what had almost happened.

"I shouldn't have pushed you away in that stall," he said in a husky, deep whisper.

She moved jerkily away from him. "Please don't remind me of the fool I was," she said tightly, avoiding his glittering eyes. "I had you mixed up with someone else in my mind," she added to salvage what she could of her pride.

His features seemed to harden even more. "And we both know who, don't we, honey?"

She didn't understand, but was too angry to ask questions. "If you're quite through, I'm hungry."

His darkening eyes traced her face, the slender lines of her body, as if the word triggered a hunger of his own.

He moved closer and she stiffened, catching the amused, curious glances of the other students on their way to and from the dining hall. "People are staring," she murmured nervously.

"Afraid they'll think we're lovers, honey?" he asked with magnificent insolence.

She reacted without thinking, her fingers flashing up toward his hard, tanned cheek. But he caught her wrist just in time to avoid the blow, holding it firm in a steely, warm grip.

"Temper, temper," he chided, as if the flash of fury amused him. "Think of the gossip it would cause."

"As if you'd ever worry about what people thought of you," she returned hotly. "It must be nice to have enough wealth and power to be above caring."

He searched her dark, dark eyes for a long time. "Your parents were poor, weren't they?" he asked in an uncommonly quiet tone.

She flushed violently. "I loved them," she muttered. "It didn't matter."

"You push yourself way too hard for a girl your age," he said. "Who are you trying to show, Teddi? What are you trying to prove? Jenna says you're studying for a major in English—what good is that going to do you as a model?"

She tugged at his imprisoning hand. "None at all," she admitted, grinding the words out, "but it'll be great when I start teaching."

"Teaching?" He stood very still, staring down at her as if he doubted the evidence of his own ears. "You?"

"Please let me go…" she asked curtly, giving up the unequal struggle.

His fingers abruptly entwined with hers, the simple action knocking every small protest, even speech, out of her mind as he drew her along the cobblestoned path beside him. She wondered at her own uncharacteristic meekness as the unfamiliar contact made music in her blood.

"You'll come home with us," he said quietly. "The last thing you need is to be alone in that damned apartment, while your dizzy aunt bed-hops across Europe, with no one about to look after you."

She knew he disliked her aunt Dilly, he'd made no secret of the fact. She'd often thought that his dislike for her aunt had extended automatically to herself, even though she was nothing like her father's sister.

"You don't have to pretend that you care what happens to me," she said coldly. "You've already made it quite clear that you don't."

His fingers tightened. "You weren't meant to hear that," he said. He glanced down at her. "I say a hell of a lot of things to Jenna to keep the issue clouded."

She blinked up at him. "I don't understand," she murmured.

He returned her searching look with a smoldering fire deep in his gray eyes that made her feel trembly. His jaw tautened. "You never have," he ground out. "You're too damned afraid of me to try."

"I'm not afraid of you!" she said, eyes flashing.

"You are," he corrected. "Because I'd want it all, or nothing, and you know that, don't you?"

She felt her knees going weak as she stared up at him, the words only half making sense in her whirling mind. One of Teddi's friends walked past, grinning at the big, handsome man holding Teddi's hand, and King grinned back. Women loved him, their eyes openly interested, covetous. But the looks they were attracting embarrassed Teddi, and she tried to pull loose.

"Don't," King murmured, tightening his warm fingers with a wicked smile. "Don't read anything into it, it's simple self-preservation. If I hold your little hand, you can't slap me with it," he added with a chuckle.

It was one of the few times she'd ever heard him laugh when they were together, and she studied his lofty face, fascinated. She was of above average height, but King towered over her. He wasn't only tall, he was broad—like a football player.

"Like what you see?" he challenged.

"I was just thinking how big they grow them in Australia," she hedged.

"I'm Australian born," he agreed. "And you're from Georgia, aren't you? I love that accent…early plantation?"

She pouted. "I have a very nice accent. Nothing like that long, twanging drawl of yours," she countered.

"A souvenir from Queensland," he agreed without rancor.

She searched his eyes. "You spent a lot of your life there," she recalled.

He nodded. "Mother was a Canadian. When she inherited the Calgary farm, we left Australia and moved to Canada. That was before Jenna was born. Dad and I spent a lot of time traveling between the two properties, so Mother and I were little more than strangers when I was younger."

"You don't let anyone get close, do you?"

He stopped at the door of the dining hall and looked down at her. "How close do you want to get, honey— within grabbing distance of my wallet?" he asked with a cold smile.

She glared up at him. "I'm not money crazy," she said proudly. She jerked her hand out of his grasp, and this time he let it go. "I have everything I need."

"Do you really?" he retorted. "Then why do you live with your aunt—why does she have to keep you?"

She wanted to tell him that she made quite enough modeling to pay her school fees and to support herself. But she hadn't seen the sense in trying to maintain an apartment of her own when she was in school nine months out of the year. Besides, she thought bitterly, Dilly was rarely at the New York apartment these days. There was always a man….

"Think what you like," she told him. "You will, anyway."

He looked down at her quietly. "Does it bother you?"

She shrugged carelessly. "You don't really know anything about me."

His eyes dropped to her soft, full mouth. "I know that underneath that perfect bone structure and bristling pride, you burn with sweet fires when you want a man to kiss you...."

Her face flamed. She moved away as he opened the door for her, standing in such a way that she had to brush against his powerful body to enter the dining hall. She glanced up at him as she eased past, her eyes telling him reluctantly how much the contact disturbed her.

"Soft little thing, aren't you?" he asked in a deep, lazy drawl, his eyes pointedly on the high thrust of her breasts as they flattened slightly against his broad chest in passing.

Teddi was grateful that Jenna was already at a table waiting for them, so that she didn't witness the strange little scene. Jenna tended to carry teasing to an embarrassing degree.

CHAPTER TWO

BREAKFAST WAS PLEASANT. It was one of the few times Teddi could remember sitting down to eat with King when he didn't go out of his way to needle her. She had the strangest impression that their fiery relationship had undergone a change while they talked earlier. She looked into his eyes and blushed, and the reaction caused an amused glint in his own eyes.

"How soon can you girls get packed?" King asked over a final cup of coffee. At a nearby table, several female students were openly watching King with every bite, their eyes dreamy.

"I'm taking a flight to New York later this afternoon," Teddi said quickly.

King watched her, reading accurately the panic in her young face. "You and I will iron out our differences this summer," he said in a tone that made her tingle all over. "In the meantime, there's no excuse for denying Jenna your company just to spite me."

It was the truth, but part of her was afraid of what settling those differences might lead to. She was nervous of men in any physical sense, and especially of King—there were scars on her emotions that she didn't want reopened.

"I've got modeling jobs—" she began.

"You can live without them for a few weeks, surely?" he taunted. "Twenty-four-hour days are only bearable for short terms," he reminded her. "You've been holding down a night job, Jenna told me, in addition to your day courses. Quite a feat, if I remember curfew regulations."

"The gates close at midnight here," Teddi murmured. She glared at Jenna, who managed to look completely innocent.

"All the same, you could use a vacation. As long as you don't spend it mooning over me," he added.

Her eyes jerked up to find him smiling in a teasing way, his eyes kind and glittering with good humor. It surprised her into smiling back, accentuating her beauty to such a degree that King just sat and stared at her until she dropped her own gaze, embarrassed.

"Besides," King added tautly, "where else have you got to go? With that nymphomaniac of an aunt, or to an apartment alone?"

"A half hour ago, you wouldn't have cared if I'd had to shack up with a bear at the local zoo," she reminded him hotly.

He cocked an eyebrow. "As I recall, Miss Cover Girl," he murmured, "the subject of bears once got us into an interesting situation."

She went fiery red, avoiding Jenna's smiling, curious gaze. "An *un*bearable situation," she murmured, laughing when King got the pun and threw back his own head.

"Please come," Jenna added, pleading. "If you're around to chaperone me, King will let me chase Blakely all over the ranch," she laughed.

"Blakely?" King frowned. "You don't, surely, mean my livestock foreman?"

Jenna peeked at him through her lashes. "I'm interested in ranching," she murmured.

"Don't get too interested in Blakely," he warned. "I've got bigger plans for you."

"Do you always try to run people's lives?" Teddi challenged.

He looked deep into her eyes. "Look out, honey, I might fancy running yours if you aren't careful."

"I'm hardly worth notice," she reminded him. "An orphan with no connections, a background of poverty, a sordid reputation…"

"Oh, hell, shut up," he growled, getting to his feet. "I've got to have the plane serviced. You two get packed."

He stormed off. Jenna giggled openly, her eyes speculative.

"Just what is going on?" she asked Teddi. "I've never seen him off balance like that."

"I have been practicing sorcery," Teddi said in a menacing whisper. "While he wasn't looking, I slipped a potion in his coffee. Any second now, your tall, blond brother is going to turn into a short, fat frog."

Jenna burst out laughing, tears rolling down her cheeks. "Oh, I can't wait to see him," she laughed. "King, with green warts!"

Teddi laughed, too, at the absurdity of fastidious King with such an affliction. He never seemed to have a hair out of place, even when he was working with the livestock.

Hours later, they were well on the way to Calgary in King's private Piper Navajo.

"I can't wait for you to meet Blakely," Jenna told her friend. "King just hired him a couple of months ago and I got to know him when I was home for that long weekend in April."

"He must be something special," Teddi murmured.

Jenna sighed. "Oh, he is. Brown eyes and red hair and

a build like a movie star. Teddi, you'll love him…but not too much, please," she added, only half teasing. "I couldn't begin to compete with you, as far as looks go."

"Don't be silly," Teddi chided. "You're lovely."

"You're a liar, but I love you just the same," came the laughing reply. Jenna leaned back in the plush seat. "King didn't chew you up too badly, did he?" she asked after a minute. Her gray eyes met Teddi's apologetically. "I could have gone through the floor when he made that nasty remark and I saw you standing in the doorway and knew you'd heard."

"King and I have been enemies for years," Teddi reminded her friend, her dark eyes wistful. "I don't know what I did to make him dislike me so, but he always has."

"It puzzles me," Jenna murmured, "that King gets along so well with everyone else. He has that arrogant streak, of course, but he's a pussycat most of the time. He's worked twenty-two-hour days to keep us solvent since Dad died. Without him the whole property would have gone down the drain." She eyed her friend. "None of which explains his hostility toward you. I couldn't believe my eyes when he went out of the dormitory after you."

"That makes two of us. I very nearly hit him."

"How exciting! What did he do?"

Teddi reddened. She was not about to admit that King had held her hand all the way to the dormitory. "He ducked," she lied.

Jenna laughed delightedly. "Just imagine, your trying to plant one on my brother. Do you know, you never used to stand up to him. When we were younger, he'd say something hurtful and you'd go off and cry, and King would go out and chew up one or two of his men." She laughed. "It got to be almost funny. The men would start getting nervous the minute you walked onto the property."

Teddi shifted restlessly. "I know. To be honest, I've been turning down your invitations lately to avoid him. I probably wouldn't have gone home with you at Easter if I hadn't been trying to shake off that friend of Dilly's who's been pursuing me."

"Would you mind very much telling me what happened at Easter?"

"I threw a feed bucket at him," Teddi blurted out.

Jenna's eyes opened wide. "You're kidding!"

Teddi's gaze dropped to her lap. "It was just a mild disagreement," she lied. "Oh, look!" she exclaimed as she looked out the window. "We must be over Alberta, look at the plains!"

Jenna peeked over her friend's shoulder and looked down through the thick cloud cover. "Could be," she murmured, checking her watch, "but we haven't been in the air quite long enough. I bet it was Saskatchewan." She got up. "I'll ask King."

Teddi's eyes followed the smaller girl while her mind went lazily back to the spring day when King had chided her about her private life just one time too many....

Jenna had slept late that morning, but the bright sun and the sounds of activity out at the stables had roused Teddi from a sound sleep. She'd put on her riding outfit and hurried down to get Happy to saddle a horse for her. Happy, one of the older hands on the huge Canadian ranch, had been one of her staunchest allies. He'd taught her to ride when King had refused to.

But Happy hadn't been in the neat stables that morning. King had. And the minute she saw him, she knew there was going to be trouble. He had a way of cocking his head to one side when he was angry that warned of storms brewing in his big body, a narrowing of one eye that meant he was holding himself on a tight rein. Teddi had been too angry herself to notice the warning signs.

"I know how to ride," she argued. "Happy taught me."

"I don't give a damn," he growled back. "The men have seen bear tracks around this spring. You don't ride alone on the ranch, is that clear?"

She felt an unreasonable hatred of him, raw because he hadn't even noticed her painfully shy flirting, her extra attention to her appearance. She had been trying to catch his eye for the first time in their turbulent acquaintance and it hadn't worked. Her temper had exploded.

"I'm not afraid of bears!" she all but screamed.

"Well, you should be," he replied tightly, his eyes roaming over her. "You don't know what a bear could do to that perfect young body."

The words had shocked her. Amazingly, now that she had his attention, she was frightened.

She backed away from him, and that had caused a quaking kind of anger to charge up in his big body. "Afraid?" he chided. "You probably know more about sex than I do, so why pretend? Just how many men have had you?"

That had been the final straw. There was a feed bucket at her elbow, and she grabbed it without thinking, intending to fling it directly at him.

He hadn't kept his hard-muscled body in shape by being careless. He stepped out of the way gracefully and before she had time to be shocked at her own behavior, he stepped forward and caught her by the wrists, roughly putting her hands behind her and pinning her against him.

"That," he growled, "was stupid. What were you trying to prove, that you don't like what you are?"

"You don't know what I am!" she cried, wounded. Her huge brown eyes had looked up at him with apprehension.

"No?" His big hands had propelled her forward until her soft, high breasts were crushed against the front of his blue-patterned cotton shirt. She smelled the fresh, laundered scent of it mingling with his cologne. It was the closest she'd ever been to him.

"You've behaved like a homeless kitten around me lately," he said in a deep, sensuous tone that aroused new sensations in Teddi's taut body. "Low-cut blouses, clinging dresses, making eyes at me every time I turn around...." He released her wrists then, and his calloused hands eased under the hem of her blouse, finding her bare back. They lingered on her silky skin, faintly abrasive, surprisingly gentle. "Come closer, little one," he murmured, watching her with calculating eyes, although she'd been too lost in his darkening gaze to notice that.

Her legs had trembled against the unfamiliar hardness of his, her breasts had tingled from a contact that burned even through the layers of fabric that separated her from his broad, hair-covered chest.

His hands were causing wild tremors all over her body as he savored the satin flesh of her back and urged her slender hips against his.

"I want your mouth, Teddi," he whispered huskily, bending, so that his smoky breath caressed her trembling lips. "And you want mine, don't you, love? You've wanted it for days, years...you've been aware of me since the day we met." His mouth had hovered over hers tantalizingly while his hands caressed her back, made mincemeat of her pride, her self-control. "You want to feel my hands touching you, don't you, Teddi?" he taunted, moving his head close, so that his mouth brushed tormentingly against hers when he spoke.

"King," she moaned, going on tiptoe to try to catch his poised, teasing mouth with her own.

He'd drawn back enough to deny her the kiss, while his hands slid insolently down over her buttocks and back up again. "Do you want me to kiss you, Teddi?" he'd asked with a mocking smile.

"Yes," she whispered achingly, "yes, please...!" Anything, she would have agreed to anything to make him kiss her, to bring the dream of years to reality, to let her know the touch and taste and aching pleasure of his hard, beautiful mouth.

"How much do you want it?" he persisted, bending to bite softly, tenderly at her mouth, catching her upper lip delicately between both of his in a caress that was blatantly arousing. "Do you ache, baby?"

"Yes," she moaned, her eyes slitted, her body liquid under his as her knees threatened to fold under her. "King, please," she half sobbed, "oh, please!"

He lifted his head, then, to study her hungry face and a look of pain had come over his features. He turned away so that she never saw whether he had to struggle to bring himself under control. She doubted it. Certainly there was no sign of emotion on his face when he turned back to her.

"Maybe for your birthday," he said with magnificent arrogance. "Or Christmas. But not now, honey, I'm a busy man."

He gave a curt laugh and she stood there like the ruins of a house—empty and alone. Her eyes had accused, hated, in the seconds that they held his.

"You're not human," she choked. "You're as cold as..."

"Only with women who leave me that way," he interrupted. "My God, you'd even give in to a man you profess to hate, you need it so much!"

She watched him walk away with her pride around her knees. She'd sworn to herself that day that she would toss herself over a cliff before she gave him the chance to humble her again. She avoided him successfully for the rest of the Easter vacation, and when she boarded the plane for Connecticut with Jenna, she hadn't even looked at him.

She sighed, watching the clouds drift by outside the window. In her mind she relived that humiliation over and over again. She wondered sometimes if she'd ever be able to forget. The incident had revived other, older memories that had been the original cause of her frigid reaction to most men. Ironically, King had been the only one to ever get so close to her, to arouse such a damning response. And he didn't even know that to Teddi, most men were poison.

"Saskatchewan," Jenna said smugly, returning to reseat herself beside her friend. "But western Saskatchewan, so it won't be too much longer before we get home." She gave Teddi a searching appraisal.

"Looking for hidden beauty?" Teddi teased.

"Actually, I asked King about that bucket you threw at him," she replied hesitantly.

Teddi's heart dipped wildly. "And?" she prompted, trying desperately for normalcy.

"I guess I should have kept my mouth shut," Jenna said with a sigh, turning toward the window. "Honestly, sometimes I think he lies awake nights thinking up new words to shock me with."

Teddi felt a shiver as she folded her hands in her lap and closed her eyes. Apparently King didn't want to be reminded any more than she did. It was just as well, King had made it perfectly clear that he despised her.

The Devereaux livestock farm, Gray Stag, was located in a green valley in the foothills of the Rocky Mountains, not far from Calgary. It had its own private landing strip and all the creature comforts any family would ever want.

The house itself was a copy of a French château, big and sprawling with a long, winding driveway and tall firs all around it. Fields of wildflowers bloomed profusely against the majestic background of the snow-capped Rockies. There was a tennis court, a heated swimming pool, and formal gardens which were the pride of the family's aging gardener. It always reminded Teddi of pictures she'd seen of rural France.

King taxied the plane toward the hangar, where a white Mercedes was parked. A petite, white-haired woman in a fashionable gray suit waved as they climbed out of the plane and onto the apron.

"Mama!" Jenna cried. She ran into the woman's outstretched arms, leaving King and Teddi to follow.

"My God, you'd think she'd been away for two years instead of two months," King growled.

Teddi glanced up at his set face, so deeply tanned and masculine that her fingers itched to touch it. She averted her eyes.

"It would be nice to have a mother to run to," she said in a tone that ached with memories.

She felt a lean, rough hand at the nape of her neck, grasping it gently in a gesture that was strangely compassionate.

"You haven't had a lot of love in your young life, have you?" he asked quietly. "It's something Jenna never lacked, we made sure of that."

"It shows," she agreed, watching her friend's warm, open smile. "She's very much an extrovert."

"My exact opposite." His eyes narrowed on the vista beyond the airport. "I don't care for most people."

"Especially me," she murmured.

His dark gray eyes pinned her. "Don't put words into my mouth. You know very little about me. You've never come close enough to find out anything."

She couldn't hold that dark gaze. "I did once," she reminded him bitterly.

"Yes, I know," he replied. His eyes sketched her profile narrowly. "I left scars, didn't I?"

She shifted her thin shoulders uncomfortably, wishing she'd never said anything in the first place. "Everyone's entitled to be foolish once or twice."

"I've wondered a lot since then what might have happened if I'd laid down with you in that soft hay," he said quietly, deliberately slowing his pace as they approached the rest of his family.

Her heart pounded erratically. "I'd have fought you," she said, her tone soft and challenging.

He looked down at her and a strange smile turned up his chiseled mouth at one corner. "Would you?" he asked in a deep, silky voice.

"You seem to think I've slept with half the men in New York, so you tell me," she shot back.

He cocked an eyebrow. "I don't know what to think about you," he admitted. "Just when I'm sure I've got you figured out, you throw me another curve. I'm beginning to think I need to take a much closer look at you, Teddi bear."

She glared up at him. "Don't call me that."

"Don't you like it?" he taunted. "You're small and soft and cuddly."

She blushed like a teenager, and hated her helpless reaction to his teasing. It was just like before. All he wanted was to make her crawl. Well, he wasn't going to do it this trip.

"Don't think you'll ever get to cuddle me," she said shortly.

"And I wouldn't bet on that, if I were you." He pulled a cigarette from his shirt pocket and lit it while he watched her. "You wanted me in the barn that morning."

She shivered at the memory of her weakness and her eyes closed briefly. "You know a lot," she countered.

"What did you expect, that I spent all my time with the cattle?" he taunted. "I know what to do with a woman, young Teddi, as you damned near found out. I can lose my head, if I'm tempted enough. You brought that about, and we both know it. Those eye-catching little glances, those low-cut dresses, those come-and-kiss-me looks you were giving me—"

"I can't possibly tell you how sorry I am about the whole thing," she ground out. "Could we please just forget it? You're safe from me this trip, I wouldn't flirt with you if my life depended on it."

"That might be better," he murmured dryly. "I live in constant fear of being seduced by one of you wild city girls."

Now that did sound like flirting, but before she could be sure, they were within earshot of the others.

"The end of the world must be near," Mary Devereaux laughed. "Are my eyes going bad, or are you two actually not arguing for once?" She eyed her son closely. "And did I actually see you smile at her?"

King cocked an eyebrow at her. "Muscle spasm," he replied without cracking a smile.

"Sure," Mary laughed. She reached out and hugged Teddi affectionately. "It's so good to have you here, Teddi.

What with King away most of the time, and Jenna's sudden interest in ranch management," she added with a pointed glance at her daughter, "I've been looking forward to a very lonely summer." She stared at the young girl. "Teddi, you aren't suddenly going to develop an interest in ranch management, are you?"

Teddi burst out laughing. "Oh, no, I don't think so."

"Thank goodness," Mary sighed. "Shall we go? I could use a cup of coffee. King, I suppose you'll drive?"

"When was the last time I let you drive me anywhere?" he mused, leading the way to the car.

"Let me think." His parent frowned. "You were six and I had to take you to the dentist when you got into it with little Sammy Blain…"

Teddi hid a smile. She linked her arm with Jenna's and brought up the rear. It was nice to be part of a family, even for a little while.

CHAPTER THREE

TEDDI'S ROOM OVERLOOKED the Rockies. It was done in blue and white, with lacy eyelet curtains at the windows and a canopied bed. This was where she always slept when she came to Gray Stag—her own little corner of the old château.

She wondered who had occupied the matching room in the original home in Burgundy. One of King's ancestors had copied the design of his wife's family home to keep that grieving lady from getting attacks of homesickness when they'd settled in Calgary. The original château dated to the eighteenth century. This one was barely a hundred years old, but it had a charm all its own.

She opened the window and breathed the flower-scented air. Everything seemed so much cleaner in Canada, so much bigger. Despite King's hostility, it was nice to be here again. Mary and Jenna more than made up for King.

Her eyes went to the soft bed. King. She remembered a night she'd spent at Gray Stag when she was seventeen, during summer vacation.

She'd been fairly terrified of King back then, nervous and uncertain when he came near with his cruel taunts. She'd never understood his dislike—she'd done nothing to him to provoke it.

But that night there was a thunderstorm, violent as only mountain thunderstorms can be. Teddi's parents had gone down in a commercial airliner on a night like this, and in her young mind she still connected disaster with violent storms. She was crying, soft little whimpers that shouldn't have been audible above the raging thunder.

But King had suddenly opened the door and come in, still fully dressed from helping work cattle in the flash flooding. His shirt was damp, carelessly unbuttoned to reveal a mat of hair and bronzed muscle that had drawn Teddi's eyes like a magnet.

He eased down onto the bed and took the frightened, weeping girl into his big arms. He murmured soft, comforting words that she didn't understand while he cradled her against his warm, damp body, his heart beating heavily under the cheek that lay on his broad chest. He held her until the tears and the thunder passed, and then he laid her back down on the pillows with a strangely tender smile.

"Okay, now?" he asked softly.

"Yes, thank you," she replied uneasily.

He stood there, looking down at her with strange dark eyes while she stared back, her eyes fixed on the sight he made, his shirt unbuttoned to the waist...it was the first time she'd been alone with a man in her bedroom at that hour of the night, and her fear must have shown. Because he suddenly turned away with a muffled curse and was gone. After that night, he was even colder, and she worked even harder at avoiding him. Something had happened while they stared at each other so intensely. She still wasn't sure what it had been, but she remembered vividly the sensations she felt when his eyes had dropped to the uncovered bodice of her gown and traced deliberately every soft line of her young breasts under the half-transparent material. The memory was like a drawn sword between them, along with all King's imagined grievances against her.

There was a sharp knock at the door and Jenna peeked

her head around it. "Come down and have something to eat," she said. "Mother's carving up a ham."

"Isn't Miss Peake here anymore?" Teddi asked as she joined her friend, remembering warmly Miss Peake's little kindnesses over the years.

"Our saintly housekeeper is visiting her sister for a few days." Jenna grinned. "She'd just die if she was here to see the size of the slices mother's getting off that ham. Mother eats like a bird, you know. Poor King!"

Teddi smiled involuntarily. "There's a lot of him to feed," she agreed.

"He gets even," Jenna assured her. "When mother's back is turned, he'll go in the kitchen and make himself a sandwich or two. He doesn't starve."

"Miss Peake was forever carrying him trays of food when he worked in the study," Teddi recalled, remembering how she'd strained for glimpses of him through that door at night.

"And he was forever complaining that there wasn't enough of it," Jenna added. "My brother has a tremendous appetite. For food, at least. Mother wants to see him married so badly, but he hardly ever takes anyone out. You'd think he doesn't know what to do with a woman, the way he avoids them."

Oh, Jenna, if you only knew, Teddi thought silently, as she remembered her own voice pleading for the touch of King's poised, taunting mouth. He knew far too much about women for a monk. Even Teddi, as inexperienced as she was, realized that.

But she didn't try to tell Jenna. It might lead to some embarrassing questions.

Teddi felt her pulse jump as they started into the spacious dining room, but if she'd hoped to find King there, she was doomed to disappointment. Only Mary was at the table, with cups of steaming coffee already poured and three places set.

"There you are." She smiled as the two girls joined her. "Isn't it a delightfully lazy day? I hope you're hungry, I've put on ham and bread and a nice salad for us."

Teddi had to muffle a giggle. There were enough pieces of bread for one sandwich apiece, and hardly enough ham to go around. And the nice salad would provide each of them with about two tablespoons. From her earliest acquaintance with Jenna, Teddi had been amused by Mary's eating habits. The fragile little woman had an appetite to match her stature, much to the chagrin of the rest of the family, and there was a good deal of moaning out of Mary's earshot. None of them would ever have said anything to hurt her feelings, but they couldn't resist a little good-natured joking among themselves.

"Don't tell me King's gone again?" Jenna asked as she and Teddi sat down, one on either side of Mary.

"Yes," Mary sighed. "To see about some kind of audit on that corporation of his in Montana. The board of directors retained an auditing firm from New York to do it."

Teddi didn't like to hear auditors mentioned. Some of her most unpleasant memories were due to one of her aunt's lovers, who was a very well-paid member of an illustrious New York firm.

"Is he going to be gone long?" Jenna wondered.

Mary shrugged. "A day or so, he said. But it's just the beginning. He may have to bring the dreadful man here as well—you know, to check the rest of the books." She caught the look on Jenna's face and laughed. "Yes, I know, this is Canada, but King reinvests some of the profits from the Montana operation into the livestock operation here, and…" She shook her head. "It's all very confusing. Ask King to explain it to you someday, I have no head for business management."

"Blakely does," Jenna murmured with a wry glance at her mother. "I could ask him."

Mary smiled at her. "I like Blakely very much. If you need an ally, my darling, you have one in me."

"Thanks, Mom," the young blonde said with a beaming smile. "It will take two of us to get around King."

"Get around King?" Mary paused with her fork in midair and stared at her daughter. "Now, Jenna…"

"Everything will be all right, I promise," came the smug reply. "Let's hurry and eat, Teddi, I want to introduce you to Blakely. You'll adore him!"

BLAKELY WOULD HAVE been adorable only to a girl who was in love with him, but he was personable and seemed to know his business. Teddi had to smother a grin at the worshipful look in Jenna's normally sensible eyes as they followed the thin, dark-eyed man around the property while the two young women were briefed on its operation. Blakely had red hair, so bright that it seemed coppery in the sun, and Teddi couldn't help but wonder what kind of children Jenna and the livestock foreman would have—blond ones or redheads. It wasn't going to be an easy thing if they were serious about each other. Jenna would never make King believe that it was she Blakely was interested in, not the millions she stood to inherit.

King. If only she could stop thinking about him! In view of his contempt for her, she should have detested him in return. But she didn't. She couldn't stop her eyes from following him whenever he was near. She felt an attraction toward him that nothing ever daunted, and she was help-less to prevent it.

She shook herself out of her troubled thoughts as Blakely mumbled something about the growth of the livestock farm.

"Originally," he informed the girls, "farms in western Canada were laid out in 65-hectare parcels. And most of the farms are scattered within a 320-kilometer strip along Canada's southern border. But these days only about 5 per-cent of the work force is employed in agriculture," he added sadly. "Although productivity is increasing among those who remain, and mechanization has aided us quite a lot. Did you know," he continued, blossoming as he elaborated on his favorite subject, "that the average output of one farm worker today provides food for over fifty people?"

"I'd give that man a raise," Teddi murmured.

Blakely stared at her until the words penetrated, then he threw back his head and laughed, delighted at the little joke.

"Forgive me," he told her, "I do tend to get carried away about farming. I love it, you see. Not just the land, or work-ing it and working with cattle on it; but the history and heritage behind it all. This was once part of the Northwest Territories," he said, sweeping his arms around to indicate the lush green valley in its summer splendor, with the tall, sharp peaks of the Rockies in the distance. "Alberta and Saskatchewan were organized out of it in 1905, but French fur traders were here long before then settling the wilder-ness. It's an exciting history, the settling of this territory, one I never tire of reading about. Or," he added sheepishly, "talking about."

"I like to talk about my part of the world, too," Teddi told him, "and I like learning about yours just as much. Please don't apologize. Think of it as cultural exchange," she added impishly.

"Thank you, Teddi," he replied with a smile.

"And now that we've got that settled," Jenna added, linking arms with the tall man, "let's see the rest of it."

Teddi followed along behind them, her eyes sweeping over the well-kept barn and stables, the white fences that kept the animals in, the huge fields of grain growing to feed the animals through the winter. It was an imposing sight. No wonder King loved it so. The scenery alone was lovely.

The next morning, Teddi went riding with Jenna and Blakely, keeping to herself, and eventually riding back alone to the ranch. It wasn't kind to tag along after them when they were so obviously falling in love and wanted to be alone.

She gave the horse to the ranch hand at the stables and walked aimlessly toward the house. Mary had driven into Calgary to shop, and there was no one to talk to. She didn't mind being alone here, though. It wasn't like being alone in that spotless New York high-rise apartment with the doors bolted and chained for safety. Here, there was help within earshot all the time. She'd never felt afraid at Gray Stag— mainly because it was King's domain, and she was afraid of nothing when King was around.

She walked into the house, idly wondering how much longer he'd be away. She was about to start up the stairs when King suddenly came down them, startling her.

He was wearing work clothes; a blue-patterned shirt open at the throat over worn jeans and dusty boots, and a straw Western hat jammed down over his blond hair at an arrogant angle.

"Where are they?" he asked without preamble.

"Your mother's gone shopping," she said uneasily.

"And Jenna?" he prodded, narrow-eyed.

She averted her gaze. "She's, uh, out riding."

"With Blakely?"

She glared at him. "What's wrong with Blakely?"

Both eyebrows went up. "Did I say anything was?"

She shifted, running her hand along the highly polished banister. "Well, no," she admitted reluctantly.

"You're always ready to expect the worst of me, aren't you?" he asked as he reached her, his eyes darkening as they slid over her face. She couldn't have imagined the picture she made, with her short, dark hair framing her face, her brown eyes like crystal, her cheeks just faintly flushed. "Your mouth is as red as a cardinal's breast."

She searched his quiet eyes, stunned at the compliment, something she'd never expected from King. King—her enemy.

He moved down another step, easing her back against the bannister with the threat of his big body. He reached down and cupped her chin with a lean, strong hand. His thumb stroked her lower lip lightly.

"How old are you now?" he asked in a deep, taut voice.

She swallowed. He was too close, too disturbing, far too masculine. He smelled of the outdoors, of a woodsy cologne and cigarettes. "I'm twenty," she said unsteadily. "I'll be twenty-one in four months."

"Too young," he murmured. "Still years too young. Do you know how old I am, Teddi?"

"You...you're thirty-three," she whispered.

"Thirty-four," he corrected. His eyes fell to her mouth and studied it for a long time. "God, what a sweet mouth!" he ground out. Then, as if the admission had annoyed him, he let her go abruptly and moved away toward the front door.

She stood staring helplessly after him, her eyes glued to the blue-patterned shirt stretched across his broad shoulders, the blond head that seemed to throw off golden lights as he passed under the chandelier. She loved the way he walked, so tall and bronzed and regal. She loved everything about him.

He turned with the doorknob in hand and looked back at her suddenly, reading with pinpoint accuracy the aching hunger she was too young to disguise.

His face hardened. His hand tightened on the doorknob. He uttered a soft curse and whirled, slamming the door shut with a booted foot as he headed straight for her.

She watched him with eyes so filled with confusion they seemed black, her face lifting as he came closer.

She didn't protest when he reached for her, crushing her soft breasts against his chest as he bent to find her mouth in one smooth, expert motion.

She felt his hard lips burrow into hers with a sense of awe, her eyes closing so that she could savor their warmth and sensuality. She stiffened involuntarily as he tried to deepen the kiss, his tongue probing at her lips.

"Let me…" he ground out, grasping the hair at the nape of her neck to tug gently, surprising a gasp from her lips. As they parted, his tongue shot past them into the soft, dark warmth of her mouth, exploring, tasting, teasing, fencing with her own tongue in an intimacy she'd never liked with other men. But King made of it a pleasure beyond bearing, a caress so sensuous that her hands reached up to grasp his hard face between them and urge him even closer.

She moaned achingly at the penetration, the suggestive intimacy as his tongue thrust gently into her soft mouth.

He reached down, half lifting her body against his so that she could feel every warm, hard line of it in total contact with her own.

"King," she whispered shakily.

He drew back for breath, dragging air into his lungs.
His eyes fairly blazed as they searched hers. "Witch," he
ground out. "Little dark-eyed witch, stop casting spells on
me, will you?"

Even as he spoke, he freed her, turned on his heel and
strode out the door. He slammed it violently behind him,
while Teddi touched her swollen mouth with nervous fingers and trembled deliciously with delayed reaction. Years
of waiting, hoping, to feel that hard, arrogant mouth on her
own, and it had finally happened. King had kissed her. The
crazy thing was that the reality had been so much more
wonderful than the dream....

CHAPTER FOUR

TEDDI WALKED AROUND in a daze for the rest of the day, absently listening to Jenna rave about Blakely while her mind lingered on the hard, possessive crush of King's mouth.

"Do you realize what you just agreed to do?" Jenna asked as they helped Mary put supper on the table.

"Ummmm?" Teddi offered with an empty smile.

Jenna grinned. "You agreed to have cowhide biscuits with grass sauce and ride a saddled chicken."

The flush appeared instantly in Teddi's cheeks and she averted her eyes to the platter of biscuits she was putting on the table. "Sorry about that," she murmured. "I guess my mind wasn't on what you were saying."

"It's been conspicuous by its absence all afternoon," came the dry reply. "Uh, that wouldn't have anything to do with King being home?"

The platter lurched precariously as it met the tabletop. "Why ever would you think that?" Teddi asked, innocent eyes dark and wide.

"Joey walked out of the office carrying his duffel bag an hour ago."

Teddi blinked.

Jenna hid a giggle behind a slender hand. "Every time King goes broody, he takes a strip off Joey. Then Joey packs his duffel bag and gives notice. The last time he did that," she continued, "was at Easter. I told you the men started getting nervous the minute you set foot on the place."

Teddi just stared, her heart beating a tattoo as she suddenly heard the front door open and close with a bang.

Mary's clear voice could be heard in the hall. "Oh, there you are, dear, the girls are putting the food on the table now."

"The computer broke down," came the harsh reply, accompanied by the sound of angry footsteps, "and we can't get a repairman here before morning. But I need those herd records *now!*"

"What are you going to do?" Mary was asking.

"Fix it," he growled. There were sounds of paper rustling, drawers opening and closing. "If I can find the repair manual...there's a home number for one of the service technicians in it. They don't give you schematics or troubleshooting info, you have to call a service technician! Before long, you'll have to call a number in Ontario in order to engage the gears of your automobile...don't keep supper, I'll be late." And the door slammed loudly.

"It's Saturday night," Teddi murmured. "Surely to goodness he doesn't expect a service technician to fly out here on a Saturday night...?"

Jenna eyed her friend patiently. "Would you say no to him?" she asked.

There was a brief pause. "I think I'd pack my duffel bag," she admitted with a grin.

Mary came through the door just then, her eyes widening at the amount of food on the table. "Gracious, what army are you girls planning to feed tonight?" she gasped, her eyes going from the platter of biscuits Teddi had made to the ham casserole, cottage-fried potatoes, green beans, sliced carrot sticks and celery and tomatoes with a dip, and the enormous banana pudding on the elegant table under the crystal chandelier.

"It'll keep until tomorrow," Jenna promised, winking at Teddi.

Mary laughed. "What a pity King's going to miss this," she murmured as she sat down and unfolded her napkin. "All his favorites. Buttering him up, Jenna?" she mused.

"Actually, it was Teddi's idea to do the casserole," came the dry reply. "I can't make one, you know. And look at these biscuits!"

"Never mind, my friend," Teddi murmured as she spooned the casserole onto her plate. "I love it, too, as it happens."

It was late, and the women were watching an old movie on TV in the den when King came in. He looked every year of his age. His thick blond hair was rumpled, and his shirt was open at the throat. His face was hard, but there was a faint satisfaction in it as he went directly to the bar and poured himself a whiskey before he dropped into his armchair with a sheaf of papers in one hand.

"I see you got the repairman, dear," Mary remarked.

"An obliging gentleman," King agreed, fingering the glass as he scanned an open folder in his lap. "I'm going to cull a few cows, and I needed these records before I made a decision on which ones to sell."

"Tomorrow is Sunday," Mary reminded him.

"Ummm," he agreed. "But Jake Harmone is driving over here tomorrow morning before church to make me an offer. Hence the urgency."

"Sell Mahitabel and I'll never speak to you again," Jenna promised him.

He looked up with the old, mischievous light in his silvery eyes as he locked glances with his sister. "Mahitabel hasn't calved in six years," he reminded her. "She's eating my grass, drinking my spring water and yielding absolutely nothing."

"She's tough," Jenna replied.

"So she is," King murmured thoughtfully. "But if we parboiled her first…"

"King!" Jenna positively shrieked. "You can't, you wouldn't!"

He burst out laughing at her horrified expression. "All right, calm down. I'll put it off another year, as I've done for the past six."

His sister breathed easier. "What a scare you gave me!"

"I'll remind you again that sentimentality and cattle raising don't mix," he remarked.

"As I found out at the tender age of twelve," Jenna said, pouting, "when my pet bull disappeared."

"He was an Angus," King reminded her.

"So? What's wrong with black Angus?" she challenged.

"Nothing, except that we run Herefords," he replied. "Your pet got in with my registered cows and they dropped half Angus calves the next spring."

"I thought they were cute," Jenna said defensively. "Little black calves with white faces."

"If you had your way, you'd make pets of every calf on the place," King murmured indulgently. His eyes shifted suddenly and met Teddi's. Something flashed briefly in the gray depths and burned so brightly that she dropped her own gaze and tried unsuccessfully to calm her wildly beating heart. Involuntarily, her mind caught and held the image of King's hard mouth taking hers, and a shimmer of pure pleasure washed over her.

"Well, the hero got the girl. As usual." Mary got up with a sigh and turned off the television. "I hate to leave good company, but that shopping spree left me dragging. Good night, my dears," she said with a motherly smile, bending to kiss Jenna's cheek as she went out the door.

"Do you still type?" King asked Teddi unexpectedly.

"Uh...yes," she stammered.

He got up from the chair with the folder in one big hand. "Come help me make a list, then."

"Aren't you going to have something to eat?" Jenna asked him, glancing curiously from King's set face to Teddi's flushed one.

"Later, honey," he said, ruffling her hair as he went out the door.

Jenna winked at Teddi, her whole face beaming with mischief as her friend followed him.

Teddi perched herself at one side of the big oak desk in King's pine-paneled study and tapped out the cattle names and lineage and herd numbers and pasture locations while he leaned back in his big chair and dictated them, ending each notation with the cow's production record. She began to realize that the names he was giving her—or rather, the numbers that seemed to pass for names for most of them— were those of cows that didn't produce calves that were up to his exacting standards.

"Animal slavery," she mumbled as he finished, and she paused to make a correction.

He raised both heavy blond eyebrows and glanced at her. "I beg your pardon?"

"Selling off cows," she explained, a tiny mischievous light in her wide brown eyes. "Poor things, what if that Mr. Harmone beats them or doesn't feed them properly?"

"Mr. Harmone," he informed her, "is going to use them as hosts for embryo transplants. They're Herefords, but they'll throw purebred black Angus calves."

She stared at him. "Sure they will," she agreed. "Shouldn't you eat something? Lack of food…"

He grimaced, getting up to toss the records on his desk. "My God, don't you know anything about cattle breeding?"

She nodded. "First you take a boy cow…"

He chuckled deeply, watching the lights play in her short, thick hair, almost blue-black in its darkness. "It's not quite that simple, darling. Suffice it to say that this new technique has a large following and Mr. Harmone is part of it. You take purebred embryos and transplant them into host cattle—like these Herefords. The result is a well-cared-for purebred calf with superior bloodlines out of a less expensive cow."

"Improving on nature?" she asked with lifted eyebrows.

"Don't women do it all the time?" he fired back, looming over her. "Lipstick, eye shadow, curlers…none of which applies to you right now, however," he conceded, studying her impossibly clear, creamy complexion, and the wide, black-lashed eyes that stared up at him.

"I don't use makeup when I'm not working," she murmured. Her eyes were as busy as his, seeking out the hard angles of his face, his imposing nose, his deep-set gray eyes, his chiseled mouth and square chin. He was so good to look at. Her first sight of him, all those years ago, had made him like a narcotic to her. She could scarcely exist without the picture of him in her mind, her heart. Her eyes fed on him.

The mention of her modeling had been enough to break the fragile peace between them. King's face had gone hard; his eyes glittered like sun on a rifle barrel.

"I saw one of those televised fashion shows you were in," he remarked curtly. "They ran it on the cable station."

Her eyes avoided his probing stare. "I can imagine what you thought of it."

"Can you? I've seen bikinis that showed less. One of the blouses you wore was quite transparent, and you wore nothing under it!"

Her face flamed. He was right, a great many of David Sethwick's creative designs for Velvet Moth were practically sheer and very sensuous. Working around designers and other models, she tended to forget that bodies were more than just mannequins to people outside the business. King had such a low opinion of Teddi, and all without foundation. She wondered how he'd react if he knew how innocent she truly was, how afraid she was of anything physical....

"High fashion very often is...risqué," she had to acknowledge, studying her well-kept nails where they rested on the typewriter keys. "And I work primarily for two designers of evening wear. It's supposed to be sexy-looking."

"You damned sure wouldn't go anywhere with me in some of those dresses," he growled.

The thought of it made chills go down her spine. It was heady to think of spending an evening with King, being escorted by him to some grand dance. She sighed unknowingly. It would never happen. Not as long as King felt the way he did about her profitable sideline. Which she ought to be pursuing even now, she reminded herself, if she was going to make enough to handle her school fees for the rest of the year. Velvet Moth would make sure she had work while she was in New York, and so would Lovewear—designers at both houses, fortunately, liked her style and her punctuality. And there was always the chance of one or two TV commercials.

"You love it, don't you?" he asked suddenly, perching

himself on the edge of the desk to study her. He was far too close. She could feel the warmth of his big body, see the buttons straining at the open throat of his shirt as he shifted, smell the outdoorsy scent of him. Being this close made her feel trembly, just as it had this afternoon when he'd reached for her....

"Love what?" she asked vaguely, looking up into his searching gray eyes.

He didn't answer for a minute, his gaze lingering on her wide, misty eyes, her full, parted lips, as if he found the sight of her at this range disconcerting. That was ridiculous, she told herself.

"Modeling," he said after a tense pause. "The glitter, the glamour, the night lights, the male adulation. You couldn't give it up if you tried, despite all that rot about becoming a teacher."

Her eyes flashed. "You don't really think I'm spending so much time in college just to improve my modeling technique?" she challenged.

"I'll admit you baffle me," he said quietly. "Why teaching?"

"Why not? It's an honorable profession," she said with deliberate nonchalance.

"Where would you teach?" he persisted. "College?"

"Grammar school," she corrected, her eyes lighting up at the mental picture she had of guiding young hands toward new pursuits. "Kindergarten, if possible."

His face underwent a remarkable change. He took a deep breath. "You like children?"

Her face beamed. "Oh, yes," she told him genuinely. "Especially when they're just old enough to reach out and begin to experience the world around them."

His chest rose and fell heavily as he stared down into

her wide, dark eyes. His tanned hand moved, touching her cheek, and she trembled at the light touch. It was amazing, the sensations he caused when he touched her. She wasn't nervous of King like this, although she still had deep fears of any man in an intimate way. It was highly unlikely, of course, that King would ever want to be intimate with her, but she couldn't help being curious about her own responses. She liked the feel of his hard, warm mouth against hers, she even liked the intimacy of his tongue. But to feel his hard fingers against her bare skin…would she panic, as she had before when one of her dates tried to go further than kisses? Part of her was insatiably curious about King in that way.

"You fascinate me," he murmured absently. His thumb brushed across her full, soft lips, parting them while he held her eyes with his. "Half woman, half child…and so exquisitely beautiful."

"I'm…not beautiful," she protested weakly. Her heart beat violently as his face moved closer.

"Oh, but you are," he breathed. His mouth poised just over hers, his warm, whiskey-scented breath mingling with hers, his eyes riveted to the curve of her lips. "I was afraid this would happen. Once wasn't enough. Not nearly enough."

His fingers tilted her chin at just the angle he wanted, and she watched, fascinated, as his hard mouth parted just before it touched hers. She waited, aching, with time stretched to the tautness of a violin string between them.

The sudden opening of the door was no less cruel than the flick of a whip. King lifted his head with a harsh jerk, his eyes almost black with frustration as he watched his sister come in with a loaded tray.

Teddi bit hard on her lip to keep from crying out, so desperately had she wanted that kiss. But she had years of practice at hiding her real feelings, and she looked quite calm when Jenna got to the desk with sandwiches and coffee.

"I thought you might be hungry," Jenna explained with a grin at her taciturn brother. "Slave driver, isn't he?" she asked Teddi.

"My God, real slices of ham," King burst out, lifting the edge of one of the sandwiches.

"Mama does skimp, doesn't she?" Jenna laughed. "This was all the ham that was left. Teddi made a ham casserole for dinner tonight and that took the rest."

King's piercing eyes swung to Teddi, lingering on her flushed face. "Ham casserole?" he murmured.

She lifted her chin. "I like it," she said defensively.

One corner of his chiseled mouth curled sensuously. "Do you?"

He knew she'd made it especially for him, the beast, but she wasn't going to let him see any reaction from her. "If you're through, I think I'll turn in," she said as she rose, muffling a yawn she didn't feel.

He hesitated just an instant, reading quite accurately the apprehension in her wide, dark eyes. "That's all I need, thanks. For tonight," he added, and she knew he wasn't talking about herd records.

"Coming up, Jenna?" Teddi asked her friend with practiced carelessness as she went toward the door.

"Right behind you. Say, Blakely and I are going into Calgary in the morning. Want to…?"

"She's going to Banff with me," King broke in.

Startled, Teddi's bright eyes shot to his face and were captured by his hard, unblinking gaze.

"I've got to talk business with a man up there tomorrow afternoon. I thought Teddi might like to see the park.

Since none of us have ever thought to take her there," he added carelessly, although the look in his eyes was anything but careless.

"I...I'd like that," Teddi heard herself saying. It was like being handed a special present without asking for it.

"You won't throw her off the mountain or anything?" Jenna teased with lifted brows.

King actually laughed. "No, I won't throw her off the mountain. Satisfied?"

"You can't be surprised that I asked," Jenna countered, escorting her friend to the door. "Only a few days ago, you hated the idea of having her here."

King studied Teddi's slight figure, letting his intent gaze move lazily up to her flushed face and thick, short hair. "That was a few days ago," he murmured.

"It's overwork," Teddi assured her puzzled friend. "Too many computer breakdowns and skipped meals." She leaned closer and said in a loud, conspiratorial whisper, "Just ask him about having Herefords produce purebred black Angus cattle."

Jenna stared, gaping, at her older brother.

He tossed his thick, blond hair back with an impatient hand. "Don't ask," he warned, "unless you want to spend the next thirty minutes having it explained to you."

Jenna chuckled, pushing Teddi out the door. "I think you'd better eat your sandwiches, brother mine, and see if it doesn't help." And she closed the door behind her before he had a chance to reply.

"King, taking you to Banff?" Jenna laughed when they were upstairs. "My gosh, miracles happen every day, don't they?"

"You aren't half as surprised as I was," Teddi said, pausing at the door to her room. "And I'm still not sure why.

Maybe he wants some privacy so he can give me the devil and I won't have any hope of rescue."

"Maybe he's mellowing," Jenna suggested.

"Maybe the chickens will give milk."

"Well, he didn't sound sarcastic or anything."

Teddi smiled wistfully. "You didn't hear him before you came in. He was giving me a scolding about that televised fashion show I was in."

"How interesting," came the amused reply. "Because when we watched it, he sat there staring like a man possessed. He didn't take his eyes off you, and he didn't say a word."

"He was probably busy trying to think up nasty things to say about it the next time he saw me," she countered, flushing.

"That wasn't how he looked," Jenna murmured thoughtfully, recalling the strange, intense look in her brother's eyes at the time.

"How did he look?"

Jenna met Teddi's curious eyes levelly. "He looked like a starving man."

Teddi turned away before Jenna could see and question the wild color in her cheeks. "It was televised before dinner, wasn't it?" she murmured. "Well, good night. See you in the morning."

"Inevitably," came the gleeful reply. "Another fascinating chapter of your ongoing war with King. I wish you two got along better," she added, suddenly serious. "I can't understand why he's so down on you. He isn't like that about another single person."

"Maybe I remind him of a woman he used to hate."

Jenna shook her head. "There aren't that many women in

his past. Very few in his present, too." She grinned. "And no one at all since Easter," she added. "I wonder why?"

"Good night!" Teddi said quickly, darting into her room.

SHE ROSE AFTER a restless night, her eyes full of dreams and hopes. It was the most exciting morning she could remember, because the day promised a whole afternoon in King's company.

Time seemed to fly as they all went to church together, and Teddi stood next to King, listening to his deep, pleasant voice as they sang hymns in the same Presbyterian church where his father and mother had married years before.

And then, church was over, and Teddi was feeling as if she could conquer the world as she sat beside King in his low-slung black Ferrari on the way to Banff. Her eyes wandered restlessly from the winding road between sky-high pines to the jagged peaks of the Rocky Mountains against an azure sky.

"It's as big as the whole world," she murmured, spellbound. "Everything out here seems gigantic, and the air is so clean."

King chuckled softly. "Cleaner than most places, thanks to our provincial government. We have stringent basic environmental standards that new developers must meet, to preserve our clean water and skies."

"Georgia has a fine environmental protection division, too," Teddi replied, "and equally stringent air and water conservation requirements. We like to think they're some of the best in the nation."

He glanced at her. "I always associate you with New York," he murmured dryly, "despite that Southern accent."

"Why, because I model?" she asked defensively. "It's just a job, King."

"A job is something one does out of necessity," he fired back without looking her way. "You model because you like the glamour of it and the excitement."

How wrong he was, she thought dejectedly. She modeled because it was the only profession she was suited to that would earn her enough to stay in school. Dilly gave her nothing toward her tuition. But, of course, King didn't know that, and probably wouldn't believe her if she told him so.

"Just don't forget," he continued coldly, "that the excitement won't last forever. Men don't necessarily marry their pretty playmates, you know."

"Now, just hold it a minute," she flared, turning in the bucket seat to glare at him. "I'm not any man's playmate, and I won't be."

"Holding out for marriage?" he asked contemptuously. "I suppose you might find a man somewhere who'd marry a girl like you."

Her eyes blazed in a face that was flushed with indignation. "It's very easy to make snap judgments about people," she reminded him. "You do prize circumstantial evidence, don't you? Although how you manage to construe modeling as prostitution is something I can't imagine!"

"It's a small world, darling," he replied, making a mockery of the endearment. "I have an acquaintance who knows a great deal about your night life."

"Night life!" she burst out. "My gosh, by the time I get back from a day of assignments in New York, the last thing I want or need is a long social calendar! All I do at night is soak my tired feet and get ready for the next day's assignments. The only time I go out is on weekends."

"Sure," he replied curtly.

"And just who is your mysterious informant?" she asked pointedly.

"I'll introduce you one of these days soon," he replied mysteriously.

"I can't wait," she returned sarcastically. She turned away, folding her arms across her chest. The blouse she wore was a camisole top that criss-crossed over her small breasts and tied at the side. Its pale blue color contrasted with the white slacks she wore, and emphasized her dark eyes and hair, her exquisite complexion. But King hadn't even noticed how she was dressed. He'd been too busy digging up insults. And she'd had such hopes of mending the conflict between them today. When he'd asked her, *told* her, about the trip to Banff, she really thought he had more than insults in mind.

She stared out the window at the incredible height of the Rockies as they traveled down the valley and across the Canadian Pacific Railway to enter Banff.

Banff was a shopper's and diner's delight, chock-full of international shops, malls and restaurants. And all around were the impossibly high, jagged peaks of the Rocky Mountains, giant stone sentinels casting their majestic shadows on the green, lush valley where the Bow River wound like a crystal ribbon.

"It's awesome," Teddi whispered, her eyes peering up toward the craggy summits that practically surrounded the valley.

"Yes, it is," King agreed. "I've lived half of my life in the shadow of the Rockies, but they still take my breath away. I can imagine how the old French fur traders felt when they saw them for the first time."

She glanced at his profile, the set of his head, the arrogant tilt of it. "One of your ancestors was a fur trader," she recalled. "So was your mother's grandfather."

"I can see the question coming," he replied dryly. "No, I don't look French, do I?"

She let her attention wander back to the sharp edges of the summits, where the timberline was clearly visible. "I didn't say anything," she protested.

"My maternal grandfather was French, Miss Curiosity," he told her, "but my paternal grandmother was Dutch. And I don't have to tell you which characteristics I inherited."

"Where are we going?" she asked, watching the small shops and restaurants whiz by as the Ferrari ate up the miles.

"I thought you might like to see the grand old lady of the mountains," he said obliquely as they crossed the bridge over the majestic Bow River.

"The who?" she asked.

"The Banff Springs Hotel," he replied. "The original hotel was built in 1888, and much of the credit for it goes to William Van Horne of the Canadian Pacific Railway, who thought that a luxury hotel would increase tourism. The CPR expanded it up until 1910, when they began to rebuild it. Unfortunately a fire destroyed part of the old building, but it was scheduled for demolition anyway, and the new hotel was completed in 1928. I think you'll find the architecture unique," he added as the gigantic hotel began to loom up in the distance. He glanced at her intrigued expression. "Three architects produced what you see, and believe me, the interior is just as impressive. No expense was spared on materials or workmanship."

"Oh, it's beautiful!" she burst out enthusiastically, fascinated by the towering structure, which reminded her of a castle.

"You should see it at night," he replied, "with all the windows blazing with light. It's quite lovely." He pulled up in the parking lot and cut the engine. "I can't imagine why none of us ever thought to bring you here before."

"There was never time," she said, reaching for the door handle.

"Or we never made time," he replied, something harsh in his deep voice.

She let him guide her into the lobby of the majestic hotel, fascinated by the fossilized stone throughout and the bronze doors to the Alhambra Dining Room, where they had coffee and pie. She felt as if her feet were barely touching the ground when they walked back to the car. King had been polite, even courteous, and not a cross word had managed to get between them.

"Where to now?" she asked as she fastened her seat belt.

"You tell me," he corrected. "Would you like to go through some of the shops in town?"

"It's Sunday," she reminded him.

"And you'll find a number of them open, just the same," he promised. "Well?"

"I'd like that," she confessed.

"Typical woman," he mused, starting the car.

"I suppose you'd rather be hunting those poor moose and elk?" she teased.

"In season, yes, ma'am," he laughed. He glanced at her. "I like to ski, too. Do you?"

"I've never learned." Her eyes flickered away from his. "Well, Jenna hasn't, either!"

"If you spent much time around me, you'd learn plenty about skiing. And other things," he added, glancing sideways with a look that said more than words.

She avoided his eyes. "According to you, there isn't anything left for me to learn."

"And maybe I need to find out how much," he said softly.

She swallowed down the urge to leap out of the car and make a run for it. "Isn't the valley beautiful?" she asked politely.

He chuckled. "Yes, it is. When we've looked through Banff, we'll drive up to Lake Louise."

He pulled the car back out into the road, turning off presently to show her the magnificent gondola lift.

"We won't stop," he said, "but it's open year-round. There's even a restaurant and gift shop up there."

Up there was a long way off, and Teddi had no head for heights. "I don't think I'd ever make a skier if you have to start up there," she murmured.

"You'll never know until you try," he chuckled. "But we'll save that for another time. And there's always cross-country skiing," he added as he pulled back out into the main road. "We'll have to do that one winter."

The statement nagged in the back of her mind while King escorted her through one shop after another, showing her Indian handicrafts, Eskimo carvings and art work by native western Canadian artists. The fur shop fascinated her, and so did the trading shop. King bought her a small carved totem that she knew she'd treasure as long as she lived, and two hours had gone by before she realized it.

They drove up to Lake Louise, traveling parallel to the Bow River on the long highway. Teddi gazed wide-eyed at the mountain scenery, drinking in fleeting glimpses of moose, mountain sheep, and craggy peaks that seemed to touch the clouds. Driving around Lake Louise was fascinating, too, she found.

"There, see the gondolas?" King nodded toward the lift.

"I'd rather look at the lake, if you don't mind," Teddi laughed, staring raptly out the window at it. "I'll bet you can hear the fish eating worms if you listen closely."

He pulled off the road and cut the engine. "Let's see," he told her, throwing his long legs out of the streamlined car.

She followed him down to the banks of the sky-blue lake and stood listening to the faint sloshing of the water at the shoreline, to the sound of the tall trees brushing each other in the breeze, to the far away baying of a hound.

She closed her eyes and she could almost see men in buckskins carrying flintlock rifles, on their way to check their trap lines. The air smelled of trees and water and bark and growing things, and her heart swelled.

"Daydreaming?"

She smiled as she opened misty eyes. "Sort of," she confessed.

"Picturing it as a site for a fashion show?" he chided.

She drew in a deep, slow breath, bending down to pick a blade of grass and worry it with her long fingers. "Actually, I was thinking about the men who settled this country," she said, "and the hardships they had to endure. There's so much history here."

"I know. I wasn't aware that you knew, however."

Her dark eyes were accusatory as they met his. "I do occasionally think of things other than expensive clothes and cameras. That part of my life exists only in New York. On campus, I'm a student and a restaurant employee. Here, I'm just me."

"Are you?" He wasn't wearing his ranch hat, and his thick, blond hair was caught by the wind, falling carelessly onto his broad forehead as he stared down at her.

She met his piercing gray eyes squarely and felt the breath pour out of her at the impact.

The old tension was back between them, as suddenly, as unexpectedly, as it had been the night before when Jenna opened the door of King's den. Her heart fluttered like a wild bird as she stood there, feeling the nearness of his big body with every nerve in her own.

His eyes dropped to her neckline where the pale blue blouse crossed over her breasts. Because of the thin camisole straps, she hadn't bothered with a bra, and she could see King's eyes, intent and curious on the thin fabric.

"This bloody thing has haunted me all afternoon," he ground out, moving a step closer, his voice deep and slow. "Are you wearing anything at all under it?"

"King!" she burst out, breathless.

"Just like a woman," he grumbled, reaching out to catch her shoulders and draw her closer, "to wear something that drives a man around the bend and then be shocked when he notices it."

"I didn't...didn't wear it to drive you around any bends," she protested.

"Didn't you, Teddi bear?" he murmured. One big hand pressed against her back, urging her close, while the other slid deftly, expertly, under one strap of the camisole blouse, making exquisite sensations where it touched the silken flesh of her shoulder, her collarbone.

"Your skin feels like velvet," he whispered. His fingers spread out, warm and hard and faintly calloused, lifting so that the blouse and her bare flesh parted company and the breeze touched her like a lover's hand.

She gasped, trembling, as his fingers edged nearer to one small, taut breast.

"Look at me," he breathed gruffly, his voice so commanding that she instantly obeyed it. "I want to watch you."

"King…" She whispered his name, not knowing if it was a protest or a plea.

"I've wanted to touch you like this until I ache with it," he whispered, letting his eyes drop to the silky blouse, deliberately lifting the edge to reveal the pale, hard-tipped breasts to his fiery eyes.

She heard his intake of breath and knew in that instant that she was lost, that he could take anything he wanted and there was no way on earth she could stop him….

Her shocked eyes met his, her lips parted under a rush of breath. His hand began to move and he watched the wildness burn in her eyes as their gazes locked. She was spellbound, her heart throbbing as she tensed, waiting helplessly for the agonizingly slow descent of his hard, teasing fingers….

CHAPTER FIVE

"Oh, gee, Mom, what a great spot for a picnic!" came the sudden, devastating cry from the car neither Teddi nor King had heard pull off the road and stop.

King jerked as if he'd been hit in the back, both hands lifting to pull Teddi's forehead to his damp chest, his broad back protecting her from prying eyes as she fought down tears of absolute frustration.

She was trembling, and his hands soothed her, although they seemed none too steady. His breathing was as erratic as hers.

"It's all right, darling," he whispered over her head. "It's all right. Hold on to me."

She clung to his shirt, hating her own weakness and his knowledge of it.

His hand smoothed the hair from her hot cheek. "I wanted it just as much as you did, little one," he whispered. "Don't be embarrassed."

"Afternoon!" a friendly voice called from nearby. "Marvelous view, isn't it?"

"Marvelous," King replied politely. "Having a picnic?"

"Sure are! Uh, on your honeymoon?" the voice mused.

King chuckled. "Not quite," he murmured, leaving the other man to draw his own conclusions.

"Lovely day for sightseeing, isn't it?" a female voice

broke in, followed by several younger voices that seemed to split the air and then faded gradually away.

"You can come up for air now," King murmured. "They're out of sight."

She swallowed nervously and lifted her head, avoiding his amused eyes as she moved away from him. "Could we get a cup of coffee somewhere, do you suppose?" she asked in an abnormally high-pitched tone.

"I could use a whiskey myself," he murmured, "but I suppose coffee will do. How about some fondue? There's a restaurant in Banff that specializes in it."

"I'd enjoy that," she said, following him back to the car. "But what about that man you were supposed to see on business?" she asked, remembering his appointment.

He looked puzzled for an instant. "Man? Business? Oh, him," he muttered. "Well, I'll see him another day. It's too bloody late now."

Which made her feel even worse, as if she'd carried him out of his way and wasted his time. He was taut as a drawn cord all the way into Banff and the sound of the radio was like a wall between them. Just for an instant she wondered if frustration could be causing his strange silence. But, then, he'd only been teasing, hadn't he? As usual.

He didn't say a word until they were seated in the fondue house drinking coffee and enjoying a special Swiss cheese fondue while music played softly around them.

She dunked her bread into the fondue, almost losing it, and noticed King watching her with a peculiar smile.

"You'd better be careful," he cautioned. "Or don't you know the tradition about fondue?"

She shook her head, her eyes dark and wide in the soft light.

"If a woman drops something in the pot," he said softly,

watching her, "she has to surrender a kiss to the men at the table."

Her cheeks began to color delicately. "And if a man does the same?"

"He's obliged to buy a round," he replied. His eyes studied her face, her soft, red mouth. "We seem fated to be interrupted at all the wrong times."

Shaken, she tried to dunk another bread cube, but her hand trembled so much as she lifted the fork that she dropped the cube squarely into the pot, which embarrassed her even more.

"If I were conceited," he murmured, fishing it out for her with his own fork, and offering it to her, "I might think you did that on purpose."

She took the cube between her lips, and saw him watching the movement with an intensity that was shattering. She averted her eyes.

"I'm afraid I don't have any illusions about the way you think of me," she said, subdued, as she sipped her hot coffee.

He finished his own bread cubes and sat back. His thick blond hair caught the light and turned silvery in it, matching the glitter of his eyes. "How do I think of you, honey?" he asked.

"As a flighty, money-mad tramp," she replied.

He fingered his coffee cup thoughtfully. "You haven't done much to satisfy my curiosity about you."

"Why bother?" she asked. "You wouldn't believe anything I said, you never have. You hated me on sight five years ago."

One corner of his disciplined mouth lifted wryly. "Not quite."

"At any rate," she continued, "you didn't want me on the

place, and I knew it. I seem to have spent most of my vacations and holidays since I met Jenna dodging either her invitations or you."

"Was that the only reason—because you thought I had it in for you?"

She looked into her coffee cup. "Of course."

"You little liar," he accused softly.

She took a large swallow of coffee. "Shouldn't we get back to the ranch now?" she asked quickly.

He caught her eyes and searched them intently. The silence between them was broken only by the soft murmur of other diners' conversations.

"I thought you were going to pass out when I started to touch you earlier," he said in a deep, hushed tone. "Why are you afraid of me?"

"I'm not," she replied firmly, avoiding his eyes. "You... you caught me by surprise, that's all."

"I rather think I did," he murmured. He didn't pursue it, but his eyes were calculating.

All the way down the road, she felt his gaze on her while a tape played soft, soothing music that helped to calm her shattered nerves. She didn't even attempt conversation. She was too shaken by her own physical reactions to him to try.

They were just a few miles down the road from Gray Stag when a thunderstorm split the skies open, and King was forced to pull over onto the shoulder because the rain obscured the road completely.

Fortunately for Teddi, there wasn't much lightning. And the sound of the rain on the roof and hood of the sports car was soothing, oddly comforting. It made the interior of the car cozy and warm and isolated.

King leaned one arm over the back of her seat, staring

openly at her, letting his eyes trace every soft line of her body in a silence that was intensified by the fury of the rain.

"Not frightened?" he asked softly, lighting a cigarette with steady fingers.

"There's no lightning," she murmured evasively.

"I remember a night when there was a lot of it," he said thoughtfully, opening a window slightly to let the smoke escape. "You were sixteen or seventeen, and I heard you crying because of the storm."

She searched his narrowed, intent eyes. "When you opened the door, it was a toss-up as to whether I was more afraid of the lightning or you."

He smiled faintly. "I realized that. It was a good thing for you that I did," he added, the smile fading. His eyes dropped to the filmy bodice of her blouse, narrowing. "There was precious little to the gown you were wearing that night. When the light hit you at a certain angle, it was transparent." His eyes lifted to catch her shocked ones. "You didn't realize that, did you? The hardest thing I've done in years was open that door and walk out. I felt as if a wall had fallen on me."

She averted her gaze to the rain splattering on the spotless hood, silently counting the drops. Her face had gone red and she couldn't look at him. She hadn't known the gown was transparent, she'd been too afraid of the storm.

"You haven't changed," he said absently, watching her. "Your body is as perfect now as it was then. Pink and creamy—"

She caught her breath, remembering his eyes on her. "Don't," she pleaded.

"Will you stop this prudish act?" he growled suddenly, flinging the cigarette out the window before he turned to catch her shoulders and drag her across the console into his hard, warm arms.

At his sudden proximity, her senses exploded, and all she could do was lie stiffly against his warm chest and stare helplessly into his blazing eyes.

"One thing's for certain," he breathed roughly as his arms tightened. "No one's going to interrupt us right now. I ache like a boy for you!"

His mouth came down on hers roughly, parting her lips. She gasped, startled by his passion. Her arms strained against him, but he was far too strong to be moved, and far too hungry. She couldn't tear her mouth away.

Suddenly, it was like that other night, the night when she was fourteen, and one of her aunt's lovers had tried to seduce her. She could still feel the thick, wet lips on hers, the roughness of his hands touching her where none of her boyfriends had dared to touch, hurting her. She'd been helpless then, too, terrified and disgusted and sick. And if her aunt hadn't suddenly come home, if he hadn't heard her key in the lock, it might have been worse than it was. But he had heard, and had let Teddi go, daring her to tell her aunt. She'd groped her way to her room, her clothes torn, her body bruised and hurt, and cried herself to sleep. Hating him. Hating all men, for the animals they became when they were woman-hungry.

And now it was that night all over again.

The wild little scream and the violent crying got through to King. He released her, drawing back quickly to look down into her pale, frightened face.

"Teddi?" he murmured huskily.

She was trembling from head to toe, huge tears rolling silently down her cheeks, her mouth trembling from the sobs that shook the rest of her.

King's dark face contorted. One big hand brushed gently at the tears, then at her tousled hair, soothing, comforting.

"It's all right," he said softly, in a voice far too tender to be King's. "It's all right, honey, it's all right. I'm not going to hurt you. I should have known, but you wouldn't tell me...here, now, stop crying."

She was as stiff as a rod while he wiped the tears away, and there was a new wariness in her big brown eyes as they met his. "I'm...I'm not that kind...of woman," she whispered brokenly. "You...treated me like a tramp...."

He caught his breath, his face hardening even as she watched. "I know."

She pushed at his chest. "Please...let me go."

He hesitated for a moment, his eyes wavering. But then he loosened his tight grip and she moved back against the door, like a small animal at bay, feeling all over again the insolence of his mouth, his tongue, the rough contempt of his hands on her body, burning even through the fabric.

He pulled a cigarette from his pocket and lit it.

She licked her suddenly dry lips. "May...may I have one, please?" she asked.

He looked surprised. "You don't smoke."

"You don't carry a bottle of liquor around with you," she said simply, trying to smile, but not succeeding.

Frowning, he pulled out a second cigarette and lit it for her. She took it without making contact with his hard fingers and dragged on it, almost choking herself before she got the hang of it.

He watched her intently, his eyes running from her untidy hair, over her pale cheeks to her mouth and lower, to her rumpled blouse.

"Why didn't you tell me in the beginning that you were a virgin?" he asked quietly, studying her.

"Because I had no idea you were going to make a pass at me," she said weakly. "And you wouldn't have believed me if I'd told you."

He sighed. "After the way you looked on the lakeshore, I just might have." He studied her flushed cheeks. "Did I hurt you?"

The flush got worse. She shook her head jerkily. "Please, can we go back to Gray Stag now?"

"Teddi..." He moved closer, and she backed against the door, her eyes impossibly wide, her body rigid in helpless reaction.

He stopped short and something like a shadow passed over his face before he turned back to the steering wheel and started the car. He glanced at her as he pulled back into the road, saw her slight figure relax visibly, and frowned thoughtfully. Then they were underway again, with only the radio to break the silence that lasted until they reached Gray Stag.

"DID HE START on you again?" Jenna asked as they went upstairs that night.

Teddi only nodded, going into her room, aware that Jenna had followed.

Jenna closed the door and sat down on Teddi's blue coverlet, her hands folded, watching her friend pause by the darkened window and stare blankly out of it.

"And what else?" Jenna pursued. "You come back home looking like a ghost, King goes out and doesn't come back... even Mother, bless her, noticed something was wrong."

"I can't talk about it," Teddi whispered. She sighed. "Jenna, I think I'd better go back to New York in the morning."

"No!" Jenna jumped to her feet and caught Teddi's

hands. There was sadness in her whole look. "You've got to tell me what happened. Did he make a pass at you?"

Teddi tried not to answer, but her own hesitation, the fright in her eyes gave her away.

"You never told him what happened to you, did you?" Jenna asked knowingly, nodding when she read the answer in Teddi's wide, haunted brown eyes.

"Tell King? Give him a stick to hit me over the head with?" Teddi moaned. "He would have accused me of tempting the man, and you know it! He thinks I'm a tramp, and that's how he treated me today."

"Oh, Teddi," Jenna said sympathetically. "I think you underestimate King all the way around. Frankly I can't see him making a pass at a woman he hates, it isn't in character. He's not a playboy, and he's much too intense for love games."

Teddi turned away. "No, he's not," she mumbled darkly. "He hates me, all right, he's shown me that. And now I've got to go away, don't you see?"

"At least wait until morning before you make any decisions," Jenna pleaded, her face worried. "I know you're upset, but sleep on it, please?"

"It won't change anything," Teddi told her.

"You don't know that." She caught Teddi by the arms and shook her gently, smiling. "Maybe King will decide to spend the rest of his life in Australia, have you considered that? Maybe he's packing right now."

Teddi couldn't help smiling, too. "I'm sure he is," she muttered. "I can just see your brother running from a woman."

"Hasn't he been running from you for years?" Jenna asked softly. "Sleep well. Things will work themselves out, truly they will. Good night."

Teddi paced the room after Jenna had left. Sleeping on it wouldn't help; she couldn't stay if King was going to treat her so shabbily. She'd wondered how she'd react to him if he ever made a pass, and now she knew. She'd panicked. But…but she hadn't down by the lake, when he'd touched her so gently, caressed her so tenderly. She hadn't been afraid, she'd wanted more. She folded her arms across her chest and sighed. If only he hadn't come on so strong, perhaps she could have given him the response he wanted. She would have held nothing from him if he'd just been gentle.

Now she was faced with going back to that empty apartment sooner than she planned. What if Dilly was there? Dilly was nobody's idea of a mother. Saddled with the responsibility of caring for her brother's child, Dilly had never liked Teddi. And when she'd broken with her boyfriend, he'd told her all sorts of lies about Teddi leading him on. That had placed a wall between them that had never come down. It never would, if Teddi knew her aunt. She'd be so glad when her education was completed and she could strike out on her own.

She put on her nightgown and got into bed. She wouldn't think about it, not about Dilly or King or the future, she told herself. But she did. And the night was the longest she'd spent in many long years.

She was up long before the rest of them the next morning, finding the kitchen deserted when she went into it to make coffee.

Normally Miss Peake would have been busy making breakfast, but everyone had managed with toast and coffee in her absence. Up until now, Teddi thought, deciding that making breakfast might, in some magical way, help her make up her mind what to do.

She dug out bacon, eggs, and butter and two frying pans

and got busy. While the bacon was frying, she made the huge cat's head biscuits that King liked, and had them ready to go in the oven when the bacon was done. While the biscuits cooked, she made a huge platter of scrambled eggs, and by then the coffee was ready as well.

She was setting the table when King walked in and stopped short in the doorway.

He was devastatingly masculine in his jeans and denim shirt. She glanced at him quickly and turned her attention back to the table, her heart beating madly.

"If you wouldn't mind calling the others," she said quietly, "I'm just putting breakfast on the table."

"You're not a servant in this house," he said curtly.

She glared back at him, and suddenly her mind was made up. "I know that, but I'd like a good breakfast before I catch my flight and as I'm sure you've noticed, Miss Peake isn't here to cook it."

"What flight?" He stood stock-still, watching her.

"My flight to New York." She turned to go back into the kitchen.

He followed, his boots making harsh thuds as he walked. "Cancel it," he said.

She glanced at him from the coffeepot, where she was filling cups. "I will not." How could she, anyway, when she hadn't made a reservation yet?

"Then I will."

She set the pot down, hard. "I won't be held prisoner!"

"I want you to stay," he said quietly.

The faint emphasis on "I" froze her. She looked into eyes that stared back with unnerving intensity, faintly bloodshot, as if he hadn't slept any better than she had.

"Why?" she asked softly. "So you can start on me all over again? Carry on where you left off yesterday?"

He drew in a slow breath, ramming his hands into his jean pockets as he leaned back against the wall and stared at her. "I found out everything I wanted to know about you yesterday," he said. "Every single thing, in the one way I could without the risk of being lied to. I didn't mean to frighten you quite so badly, but I wanted answers you wouldn't have given me any other way."

She stiffened. "You mean you did that on purpose?"

He nodded solemnly. "It was a revelation. I had a feeling that you weren't half as sophisticated as I'd given you credit for being. The first time I kissed you, I had to force you to open your mouth—hardly the response of a woman who knows much about kissing," he added with a faint smile. "And you were far too devastated by what happened at the lake, as if it was something totally new. It all added up to one thing. When I kissed you on the way home, the way you reacted clinched it. What I didn't bargain for," he added on a weary sigh, "was the fear. Surely to God you knew I wouldn't force you?"

"No," she admitted, turning back to the coffeepot. "I didn't know that. You...you were so rough."

"Someday you might understand why," he told her. "But I don't think I'll try to explain it right now."

He was across the room in three long strides, his nearness sudden enough to be startling. She could feel the heat from his body, feel his warm, smoky breath stirring the hair at her temples, but still he didn't touch her.

She looked up apprehensively, helpless in the pull of his silvery eyes.

"I don't want you to go," he said quietly. "Now that I know the truth, I'll never handle you so roughly again."

Kindness from him was so new that it was startling. "But we're enemies," she whispered.

A muscle flinched in his square jaw. "We were," he agreed.

"You don't even like me," she persisted. "Why keep me around to irritate you even more?"

His face relaxed a little. One big, long-fingered hand came out of his pocket to touch, gently, the soft line of her cheek. "Because, little one," he murmured, "I like the way it makes me feel when I touch you."

Her cheeks flamed. Her lips parted. "Don't…"

He bent, brushing his lips over her forehead, her eyelids, her eyebrows in a silent caress that tingled with sensation. The whispery touch made her knees feel rubbery.

"You see?" he asked softly, drawing back to catch her stunned expression. "I'm not always rough."

She gazed up at him, fascinated, her eyes wide and very dark and curious.

His breath came roughly as he met that look, and like a man in a trance, his big hands came up to cup her face and hold it up to his.

"Come close," he breathed, bending toward her again. "I won't hurt you."

She obeyed him because the temptation was too much to resist. She loved the feel of his big body against hers, its strength and warmth; she loved the touch of his calloused hands against the tender skin of her face. She loved so much about him….

He brushed his mouth tenderly over hers, smoothing it, teasing it, and she caught her breath at the exquisite sensation and drew back an inch.

"Don't draw away," he murmured, his thumbs caressing the corners of her mouth. "It won't be like yesterday. Come here, darling."

And this time, he made it sound like an endearment.

His mouth pressed softly, gently against hers, not forcing it open, not exerting any kind of pressure at all. It was the gentlest kind of kiss, and everything womanly in her responded wildly to it.

She eased up on her tiptoes, her fingers resting against his warm chest, feeling the rise and fall of his heavy breathing. Her eyes closed as she increased the pressure of her own mouth, wanting something more, something…more!

"Please…please," she begged, uncertain herself what she was asking of him.

"Are you sure?" he whispered against her pleading mouth. "It won't be this tender if I kiss you the way you're asking to be kissed."

Her eyes lazily slid open and looked up into his. "Oh, yes," she breathed shakily, "I'm sure…"

His fingers tightened at the sides of her head, his own eyes slitted and fairly blazed with hunger. "Open your mouth for me, darling," he whispered, and she felt his own lips parting even as he spoke, felt the moist insistence of them on her yielding mouth. Her eyes closed. The world began to spin around deliciously as she felt his tongue caressing the inner sweetness of her lips….

This slow, sweet ardor was a world away from the rough passion of yesterday, even though he was hungry, and the hard crush of his mouth showed how hungry. But there was enough restraint in him to make her feel protected, secure in the warmth of his arms as he rocked her gently against his big body.

The sound of a door slamming brought his head up with a gruff curse. He drew in a steadying breath and reluctantly let her go. "I'm beginning to think there's no privacy in the world anymore," he muttered darkly.

Remembering their bad luck yesterday and the day before, she couldn't hold back a smile.

He shook her gently by the waist. "Think it's funny?" His eyes gleamed wickedly. "Come riding with me. If you dare."

"I don't know," she murmured thoughtfully, surprised at their suddenly easy relationship. "Isn't it supposed to be terribly dangerous going off into the woods with men?" She peeked up at him through impossibly long, thick lashes.

He caught his breath at the look, his fingers tightening. "Only for women who look like you do," he returned curtly. "Teddi…"

"Teddi, are you in there?" Jenna called suddenly.

King let go just as the door opened and Jenna walked in, her face beaming, her long hair swinging gaily. She stopped short at the sight of her taciturn brother and her flushed friend.

"Scrambled eggs at twenty paces?" Jenna guessed, looking from one to the other. "Or is it a duel with crossed forks?"

King smiled faintly. "Not quite. Here, I'll carry this in." He took up the platter of eggs and went into the dining room with it, leaving the girls to bring the coffee.

"Well?" Jenna prodded in an impatient whisper.

"We're going riding," Teddi said, shaking her head. "I don't ever expect to understand your brother."

"Oh, I think you might, someday," Jenna replied knowingly as they went through into the dining room, where Mary and King were already seated.

All through breakfast, Teddi felt his gaze. Once, she looked up from her cup of coffee and stared straight into his steady gray eyes. She didn't move and neither did he, and the air between them sizzled with emotion. He was, she thought wildly, such an impossibly attractive man. She wanted the wildest things—to sit down in his lap, and twine her fingers through that thick, blond hair, to trace his chiseled mouth and feather kisses all over his face. Her heart thudded furiously as she read the exact same hunger in his eyes, silver eyes that seemed to see right into her mind.

"Teddi, that was just delicious," Mary said, bringing her back to reality as she laid her fork down with a smile. "I didn't realize until this minute just how much I miss Miss Peake. Thank you."

"You're very welcome," Teddi replied, trying not to let the exploding emotions she was feeling show in her voice.

"At least the biscuits don't bounce," King observed, leaning back and cocking an amused eyebrow at her.

"King, what a thing to say!" Mary chided. "Why, I thought Teddi's first efforts were…admirable," she said, searching for a polite way to describe Teddi's attempts to make the same biscuits several years earlier.

"I've no quarrel with that," King replied. "They were admirable, all right." He stood up, flexing his broad shoulders absently. "But the biscuits still bounced."

Teddi couldn't repress a smile. "It wouldn't have been so bad if that Oklahoma cattleman hadn't been at the table," she murmured.

"And especially," Jenna couldn't resist adding, "after King had just been bragging about the delicious food Miss Peake was known for, unaware that Teddi had just had her first lesson in biscuit making."

"They *looked* lovely," Mary interrupted loyally.

"And now they're good enough to enter in bake-offs." Jenna smiled.

"Well, I get lots of practice," Teddi reminded her. "Since there aren't any modeling jobs to be had near the college,

I work a split-shift at a restaurant," she told Mary. "My classes don't begin until late morning, so I'm up baking biscuits at 5:00 a.m. Then I go back and work another four hours after classes."

"What the devil for?" King demanded. "Your aunt supports you and pays your tuition. Do you need to kill yourself for spending money?"

"What do you mean, Dilly pays—" Jenna began hotly, until Teddi almost knocked over a chair trying to silence her.

"Never mind, Jenna," she said firmly, silently daring her friend to say another word. If King wanted to believe she was a girl who had to have money for frivolities, and a freeloader to boot, let him, she didn't care. "Excuse me," she said without meeting his eyes, and, putting down her napkin, left the room.

King caught up with her at the staircase, reaching out with a firm but gentle hand to catch her as she started up the steps toward her room.

"I didn't mean that the way you took it," he said before she could speak. His face looked harder than ever, his big body taut and poised, one booted foot on the step she was standing on.

She met his eyes, her look wary and uncertain. "I still have to have clothes to wear to classes," she said quietly. "And on some modeling assignments, I have to have my own wardrobe."

He drew in a deep breath. "And your aunt's generosity doesn't extend that far?"

He wouldn't have believed the extent of her aunt's "generosity," she thought bitterly, remembering that she had to buy her own clothes, pay her own tuition, and manage transportation to and from college. She was practically pen-

niless after all that. But an education would give her the
means to support herself, and she only had another year
to go. Just one more year. Then she'd be totally indepen-
dent of Dilly.

The hand on her arm was suddenly caressing, drawing
her back down beside him. "We have a truce, remember?"
he asked in a deep, lazy tone. "It shocked me to think of
your doing something less glamorous than modeling. It always has. You don't look like a cook, darling."

"The biscuits prove I am one, though," she reminded him
with a faint smile. "They don't bounce anymore."

He watched the light come back into her wide, dark eyes,
and nodded. "So they don't. Come on. We'll ride up to the
gate and back over by the Johnson property."

"Where all those gorgeous blue spruces are?" she asked.

"You always loved blue spruce, didn't you?" he laughed.

She nodded.

He smiled. "Still an outdoor girl, aren't you? Do you
miss the city?"

She looked up at his rugged face under its shock of
blond-streaked hair and saw blatant curiosity in his eyes.
"No," she said truthfully. "I don't miss it at all."

He stared down at her so intensely that she felt as though
her heart would run away with her. But a minute later, he
tore his eyes away from hers and led her out the door.

CHAPTER SIX

RIDING AROUND GRAY STAG was one of Teddi's favorite recreations anytime, but riding with King beside her was a taste of heaven.

He looked magnificent in the saddle, she thought dreamily, glancing at the tall, broad-shouldered man beside her. In his well-fitting jeans and shirt, with a wide-brimmed hat cocked over one eye, shading his hard face, he was handsome enough to make any movie cowboy envious.

He took a draw from his cigarette and turned his head, catching her staring at him. One corner of his mouth curled and he chuckled softly at her embarrassment.

"The, uh, the scenery is lovely through here," she said, clearing her throat nervously.

"So are you, little one," he murmured appreciatively. "I don't mind if you look at me, Teddi. There's nothing to be embarrassed about."

He knew too much about women, she thought half angrily, trying to hold back a grin. She lost, and laughter burst out of her like the sun out of a thundercloud.

He reined in his horse and just looked at her, as if the gleeful, silvery laughter fascinated him. With the sun glinting off her dark hair, and the laughter making lights in her wide brown eyes, she was a sight to stop traffic.

"You make me feel about thirteen," she accused when

she stopped to catch her breath. "And I do wish you'd stop making fun of me. It's not fair."

"I'm not making fun of you," he denied, smiling faintly. "I just like watching you blush, darling."

"Beast," she said, pouting.

He chuckled, urging his mount into a trot alongside her. "Have you seen my new Arabians?" he asked.

"No, we started that way, but Jenna and Blakely got sidetracked…"

His face hardened. "They're doing a lot of that lately," he muttered. "Blakely's slacking up on the job."

"King, he's a nice man," she began hesitantly, wary of disrupting the uneasy truce between them.

His cold gray eyes cut into hers. "You know how Jenna likes to spend money," he said curtly. "How long do you think the boy could support her tastes on his salary? Even if I gave him a tract in the Valley and helped him get started, it would be a hell of a job getting a foothold. He'd need a wife who could work alongside him, support him. Can you see my sister buckling down to that kind of drudgery, at her age?"

"I think Jenna is a lot like you," she said after a minute, choosing her words carefully. "I think she could do anything she wanted to do. And she loves Blakely."

"She's infatuated with him," he corrected. "Girls your age don't know what love is."

She averted her eyes. "Don't we?" she asked with faint bitterness, remembering all the sleepless nights she'd had because of the heartless man riding beside her.

"The fact is, Teddi bear," he concluded, "Jenna is my sister, and it's a family problem."

She felt as if he'd hit her. Always an outsider, was that to be her destiny? "Thanks for reminding me that I'm not allowed a voice in your family matters," she said with cold dignity, refusing to look at him. "If you don't mind, I think I'll go on alone. I don't like the company I'm keeping." She wheeled her horse and rode back down the wide trail under the mammoth pines and spruces, along the wide bend in the river.

King caught up with her there and reached out to catch the reins and jerk her mount to a halt. "Get down," he said.

She didn't move. He dismounted gracefully, his eyes blazing, and jerked her down from the saddle into his hard arms.

"I want to go home," she burst out, seconds away from tears.

"Home is where I am," he said in a goading undertone. "Or haven't you worked that out yet?"

Before she could come up with any sane reply, he bent his head and took her mouth.

She barely felt him lift her into his arms. Her eyes were closed; her whole being was centered around the feel of his warm, hard mouth stroking between her full lips, preparing it, opening it to the piercing intimacy of his tongue.

She drank in the scent of him, the woodsy, smoky mingling of soap and cologne and tobacco, the hardness of his big body where her soft breasts were crushed into it as he carried her.

She felt herself being lowered, but she didn't open her eyes. She was too lost in the slow, tender ardor of his mouth to care where they were. She felt the pine straw under her back, heard the sounds of wind and bubbling river water mingling in her dazed ears as she felt the warmth of him all the way down the length of her tingling body.

It was only when she felt his fingers brushing lightly over her breast that her eyes flew open.

But he held her there with gentle firmness, controlled her with the weight of his body, one powerful leg thrown across hers to keep her from moving away.

"Let me," he said softly, holding her eyes as surely as he held her body, his fingers trespassing over her small, taut breasts as if they had every right in the world to be there.

"Don't," she pleaded in a choked whisper. Her wide, dark eyes pleaded with his blazing gray ones in a silence that magnified the sound of his fingers brushing over the cotton of her blouse.

"Why?" he asked.

"It's so intimate," she managed, hating the helpless reaction of her body that was telling him blatantly how much she was enjoying it.

He bent his blond head and brushed his mouth over her eyelids, forcing them shut. "Don't look at me with those accusing eyes," he whispered. "I'm not going to hurt you. I only want the feel of you, the softness of you under my hands. I want to show you how it can be between a man and a woman."

"You...you just want to humiliate me again, the way you did that day...in the barn," she choked.

She felt him grow taut before his mouth touched her cheek, her neck just below her ear. "That's not the reason," he whispered gruffly. "If you need one, it's because I'm starving for you, is that blunt enough?"

He lifted his head and she opened her eyes, watching the hard mouth poised over hers, feeling the banked tension in his body. "Don't...don't force me," she whispered apprehensively. "Don't...be rough."

"I'll cherish you, if you'll lie still and let me," he breathed against her mouth. "All you have to say is 'no,' darling." His heavy blond eyebrows drew together as his lips fitted themselves exactly to hers, pressing them gently apart. His big hands cupped her face, holding it just where he wanted it, while he kissed her as if he'd die trying to get enough of her soft, tremulous mouth. She found herself soothed by his controlled ardor. She relaxed against him, letting herself sink into the pine straw.

"You see?" he asked, lifting his mouth to brush it over her face in slow, soft kisses that lit a fire in her blood. "I'm not going to pounce on you."

"You know so much about women," she murmured, "and I know so little about men. We're hardly matched."

His lips tugged into a faint smile. He rested his weight on his elbow and studied her flushed face, her lazy, sensuous eyes. His gaze dropped to her blouse and he eased one finger under the edge of the neckline where it plunged into the narrow space between her small breasts.

He watched the helpless reaction in her eyes as he touched her bare flesh, easing his warm, faintly calloused fingers onto the soft, white swell under the wispy lace of her bra.

"You feel so exquisitely soft," he whispered, his fingers slow and gentle, edging toward the taut peak.

Her nails bit into his upper arms and her breath caught. Nothing in her life had been like this, no man had ever touched her this way—it was so different from that nightmare attack of her youth, so caring and tender.

She felt herself go taut, and strange tinglings made her body tremble with anticipation.

"Easy, darling," he whispered softly, leaning close to brush his mouth lightly against hers as his fingers moved again, gentling her. "This is part of it. I'm not going to hurt you. Just relax against me and let it happen."

Her eyes looked straight up into his. "King, this is…the

first time..." she whispered brokenly, trying to tell him, to make him understand the devastating experience it was.

But he seemed to know it already, smiling down at her as he moved, placing his warm mouth over her lips, increasing the pressure gently as his hand eased down, and then up, swallowing her, and she cried out involuntarily at the unexpected surge of pleasure.

He caught his own breath at the wild little sound, drawing back a whisper to look at her. "Magic," he murmured gruffly. "What we do to each other is magic. Buds opening in the sun..."

She felt the violent shudder of his heart against her body, the rasp of his breath, as he kissed her again, deeply this time. She felt new sensations, wild, delicious surges of pleasure that worked their witchcraft on every tingling nerve. Her hands slid up his arms, feeling him, caressing him. They went around his neck and buried themselves in the thick, cool strands of his hair, to keep him close.

She was vaguely aware that both his hands were under her blouse, but she wasn't aware of what they were doing until she felt them against her bare skin, cupping her, molding her, rough and tender and warm, and her eyes flew open and looked straight up into his.

His tanned face looked strained, his eyes narrow and glittering as they read hers. "You fit my hands as if you'd been created for them," he said in a voice she didn't recognize.

She flushed, her lips parting on an unsteady breath.

He looked down at the blouse, under which his hands were outlined as he touched her. "I want to look at you, Teddi," he said quietly.

The thought of his eyes on her bareness was enough to bring her heart into her throat. She wanted that. The breeze on her skin, his eyes seeing her. She wanted him with a suddenness that startled her, all her untouched emotions roused to the point of pain as he caressed her.

"Frightened, little virgin?" he asked softly. "You know I won't hurt you."

"Oh, yes, I know," she said. She reached up and touched his face, daringly, her fingertips tracing the hard line of his mouth, his straight, arrogant nose, pushing back a shock of thick, sun-streaked hair from his broad forehead.

"Do you want it?" he asked quietly.

She touched his mouth, fascinated with it. "If I don't say no right now," she confessed honestly, "I won't be able to. You make me feel as if I'm burning up," she whispered.

"You make me feel the same way," he admitted, yielding reluctantly to the plea in her eyes. He drew his hands away from her body with a heavy sigh, and leaned them on either side of her head. His darkened eyes searched hers. "This is the first time for me, too, did you know?"

She smiled lazily, breathing more steadily now. "Pull the other one, Great White Rancher," she teased.

He grinned back, tugging at a lock of her short hair. "I'm serious. You're the first virgin I've made love to since I was sixteen. And this," he added wickedly, "is the first time in years that I've had to stop."

She searched his eyes, loving him, aching for more than just physical contact. She would have given anything for his love. She sighed. "I'm sorry."

"There's no need." He traced one of her thin eyebrows with a lazy finger. "Teddi, haven't you ever wanted a man?"

She swallowed. She was tempted to tell him all of it, nightmare and all, but this wasn't the time. It would spoil things between them. "No," she said after a minute. "At least, not before you."

He leaned his forehead against hers with a rough sigh. "Oh, honey, what a thing to admit to a man," he ground out. "Can't you tell how much I want you?"

It was hard to miss, as close as he was, and she felt faintly embarrassed by the knowledge. "I...don't imagine you have this problem too often," she murmured.

He drew away and stared down at her as if he had immediate fears for her sanity, and she flushed beet-red.

"I mean," she corrected, avoiding his gaze, "I don't imagine that many women say 'no' to you."

"We won't talk about other women," he said firmly. "I'm not a playboy, if that's what you're insinuating."

"You'd hardly have time to be, the way you push yourself here at the ranch," she agreed, glancing up at him. "You work much too hard."

He toyed with a strand of her hair. "Habit, darling," he admitted, and the endearment sounded genuine. "I've always had to work hard. In the early days, if I'd allowed myself much time for recreation, everything we had would have gone on the auction block. I had Mother and Jenna to think about after my father died, and three properties to manage. I had to keep everything going."

"And you've made a success of all of them," she said. Her fingers touched the silky hair at his temples. "It's made you hard, though."

"Business is ruthless, little one, didn't you know?"

"Yes, I know," she murmured, remembering her own hard knocks in the world of modeling when she'd first entered it.

"Your own life hasn't been easy," he remarked.

"It wasn't so bad, after I got to boarding school," she lied. A smile touched her mouth. "And I had Jenna to talk to."

His face seemed to harden. "When I wasn't making

things difficult for you, you mean. I've been a brute to you at times. But you can't know the pressures I was under, the way it's been with me." His darkening eyes met her puzzled ones and dropped to her mouth. "Kiss me," he said gruffly, bending. "Kiss me the way you wanted to that morning in the stables when I teased you."

Without even thinking, she locked her hands behind his head and dragged it down to hers, letting her mouth tell him how hungry she'd been, and still was, holding him close, close....

"Don't you like to taste me?" he murmured against her mouth.

"I am," she murmured back.

He rubbed his nose against hers. "I'm going to have to teach you how to kiss, I can see that right now."

"I know how," she protested.

"Little girl kisses," he scoffed with a wicked gleam in his eyes. "Not half intimate enough. I like it like this, Teddi..." He caught her cheeks and teased her lips with his until they parted hungrily. His tongue shot past them, and she clutched him as he taught her things she'd never known about the way people kissed. He didn't just use his lips; she felt the gentle thrust of his tongue, the nibbling pressure of lips and teeth as he tormented her until she thought she'd go mad.

"Please, King," she whispered brokenly, her nails biting into his back, her eyes riveted to his mouth. "Please, please...!"

"No holding back this time," he growled as his mouth took hers fully. "Kiss me."

And she kissed him back as hungrily as a new wife, as passionately as a woman who'd just found the love of her life. With a sense of awe, she felt the full weight of his body settling over hers until they were locked together, breast to breast, thigh to thigh, hip to hip, and she clung as the unfamiliar contact burned the most exquisite sensations into her reeling mind.

"King," she whispered into his devouring mouth.

"Darling," he whispered back on a hard groan, shifting as he felt the soft, involuntary movement of her young body, surprising a sweet little cry from her throat.

She felt herself trembling. Incredibly, so was he, and even as she felt her body yielding everything he was demanding, he suddenly stiffened and, with a muffled curse, rolled away from her. He lay breathing roughly on his back, one knee drawn up between them, his forearms over his face.

"King…?" she asked, concerned at the rigidity of his big body.

"Go walk around for a minute, love," he said in a taut, aching tone, "and give me a little while to lie here and curse my own stupidity. Go on," he added when she hesitated.

She got up shakily and walked over to the bank of the river, watching it run lazily between the banks while her heartbeat slowly calmed. Her back against a tree at the edge, she tore off a bit of bark and sailed it down into the water, her eyes drifting from the majestic pines to the mountains beyond.

She felt rather than saw him behind her a little bit later, and she dropped her eyes to the ground.

"Embarrassed?" he asked gently as he lit a cigarette.

"A little," she admitted quietly. "I…didn't know, you see."

He laughed softly, drawing her close beside him with a protective arm around her shoulders. "We're both human," he murmured. "And together, we're volatile. I should have expected it."

She looked up at him shyly. "I wasn't teasing…"

"Don't you think I know that?" His eyes searched hers quietly. "It was beautiful. Not some sordid roll in the hay, not lust. I've never been that gentle with a woman in my life—or that intent on pleasing one. You're...very special, little one," he added, frowning. "You make me vulnerable in ways I couldn't have imagined."

She dropped her eyes to his chest, drinking in the sound of his deep, tender voice, the words that revealed he had some kind of feeling for her, after all.

"I thought it was the other way around," she whispered.

His mouth brushed against her forehead. "You can't imagine what it did to me," he breathed, "touching you that way, knowing that no other man ever had." He caught his breath and hugged her close for an instant before he let her go and moved away to retrieve his hat from the ground, where it had fallen an eternity ago.

"As much as I hate the thought," he said, "I'm a working man. And to make it all worse, I've got that bloody accountant coming this afternoon." His eyes darted to catch hers and he looked faintly irritated. "There's something you need to know about him before he gets here."

"What?" she asked, smiling.

He stared at her, captivated by the radiance of her face. "No," he said. "Not yet. I'll tell you later. Come on, tiger, let's go home."

The ride back was quiet, and Teddi didn't admit to herself how much she was hoping that when he helped her down in the stables, he'd kiss her just once more. But when they reached the huge barn where the horses were quartered, Blakely and Jenna were just coming from the house, and Teddi felt her heart sink.

"There you are," Jenna said, clinging to Blakely's hand and laughing as if she had the sun captured inside her.

"Some man is here to see you, King. Mother drove into Calgary to pick him up, and they've just come back."

King nodded. "The accountant," he said with a strangely secretive glance at Teddi. "Well, let's go in. You might as well all be introduced at once. He's going to be here for a few days."

Teddi dismounted by herself and fell into step with Jenna and Blakely while one of the ranch hands took the horses away. None of them could keep up with King's long strides; he was walking like a man with a distasteful goal ahead.

"Here's King, now," Mary was saying as they walked into the living room.

The visitor stood up, lean and dark and brown-haired, smiling crookedly when he saw Teddi. She got a good look at him at the same time, and all the bad luck in the world seemed to descend on her at once. This wasn't just any accountant. This was Bruce Billingsly, who'd hounded her so single-mindedly at the beginning of the year that she'd even risked King's contempt and accepted an invitation from Jenna at Easter. Bruce, who wouldn't take no for an answer.

So now she knew who King's secret informant was, who'd been telling him lies about her life, her work. She knew who'd helped to poison his mind against her. And here was the culprit in person, with a gleam in his eye telling her clearly that he had more mischief in mind.

Her wary eyes turned to King, who was watching the silent exchange with a cold scrutiny.

"Small world, Teddi," Bruce laughed, moving close to bend and kiss her on the cheek, to her amazed indignation. "How do you do, Miss Devereaux, Blakely? Good to see you again, King, but," he added, with a raised eyebrow as he drew a rigid Teddi to his side, "what's my girl doing here?"

CHAPTER SEVEN

THERE WAS A small flash of emotion in King's gray eyes that no one seemed to catch except Teddi. When he turned to Bruce Billingsly, there was nothing in his expression except a trace of mockery.

"As I told you before," he told Teddi over Bruce's shoulder, "we have a mutual acquaintance."

"Sure. Me," Bruce said with a grin. "Oh, I've been singing your praises for the past several months, honey. King didn't know much about your modeling career, but I filled him in."

I'll just bet you did, Teddi thought miserably, remembering how she'd tried to elude her aunt's boyfriend. He was like so many of Dilly's other pickups, arrogant, a little conceited, and money-hungry as well. Since he couldn't land Dilly, he'd set his sights on Teddi, with a lot of enthusiasm and no success at all. And apparently when he realized that King had a passing acquaintance with her, he decided to make sure that nothing could develop in that quarter while he was pursuing her. He'd even shown up at college once or twice, and she'd had a time trying to shoo him away.

Teddi's apprehensive eyes looked up into King's and read the disgust and contempt there. Bruce's arrival had killed the trust that had been growing so delicately between them. The beautiful morning would become a memory, there would never be a repeat of it. She saw that in King's hard face. It was as if he'd been looking for an excuse, a weapon. And now he had it.

"Aren't you glad to see me, Teddi?" Bruce, grinning, hugged her.

King stabbed his hands into his jean pockets. "You didn't tell me about your budding romance, darling," he said, and it didn't sound like an endearment anymore. "But now that Billingsly is here, perhaps you'll have time to pursue it. When," he added with a cold smile for Bruce, "he's through getting my books in order. And there's no time like the present. Shall we get to it?"

"But, King, he's only just arrived," Mary protested, her sense of hospitality outraged.

"He didn't come here for a social gathering, Mother," he reminded her. "Billingsly?"

Bruce knew the whip in that deep voice, apparently. "I'm ready," he lied, letting go of Teddi reluctantly. "I'll see you later, honey, we've got a lot to talk about."

"Indeed we have," Teddi said with a venomous smile, her dark eyes flashing.

King didn't even look her way, and his back was arrow-straight as he led the shorter man out of the room.

"What was that all about?" Jenna asked, while Blakely and her mother discussed ranch business.

"I told you about him," Teddi moaned. "The one who chased me until I couldn't stay in New York at all for being hounded?"

"That's him?" Jenna gasped. "Here?"

"Here, though heaven only knows how. He works for the firm that does King's accounting, I suppose," she said miserably. "Now that I think of it, he told me he knew King when he was running after me, but I never asked how. I should have realized…"

"That's the man who came up to college looking for you," Jenna burst out, remembering. "Holy mackerel!"

"He just wouldn't take no for an answer. I thought that when I came up here at Easter I'd finally gotten rid of him," she said with a wan smile. "Oh, Jenna, what am I going to do? King believes him, he really believes there's something between us. I couldn't even push the silly man away, I was too shocked at seeing him here, and heaven only knows what lies he's been telling King about me! And King will believe every word," she added miserably.

Jenna was beginning to add things up. The look on Teddi's face when she and King had ridden in, the very tender light in her brother's eyes, the slight swell of Teddi's lower lip, the pine straw in her hair—it all began to make sense.

"Just what were you and King doing in the woods besides discussing international economics and the future of democracy?" Jenna asked, tongue in cheek.

Teddi blushed, and Jenna had the answer she wanted. She laughed delightedly.

"Now I know why King's been so hard to live with," she murmured. "Mother said he'd been horrible since Easter. Something happened then, too, didn't it, after you threw that feed bucket at him? Oh, my friend—" her gray eyes lit up "—if you knew how I've dreamed of having you for a sister-in-law...."

"It isn't like that," Teddi protested, embarrassed. "And you mustn't say anything. Oh, please, Jenna, you can't!"

There was a long, heartfelt sigh. "All right," came the grudging promise, "I'll keep quiet. But you do care for him, don't you?"

The dark eyes fell. "Yes," she admitted quietly. If caring could be described as a passionate obsession that hadn't waned in almost six years, then, yes, it was definitely caring.

"And King?" Jenna prodded.

She shrugged. "Who knows what he thinks? It doesn't matter now, anyway. He's always believed the worst of me, and now here's Bruce to feed him some of the most delicious lies he's ever tasted. He'll be overjoyed."

"Stop that," Jenna said sternly. "If King feels something for you himself, what makes you think he's going to believe Bruce? He's intelligent enough to know pique and hurt masculine pride when he sees them. If Bruce is just out for revenge, he'll see that, too."

"Will he?" Teddi said and shrugged. "Let's go and make some sandwiches. I imagine we'll have hungry mouths to feed any minute."

"Might as well, I suppose." Jenna looked worriedly toward Blakely and her mother. "Oh, Mother, we're going to make lunch!"

"Can I help?" Mary offered.

"No, dear, you talk to Blakely," Jenna encouraged, with a pointed look at Blakely, who reddened slightly. "It will only take a few minutes."

"What's going on back there?" Teddi whispered when they were out of earshot.

Jenna took a deep breath. "Blakely's going to ask her advice about how to deal with King. He...he wants to marry me," she added, faltering. Her eyes closed blissfully. "Teddi, he wants to marry me!" She looked as if she had every single blessing in the world as she said it.

If Teddi had any doubts about her friend's emotional involvement with Blakely, that settled them.

"Can I help?" she asked her friend.

"I may have to call on every single friend I have in the

world and all my acquaintances to get around King," Jenna said miserably. "He'll say I'm too young, that Blakely won't be able to give me what I want, that I won't settle..."

All of which was just what King had told Teddi, and she had to look away to keep her best friend from reading it in her expressive face.

"I love him," Jenna said stubbornly. "If I have to draw water from a well and make my own clothes, I'll do it, as long as I can live with him. That's all I want in the world. And I'll get it," she added with a stubborn set to her jaw. "You just watch me!"

"I believe you," Teddi assured her with a laugh. She was a lot like King, and if anybody had a chance of holding out against him, it was Jenna.

THE MEN ATE their sandwiches in the study, so Teddi was spared a confrontation. But when they sat down to dinner that night, it was as close to civilized warfare as Teddi had ever come.

Bruce sat across from her, his eyes resting appreciatively on the soft white shirtwaist dress she'd donned. King glared at her from the head of the table, his eyes as cold as winter. She felt like a human sacrifice, and Jenna's evident amusement didn't help a bit. Mary, blissfully oblivious of the undercurrents around her, chatted enthusiastically about an upcoming art exhibit in Calgary.

"I thought you'd be working this summer, Teddi," Bruce murmured when there was a pause in the conversation. "I asked for a local assignment in New York for that reason."

Teddi met his eyes coolly. "Did you?" she muttered, hating him for what he'd done to her fragile relationship with King. "I thought I'd made it quite clear that I didn't have time for a lot of nightlife."

"Pull the other one, honey," he laughed, his eyes calculating as he measured King's interest. "I've seen you in nightclubs all over New York."

Teddi's eyes dilated. "You most certainly have not!" she cried.

"Sure, if that's the way you want it," he agreed, making it sound as if he was covering up for her. "It doesn't matter, you know," he added in a demoralized tone. "I know I couldn't compete with the kind of money your escorts had. I'm just a working man."

Teddi's fingers clenched on her fork, and just for one wild second, she contemplated the effect of throwing her plate across the table at him. His eyes were laughing at her. He knew what he was doing, and she realized all at once that her first impression had been right. He was going to crucify her for the blow she'd dealt his masculine pride. If he couldn't have her, no other man was going to, especially not King.

"I don't need to date rich men," she bit off.

"You don't?" Bruce asked innocently. "But, sweet, Dilly doesn't give you a penny toward your education. You've got to get money somewhere."

He was planting deadly seeds and finding fertile ground in King's already suspicious mind.

"I make enough to support myself," Teddi said.

"You must, if you can take the whole summer off for a vacation," Bruce said with an insinuating look toward King. "Or are you up here on a 'fishing' trip?"

King's expression was one of pure fury.

With a mighty effort, Teddi lifted her coffee cup to her lips and managed not to burst into tears. It was like having an invisible knife take the skin off an inch at a time, and nobody could see the wounds. Especially not King, who got to his feet and tossed his napkin down.

"If you're through, Billingsly?" he asked with maddening carelessness, leading the way out of the dining room.

Teddi watched him go, aware of Bruce's triumphant smile as he followed. The light went out of her eyes, her soul, at that moment, because she knew King had believed Bruce. All that she had kept from him was suddenly out in the open. Now King knew that she was responsible for her own educational expenses, her living expenses, that Dilly didn't help out—and he believed one more thing, that she needed money. He would inevitably come to the conclusion that she had been trying to trap him, especially since she'd come to Gray Stag instead of going back to New York during summer vacation. He would fit those puzzle pieces together, along with what Bruce had let drop about her so-called "dates" with wealthy men—a lie if there ever was one—and her indifference to working men. And when he put all that together, he was going to have a false picture of a penniless young woman out to catch a wealthy man any way she could. The fact that she flirted with him at Easter would take on new meaning. And there was nothing, absolutely nothing she could do to convince him that he was wrong, because now he'd think she was a liar. Chances were good that he'd also doubt her innocence, think it was part of the act, part of her plan to trap him into marriage. She felt tears welling up in her eyes.

"Coffee's hot!" she said as she put her cup down with a laugh, hoping to explain her sudden tears.

"Suppose we take the pot in there," Jenna suggested icily, "and pour it over Mr. Billingsly's head? What a bunch of rot! And my big, dumb brother sitting there looking as if he believed every word! Men are the stupidest...!"

"What an excellent suggestion," Mary said, her usually kind face drawn into taut lines. "And I'll have the daily maid put him in the green guest room. It has the lumpy mattress, remember?" she added with a malicious smile.

"Mother, you're a jewel." Jenna grinned.

"I think I'll go look for a few rocks to tuck in among the lumps," Teddi said with a wan smile. "See you later."

She walked out, a slim, dejected figure, and two pairs of pained, sympathetic eyes followed her.

She was expecting King to confront her, and minutes later he found her in the moonlit garden behind the house and paused just in front of her.

"Bruce told me what good friends you two were," he mocked. His darkening gray eyes cut at her as he spoke. "I never knew until today whether to believe him."

"But this evening's performance convinced you," she replied.

"I beg your pardon?"

"Never mind," she said, turning dejectedly away. "Naturally you believed every word he said, it only confirmed your own sterling opinion of me."

"Aren't you going to deny it?" he challenged.

"No," she replied stiffly. "I can't see that it makes that much difference."

He stared at her small, stiff back, his eyes doubtful, uncertain. But she didn't turn, and she missed the expression that crossed his hard face.

"Think how fortunate you were to have been saved from me in the nick of time," she said over her shoulder as she started toward the house. "Good old Bruce, he's a knight, he is."

"How much of that innocence was an act?" he asked coldly.

She'd known that question would come, and she was ready for it. If he wanted to believe lies, she'd give him some more, the beast! "All of it, darling," she taunted, batting her eyelashes at him, while her heart splintered in her chest. "That's what you believe, isn't it, and Kingston Devereaux never makes mistakes about women," she reminded him, using his own words.

She walked away and left him standing there. What good would it have done to contradict Bruce, anyway? She consoled herself. The morning had only been a dream.

IN THE DAYS that followed, Bruce dogged her every step. The only good thing about it was that King kept his nose to the grindstone, with a single-mindedness that raised Jenna's pale eyebrows.

The time inevitably came when she and Bruce confronted each other, unexpectedly one morning when Jenna and Blakely had invited Teddi to go for a swim. She'd rushed to get away from Bruce's hot eyes and King's cold ones, hurriedly donning her pale yellow two-piece suit and throwing a sundress over it.

A long whistle met her as she came down the staircase to find Bruce lounging against the study door, watching her.

"You get lovelier by the day," he told her. "Teddi, when are you going to stop avoiding me?"

"Never," she told him bluntly. "Look, I don't want to hurt your feelings, but I've told you until I'm blue in the face that I don't feel that way about you! Why can't you just leave me alone?"

"Because I learned young that a man can get anything he wants if he keeps after it long enough," he replied confidently.

"Not people," she replied. "Not ever people. You can't force people to love, Bruce."

The grin widened. "Who's talking about love?" he murmured, eyeing her body.

She stiffened. "I'm not ready for that kind of relationship with any man."

"So you said," he murmured, "but there's fire under all that ice, I'd bet my right arm on it. I could make you change your mind. There's never been a woman I couldn't get," he added with hateful confidence.

"Meet number one," she hurled back, tired of arguing. "I don't want you. Can't you get that through your thick skull!"

"Who do you want, the cattle baron?" he growled. "It won't work, Teddi. I'm not handing you over to him without a fight. I saw you first."

"What are you talking about?"

"I've told King things about you," he said huskily. "None of it very flattering, but he believed it. I can make it even worse if you don't play ball. You're my girl, and I'm not giving you up."

"Look, will you just leave me alone?" she burst out, feeling her control snap.

"I can't," he murmured. His eyes leered at her. "You're a knockout, do you know? You drive me wild," he concluded, and his desire found expression in his eyes as he moved forward. He caught her before she could react and dragged her into his arms, emotion clouding his eyes as he forced her to be still, despite her struggles.

"Turn me loose," she ground out, trying to find enough space to kick his shin.

"Not on your life," he grumbled, bruising her with his tight hold. "You threw me over at Easter. You tore my pride to shreds. Wouldn't even let me get close, give me a chance to get to know you. Well, here I am and here you are, and this time you're going to spend some time with me or I'll ruin you with your rich friends. I didn't have old Mr. Murray send me out here to do King's books for nothing..."

"Think so?" she asked. She dipped suddenly and brought her foot down sharply on his instep.

He cried out, and she tore away from him, breathing hard, her hair and eyes wild.

It was at that moment that King came in the door. His sharp eyes went from Teddi's disheveled appearance to his accountant's pained expression. Immediately, he jumped to his own conclusions.

"I'll remind you that you're working on my time," King told Bruce with barely controlled anger. "That doesn't allow you the luxury of flirting with Teddi. Clear?"

Bruce shrugged, shooting a lightning glance at Teddi. "Whatever you say, Mr. Devereaux. My fault. I shouldn't have let myself be tempted," he added damningly as he turned and went back into the study.

"Leave him alone," King told her coldly, his eyes contemptuous as they ran the length of her body. "I should have followed my instincts and let you go to New York in the first place. We're a small community here, with old-fashioned moral values. If I catch you playing around with your boyfriend under my roof, you'll both go out on your ears."

And before she could voice the furious reply her mind was forming, he followed Bruce into the study and slammed the door in her face.

Minutes later, she was fuming in the cold, clear water of the river.

"King again?" Jenna asked as soon as Blakely left them to dress in the secluded shade of some nearby bushes.

"However did you guess?" Teddi asked with a weary sigh.

"Oh, I'm getting quite good at mind reading," came the amused reply. "He's giving you a rough time about Bruce, huh? The idiot. He's just impossible lately. Ever since Bruce came, in fact." She glanced at Teddi. "Doesn't he act jealous, though?" she mused.

Teddi's face was suffused with color. "King? Jealous of me?"

"Why don't you tell him the truth?" Jenna asked as they climbed out of the water. She paused and turned to face her friend. "Teddi, what have you got to lose?"

"My self-respect, my pride, my—"

"You can do without those. But can you do without King?"

Teddi let her eyes drop to the ground, where the sun shining through the leaves was making shadow patterns. "I've done very well without him for almost six years," she murmured.

"He feels something," Jenna said quietly. "We both know that. But unless you make him see the truth, he's very likely to wall his emotions up for good where you're concerned."

That was possible. And he had felt something, Teddi knew that better than her friend did, remembering the hunger of his hard mouth, the urgency of his body against hers that magic morning in the woods. King had dashed her pride to slivers once—could she take it if he did that again? On the other hand, no one achieved anything worthwhile without courage. There were no great rewards without great risks.

She took a deep breath. "Well, I can't look any worse in his eyes than I already do, can I?" she asked with a whimsical smile.

"He was going out to check the stock this morning after

he finished with Bruce," Jenna murmured. "You might find him in the stables."

"What a smelly place to chase a man," Teddi grumbled.

"At least it's private," Jenna laughed. "Uh, Blakely and I discovered that early on. Now, get out there and fight. Just remember one thing—you catch more flies with honey than you can with vinegar."

Teddi sighed. "There's just one thing wrong with that philosophy."

"What's that?"

Teddi gave her a mischievous glance. "Who's going to hold King while I smear honey on him?"

Jenna simply threw up her hands.

THE WALK TO the stables was the longest Teddi ever remembered making. Several times she almost decided to turn and go back to the house. The "what-ifs" drove her wild. What if he didn't believe her? What if she told him how much she loved him, and he laughed at her? What if she threw her arms around him, and he pushed her away? It was insane, this idea of Jenna's. She felt a sense of foreboding. There was still time, she could turn back. But what if she did, and King turned away from her forever?

Resolutely she forced herself not to worry about her still-damp hair, about her bareness under the sundress. In her haste, she had thrown on the dress, leaving her wet bathing suit with Jenna.

She entered the dimly lit barn, blinking her eyes to adjust them to the darkness inside. Her gaze lit on a shadow that moved into view out of one of the neat hay-filled stalls.

It was King, denim-clad and powerful looking, and as unyielding as the walls.

"Looking for your lover?" he asked in a mocking tone.

"No, actually I was looking for you," she said before her courage deserted her.

He lifted his head, looking down at her with his lips slightly pursed, studying her slender young body, which was only barely covered by the yellow-and-white gingham dress. It was a seductive little coverup, held over her breasts by a narrow band of elastic, elasticized at the waist, barely brushing her knees at the hem. Her feet were encased in strappy little white sandals. The picture she made was one of sunny innocence, joyful youth.

A glimmer of passion appeared in King's hard face as he looked at her, and that tiny chink in his armor gave her enough nerve to approach him. He wasn't indifferent to her, that was certain enough. And all her small doubts were instantly erased when she pressed her hands against his damp shirt front and moved close. His heart was beating too hard, his broad chest rising and falling much too rapidly for a calm man. The tautness of his body gave her answers to questions she wouldn't have dared ask.

"Now will you listen to me?" she asked, looking up into darkening, stormy eyes. Her hands flattened against his shirt, faintly caressing. "Bruce is just getting even with me. Earlier this year, he wanted to date me and I wouldn't go out with him. It hurt his pride, and now he's out for revenge. I don't want Bruce. I…I want you, King," she breathed, going on tiptoe to brush her lips against his throat, his chin, the corner of his mouth. Bold with new confidence, feeling for the first time like a whole woman instead of a frightened girl, she reached up to lock her fingers in his thick hair and pressed her hungry lips against his hard, unyielding mouth.

"Oh, kiss me," she breathed achingly, pressing closer to his hard, taut body with a hunger that flared like a match thrown into dry wood. "Kiss me!"

Steely fingers suddenly bit into her arms and tore loose her grip on him. He thrust her from him with a force that almost tripped her. She caught her balance, staring at him with wide, apprehensive eyes.

"Don't you ever," he said in a voice like a razor's edge, "try that with me again! My God, everything he said about you was the truth, wasn't it?" His accusing eyes swept over her. "This is the real you, isn't it, darling? Eager, willing, wanton...and there I was, treating you like porcelain because I didn't want to frighten you. Frighten you! How much do you get for a night, Teddi?" he asked with a half smile that sickened her. "Maybe we can work something out."

Devastated, she wrapped her arms around her trembling body and turned to leave.

"No comeback?" he taunted. "What's the matter, are you holding out for a ring? No chance, honey. You'll have to ply your wiles on some other rich rancher. I just went off the market!"

She turned at the entrance to the barn and looked back at him. "First blood to you, Mr. Devereaux," she said with cool pride. "You're wrong about me. You always have been. You'll believe anything you're told, as long as it's something bad, won't you? Well, I'm no more a hooker than you are a gentleman, and someday you'll find that out. Not that it will make any difference to me. Rich or not, I want no part of a man who's morally blind."

And she turned and walked away.

KING DIDN'T COME in for dinner that night, and Teddi pleaded a splitting headache and stayed in her room that night. The headache was real enough, she told herself—six foot three with blond hair and gray eyes and the farsightedness of a mole.

She'd just pulled on a long yellow cotton nightgown when there was a knock at her door.

She stared at it blankly. "Who's there?"

There was no answer. Maybe…she brightened. Maybe it was King; maybe he'd had second thoughts and had finally decided to listen. She went to the door and pulled it open. Bruce, in his robe, stood outside grinning at her.

She tried to shut the door, but he wouldn't let her. He forced her back into the room, leaving the door carefully open, like a man with a master plan who wouldn't brook interference.

"What do you think you're doing?" she cried, struggling with him as he forced her back against the bed.

"It's called the coup de grace, darling," he said in an undertone, abruptly pushing her back onto the bedcovers just before he threw himself down beside her and buried his face in her throat. "Guess who's coming up the stairs?"

She pushed futilely at him, barely avoiding his hot mouth as it went across her cheek and tried to catch her lips.

She cringed when she heard the door suddenly open even farther. Turning her head, she saw King standing in the doorway, watching with condemning eyes.

Bruce sat up and ran a hand through his disheveled hair, grinning at King.

"Sorry about that," he told his employer. "We got carried away and forgot to close the door."

King glanced from the younger man, clad only in a robe, to Teddi dressed in the semisheer cotton nightgown. The contempt in his face was unbearable.

"I'll expect you both to be packed and out of here by tomorrow morning," King said in a quiet, very controlled tone.

Bruce gaped at him, as if he hadn't expected anything so drastic. "But, King... Mr. Devereaux...what will I tell my firm?"

"That's your affair," King said coldly. "I'll let you explain it after I've given them the bare facts and requested another accountant. I warned you about playing around under my roof. You might have listened."

"But—!" Bruce cut short his protest when the door slammed shut.

He stared at it, bug-eyed. "He didn't mean that, surely!"

"Of course he meant it," Teddi said numbly. She got off the bed and tugged on her thick toweling robe. She felt her world ending with a sense of quiet inevitability.

"I didn't think he'd react like that," Bruce choked out. "I just wanted to make sure he didn't snap you up before I had one more chance, that's all."

"Snap me up." Teddi laughed bitterly, shoving her hands in the deep pockets of her robe. "He's hated me for five years. He's always believed I was some sort of nymphomaniac. You only confirmed his darkest suspicions. But it backfired, didn't it?"

He sighed wearily. "I feel sick," he mumbled. "I've got car payments, my rent's due...and when the firm finds out I've been sent back, I may lose my job."

"I'm sorry," she said, "but you did bring it on yourself. I told you how I felt. You just wouldn't listen. Would you please go?"

He looked up, noticing for the first time the tears running down her pale cheeks, the horrible expression in her eyes. "You love him," he said with dawning realization.

She hunched her drooped shoulders. "I had a tiny chance before you came. Now there's no chance at all. I hope life is as empty for you as you've just made it for me," she added with a flash of spirit.

He seemed to shrink before her eyes. "If it's any consolation, I feel like a prize idiot. I meant to upset the cart, any way I could, because I wanted you to notice me. I couldn't compete with King—who could? And the way he looked at you...well, I thought if I could get the competition out of the way, I might still have a chance." He met her eyes, and there was a sadness in his. "I've never felt this way about a woman. You were like an obsession." He sighed. "At any rate, I am sorry, for what good it does."

"Not very much, I'm afraid," she said honestly.

"As I thought. Well...good night. I'll see you in the morning. Perhaps if I explained to King...?"

She smiled sadly. "He wouldn't listen," she replied. "When he makes up his mind, that's it."

"I really am sorry," he added just before he left the room.

But she didn't reply. What else was there to say?

IT WAS LATE before she finally got to sleep, and she dragged out of bed the next morning with eyes that were red from the combination of tears and insomnia. She packed before she went downstairs, knowing that King had meant every word of that terse command the night before.

She went into the dining room at the usual time for breakfast, expecting and hoping to see King already gone. But he was sitting at the table by himself, a cup of coffee in front of him, and nothing else.

She moved into the room with a bravado she didn't feel, elegant in her white pleated skirt, white gauze blouse and black bolero jacket.

"Could I have a cup of coffee?" she asked, intimidated by the expression on his hard face, the glittering anger in his deep-set eyes. He was wearing brown denims with a pullover beige shirt, and despite his fair hair, he looked dark and foreboding.

"Help yourself, darling," he said coldly.

She sat down as far away from him as she could get and poured herself a cup of black coffee from the pot on the warmer. The mahogany dining table was long, and she felt uncomfortable seated at one end in her brocade-upholstered chair. She glanced from the crystal prisms of the chandelier to King, silhouetted against the drawn pale jade curtains at the window behind him.

"Is...is Jenna coming down?" she asked falteringly.

"She and Mother have already been down," he said curtly. "I asked them to stay upstairs until you left. I've told my sister that if she continues her friendship with you, I'll send her young Blakely to the Australian property for an indefinite stay."

The pure chauvinism of the remark made her bristle. "In chains?" she asked with a cool smile. "Or perhaps you thought you'd make him swim the Pacific while you rowed alongside yelling suggestions?"

His face went harder. "My family's business is no longer any of your concern," he said remotely. "Your friend should be down any minute. I've lent him a vehicle to drive you into Calgary. I'll have it picked up later."

She stared into her coffee, too drained of emotion to even cry. Not only was she losing King, but Jenna was to be forbidden any contact with her. Her only friend....

"Do you have enough money to get to New York?" he asked with casual politeness.

"Yes," she bit off.

He finished his coffee and set the cup down firmly. "How is he in bed?" he asked, lashing out unexpectedly.

Her eyes jerked up and she glared at him with pain and anger in every line of her pale face. "Just great, thanks!" she threw at him. "He could give you lessons!"

"You little tramp!" he breathed. He was on his feet before she could move, reaching down to drag her out of the chair and up into his hard arms.

"Put me down!" she cried, fighting. But he was strong—much stronger than Bruce had been. He carried her, squirming, into his study and kicked the door shut behind them without even breaking stride.

He threw her down onto the long, leather sofa and stood over her, breathing roughly, his face livid with barely leashed fury.

He paused just long enough to rip off the knit shirt, baring a chest with bronzed muscles under a thick wedge of curling dark blond hair, before he came down beside her.

"Go ahead, darling, fight me," he ground out, controlling her struggles easily as his mouth crushed down on hers. "It'll just make it that much more intense when I make you submit."

She felt his hands on her body, careless of hurting her, while she tried vainly to push him away, to free herself. She loved him, but what he was doing to her was monstrous. Her mind reeled back to that long-ago night, to the feel of that drunken beast's cruel hands, the hot searching of his mouth. She cried out, but King didn't seem to hear.

He dragged her blouse away from her skirt, and his hands went roughly under it, easily disposing of the lacy obstacles, to find her bare, soft flesh with rough fingers.

It was just like that long-ago night, and she was fighting suddenly for all she was worth, mindlessly fighting in a blind fury, sobbing, crying, her face contorted into a mask of panic-stricken terror.

His hands were busy again, on the buttons of her blouse, and before she could stop him, the fabric was suddenly out of the way, and King drew back. He held her by the wrists, his eyes cloudy as he studied her writhing body, her white face, her wide, frightened eyes.

He stood poised there, like a man barely able to think at all, staring down at her half-nude body, bare from the waist up where her blouse was pushed aside. For an instant, his gaze was riveted to the soft mounds of her breasts and he dragged in breaths like a man dying of oxygen deprivation. Did she imagine it, or was there a softening in his face, did his steely fingers relax just a little where they were biting into her wrists?

"Please," she whispered brokenly. "Please, King, don't hurt me!"

Something snapped in him at the husky sob of her voice. He looked back up at her face, and she watched the conflicting emotions war in his eyes.

"Teddi?" he murmured, seeming to snap back to sanity as he realized how frightened she was.

He let her go all at once and watched, frozen, as she dragged her blouse around herself and huddled into the corner of the sofa, crying like a terrified child in the dark, in little breathless, broken sobs that echoed through the room.

"I wouldn't have forced you," he managed tautly, his eyes never leaving her. "Must you have hysterics every time I touch you?"

"I was fourteen," she said in a strangled voice. "Dilly was going with a decorator who…who took a fancy to me. One night they had a terrible argument and she…she stormed out of the apartment and didn't come back. He'd been drinking, and I thought I'd be safer if I went to my room." She laughed brokenly, avoiding his eyes. "I almost made it. He caught me at the door and dragged me back to the couch and tore half my clothes off." Her eyes closed and she cringed. "He was like a wild animal. He hurt me terribly…hands all over me, horrible wet kisses…and just before he tried to force me, he heard Dilly at the door." She shivered at the memory. She couldn't even look at King. It would have been a revelation to her if she had, because his features had taken on the look of a man being dragged apart by a team of horses.

She swallowed. "He thought he was irresistible, you see, and it made him angry that I fought. He slapped me around quite a lot, and then dared me to tell Dilly. She didn't even question the marks on me," she added with a bitter smile.

She managed to fasten her blouse in the silence that followed. "I've never slept with Bruce," she said finally. "I've never slept with any man. Just the thought of it…terrifies me. I…I thought for a little while that I might be able to accept more than kisses…with you, at least," she whispered. "But not anymore." She stood up, turning toward the door.

"That was why you were so frightened of me in the car on the way back from Banff," he said quietly.

"Yes," she told him. "I…I suppose the scars go pretty deep. He was…quite brutal."

"Teddi!"

She paused with her hand on the doorknob, but she couldn't look at him. "I'll go with Bruce," she said with gentle pride. "And if you still want me to keep away from Jenna, I will."

"Oh, God, don't turn the knife!" he said in a barely audible tone. He started toward her, but she opened the door and moved quickly away from him.

He flinched. "I won't hurt you," he said, hesitating.

"So you promised me once before," she reminded him,

choking on the word. "I think I'd die if you touched me again. Please…all I want is to get away from you!"

She turned, oblivious of the look on his face, and ran all the way upstairs to her room. She didn't leave it until she heard Jenna's concerned voice on the other side. She opened the door and ran straight into her friend's outstretched arms.

CHAPTER EIGHT

THE ONLY GOOD thing about Teddi's abrupt arrival in New York was that Dilly was still away. There was a curt little note on the coffee table telling her that her aunt would most likely be away until late September.

Teddi called her agency first thing, and was pleased to hear that they had work for her right away.

"Velvet Moth is having a showing Saturday for buyers and the press," Mandy burst out enthusiastically. "I told Mr. Sethwick that you were out of town, but he insisted that he only wanted you to do his new gown. He calls it the 'firemist special,'" she added, teasing. "If you accept, you'll need a fitting at Jomar's in the morning at ten. And Lovewear wants a girl for a millinery ad, if you're interested in a go-see. There's an open call Thursday morning at nine, there. I've got a weather permitting for a soft drink commercial as well—you'd fit the client's requirements very well."

A weather permitting assignment would mean a cancellation fee if it fell through, and Teddi jumped at it. It would mean more exposure, too. But she was cautious.

"Who's shooting it?" she asked quickly before she accepted.

"Ronnie, remember him?" came the laughing reply from her agent.

"As long as it's not that crazy Irishman," Teddi said with

a relieved sigh. "Do you remember, he made me jump the wall in that hosiery commercial he was shooting no less than fifty times? I was a nervous wreck when we finished, and it cost me twelve pair of hose because of the snags!"

"I hear he's given up fashion photography and gone into films," Mandy told her.

"And next thing," Teddi murmured, "we'll hear about a film producer going bankrupt on retakes."

Mandy giggled. "No doubt. Well, I'll get back to you on the commercial, and keep in touch tomorrow. Welcome back, by the way. How was Canada?"

"Cold," Teddi said without further ado, and hung up.

The next few days went by in a flash. She made sure that she didn't have time to think about King. Mandy outdid herself in bookings. Teddi did two commercials, the Velvet Moth fashion show, a photography session for the millinery ad and three photographic sessions for other ads. By the end of the week, she was exhausted. She spent Sunday with her feet in a hot tub of water and counted her blessings. She'd made enough to pay next semester's fees and would have just enough left over when all the checks came to pay her airfare back to school.

The slump season in the fashion industry was just down the road, but if she worked a little harder, she might save up a nest egg to carry her through the rest of the year. And the restaurant job near the college would keep her in clothes and incidentals.

That night, her dreams were wild and disturbed and full of King. She woke up at four in the morning crying, and got up to make coffee. Would she ever forget his cruelty to her, the cheap way he'd treated her? Would she ever stop thinking about the way it had been that morning they went riding, when, for the first time, she wasn't afraid, when she was able to give, to open her heart, to love him?

She got dressed in slacks and a loose white blouse with high-heeled sandals and waited impatiently for the agency to open so that she could call Mandy and see if there were any jobs for her. She took a long time over her makeup, did her nails carefully, packed her carryall with the essentials of her trade—brush, comb, makeup, tissues, shoes, hairpieces and clothes, anything she might need during a shooting— and wandered around the living room of the apartment to watch the sun rise over the sleeping city.

Why, oh, why did King always have to think the worst of her? She still cringed at the memory of his hands hurting her, his eyes contemptuous as they stared down at her bareness. It hadn't all been contempt, she reminded herself. For an instant he had seemed to be awed by her, savagely hungry for the sight and feel of her. Of course, any man could feel desire in those circumstances, it meant nothing. The thing that puzzled her was his unreasonable anger about Bruce. Jealousy would explain such fury, but King wasn't jealous of her, how could he be when he thought so little of her? But…why had he fired Bruce? Since his contempt was mainly for her, why punish a man he thought she'd tempted?

She sipped her lukewarm coffee with a grimace of distaste. How hard it was to kill hope, she thought miserably. All the way to the airport, with Bruce contrite and worried beside her, she'd hoped against hope that King would come after her. But he hadn't. She hadn't seen him again after she left the study. When she'd gone downstairs, leaving Jenna behind, Bruce had been waiting, quiet and subdued, and King hadn't even stayed around long enough to say goodbye.

Even the first few days she'd been home, she wondered if King might call. But he hadn't. Why should he? she asked herself, laughing aloud at her own idiocy. He didn't care. If he felt anything now, it was probably guilt over his treatment of her—if his hatred would permit that. At least now that he knew the truth, perhaps he thought less harshly of her.

King. Her eyes pictured him and closed on a new wave of tears. Would she ever get used to being apart from him? Every day she lived was filled with that kind of loneliness that only those who love in vain understand. It had always been King, from the time she was fifteen and got her first look at him. There'd been boys she dated, but none of them could hold her interest. King was so much a man, so far removed from ordinary men. Now she couldn't settle for less.

Angrily, she dashed away the tears and got to her feet. What she needed, she decided, was another cup of hot coffee.

Mandy called an hour later, full of enthusiasm. "Love-wear wants you at nine," she told Teddi. "Can you make it? It's for an interview on three commercials for their new line of jeans!"

"Can I make it? Are you kidding?" Teddi laughed. "I'll crawl there on my knees if I can't catch a cab. Thanks, Mandy!"

She snatched up her portfolio with the composites safely tucked away inside, and paused just long enough to grab her small shoulder bag before she rushed into the elevator, cursing the incredibly high heels that she couldn't take time to change.

She darted through the door and out onto the sidewalk, making a wild dash for the first cab she saw pulling up at the curb. She misjudged the step, and in an incredible se-

DIANA PALMER   283

ries of stumbles, worsened by the high heels, she managed
to land herself just past the cab's front bumper, right in the
path of an oncoming car.

Wide-eyed, helpless, she could see the disaster coming,
but there was nothing in the world she could do in that split
second to save herself. Like a spectator watching her own
body, she observed with an inhuman calmness. Then she
felt a sudden cold emptiness, numbness, and screams followed her down into the darkness.

CHAPTER NINE

THE NEXT FEW hours went by in a haze of terrible pain, urgent voices, movement and sirens, followed by visions of white clothing and silvery metal and, finally, complete numbness.

When she regained full consciousness, she was aware of pain in her face and her right leg and a bruised feeling over most of her body. Added to it all, she had a splitting headache.

Her eyes opened slowly, staring up at a small, dark-eyed nurse who was taking her blood pressure. There was a thermometer in her mouth, and she watched the nurse take it out and read it.

"Hi," the nurse said gently. "Feel up to a few questions now?"

"I think…so." Teddi's hands went to her face, and she felt a thick padding of bandages from her temple to her chin.

"It's all right," the nurse said quickly. "Nothing that won't heal."

Teddi swallowed. "What else?" she asked, turning to notice for the first time the bandages on her right leg where the covers were disheveled.

"Dr. Forbes will tell you all about it," she was assured, "when he makes his rounds in about—" the nurse checked her watch "—thirty minutes. But for now, I'm going to send down someone from admissions and let them get their information, if you're sure you're up to it?"

"Yes, I'm…I'm fine," she said without any conviction. Her face and leg were obviously damaged in some way, and she could only guess at the rest of her injuries. She felt bruised all over.

"Just…one thing," she said before the nurse left. "I was on my way to an interview… I never made it, but could someone call the Amanda Roman Talent Agency and tell them where I am? I'm a model."

"Sure," the nurse assured her with a gentle smile. "I'll do it myself. What is your name, by the way? Did you know, you weren't even carrying any identification on you?"

"Left my wallet at home again," Teddi groaned. "Well, no harm done. I'm Teddi Whitehall."

"I'll make the call right now," the nurse said, and she was gone.

Time dragged horribly until Dr. Forbes, a kind, white-haired gentleman, walked in to tell her what was wrong.

"Your leg was badly lacerated," he began quietly, seating himself on the edge of the bed. "We had to do some cosmetic surgery as we repaired the damage. That's why your thigh may feel a bit uncomfortable. That's where we took a patch of skin for the graft. Not to worry, it'll grow back quickly enough. The same can be done for your face when the stitches come out, if you think you want that. The scar will heal completely, in time, without it," he added, watching her face grow white.

"My…my leg?" she whispered.

He drew in a slow breath. "My dear, there's just no simple way to put it. We can repair flesh and bone, to a degree, and cosmetic surgery will put it nearly right again. But we can't make it as good as new, you understand. Those ligaments are going to take a long time to heal. You may be left with a slight limp. Of course, further surgery can be performed, if necessary."

"Of course," she murmured, barely hearing him.

"And you have a concussion," he added with a faint smile, "as you've probably suspected if your head is throbbing as much as I expect."

"It is uncomfortable," she agreed, touching it.

"I'll have the nurse give you something for it." He patted her hand. "Don't worry about it today. Give yourself time to adjust to the shock. I realize it must seem like the end of the world to a beautiful woman such as yourself, and a model as well. But you know, in the long run, most changes are beneficial, regardless of the disasters they might seem at first. The difficulty is not in situations, my dear, but in our attitude toward them. Your scars will fade before you realize it. A few weeks from now, you'll be moving around quite well."

She nodded, her mind whirling with shock. What was she going to do? The hospital bill would be formidable, and it was clear that she'd be out of work for several weeks if not longer with these disfiguring marks. How could she cope?

"Bear in mind what I said," he told her, rising. "We'll keep you here another day or so, and then you'll have to be careful about getting around, not putting too much pressure on that leg. Once you're home, you'll do very well, I'm sure."

"Yes," she agreed. "Thank you."

When he was gone, she huddled under the bedcovers, staring at the blank television set and the empty bed in the semiprivate room. Teddi couldn't ever remember feeling so alone. She was hurt, deserted, with no one to care about her. They'd asked if she wanted them to notify anyone besides

Mandy. But she'd said no. There was no one to tell. Dilly would only be irritated at the interruption. King didn't care, and he'd forbidden her to call Jenna. She burst into tears, burying her face in her hands. She'd always been strong, because she'd had to be. But for a moment, she gave in to grief. Everything seemed so hopeless.

The next morning, things looked no brighter, but Teddi was beginning to think she might cope better a little further down the road. Toward that end, she asked about being released from the hospital. In the first place, she explained to Dr. Forbes, she just didn't have the funds to cover a long hospital stay and she had no insurance. In the second place, she'd feel much more comfortable in familiar surroundings.

"Well," he frowned thoughtfully, staring at her with his thin lips pursed, "is there someone there to look after you? You won't be able to do much walking, you know, and those dressings will need to be changed."

"Oh, my aunt will be there," she assured him, cringing mentally at the deliberate lie.

He considered the matter for a minute. "All right," he agreed finally. "But you'll need to come to my office in a week and have those stitches removed."

"I'll be there with bells on," she promised.

"Just call my office and make an appointment," he advised. "Now, look me straight in the eye and promise me you'll stay in bed for at least three more days before you try to get up and run road races."

She looked him in the eye and promised. It was a shame that she burst into a giggle on the last word.

It was hard-going alone in the apartment. She could barely hobble to the kitchen, even with the aid of a walking stick, and every step hurt like the devil. If it hadn't been for a friendly neighborhood grocery that delivered, she probably would have starved to death. Dilly hadn't left any food in the place, and the meager supplies Teddi had gotten in when she arrived had dwindled to a carton of spoiled milk and some stale bread.

Despite her diminished finances, Teddi gave the delivery boy a large tip after he was kind enough to not only put the groceries away for her, but fix her some soup and coffee as well.

"After all," she coaxed when he tried to give it back, "without you I'd have starved."

"Oh, I doubt that," he replied with a grin.

She finished her coffee after he'd left and leaned back against the sofa. As she thought of the assignments she was probably missing, tears misted her eyes. Her fingers went to the bandage on her cheek. She'd mustered enough courage that morning to change it, and had cried bitterly at the sight of the red antiseptic-smeared gashes with their ugly black stitches. She looked like an advertisement for a horror movie.

She was so wrapped up in her morose reflections that it was several moments before she realized the phone was ringing. She stretched over to pick up the receiver.

"Hello?"

"Teddi!" Jenna cried, relieved. "My gosh, I thought I'd never find you! I've been calling the apartment every morning for days looking for you. Where were you, what's going on?"

"I've been…working," Teddi murmured. "How are you?" she asked, fighting down tears at the sound of her friend's voice.

"I'd be fine if I were an only child," came the grumbling reply. "King's been just awful. Oh, Teddi, what did he say to you? Do you know he got stone-drunk the night you left and couldn't lift his head the next morning? He left suddenly for Australia that afternoon…but never mind that, your agency said something about an accident. I called there in desperation, you see…"

"I flung myself under a Cadillac," Teddi murmured, drying her tears on the hem of her blouse.

"You what?"

"I stumbled off the curb in my mad dash for a cab," Teddi said sheepishly. "I was rushing to an interview when I slipped and did a balletic routine—totally impromptu, you understand—under the wheels of a bright yellow Caddie. Didn't I have good taste?"

"Are you all right?" Jenna persisted. "Why were you in the hospital?"

"I mangled my leg and got a few cuts and bruises. Other than that, I'm my usual self."

"Are you there alone? Is Dilly home?"

"Heavens no, thank goodness," she replied with a sigh. "Gosh, it's good to hear your voice. I was getting maudlin, sitting here by myself."

"Are you sure it's only some cuts and bruises?" Jenna asked shrewdly, knowing from long acquaintance how her friend tended to minimize things.

"Only!" Teddi laughed. "It's my right leg, you know, the one I kick people with!"

"You know what I mean. And where are the cuts? And what did you mean about your leg being mangled?"

"Nothing much," Teddi lied. "I'll be fine in a few days."

"Come up here and stay with me. I'll look after you."

"No!" Teddi said quickly, visions of King appearing before her eyes.

"He's just come back from Australia," Jenna said, reading the other girl's mind. "Subdued, quiet, hardly the same man who left here the day after you did. The men are shaking in their boots, waiting for the explosion. Whatever he did or said, Teddi, it's hurt him, too."

"You're sweet to offer," Teddi said, "but I can't possibly leave right now. I've got to be here if my agency calls. I could still model hands, you know, or lips."

"Oh," murmured her blissfully ignorant friend. "Are you telling me the truth?"

"Truly I am. Look, how are you and Blakely getting along?"

"Blakely has decided that I am worth fighting King for," she informed Teddi smugly. "He has told King that he is marrying me in December, whether King likes it or not, and if he can't work on Gray Stag, there are lots of other properties around the area that will hire him. How about that?"

"I'm so happy for you," she said genuinely. "Can I come to the wedding?"

"Silly, you're going to be maid of honor. So do hurry up and heal, won't you?"

"With all possible speed," Teddi promised.

HOURS LATER, REFLECTING on that conversation while she curled up on the sofa in her fluffy blue bathrobe with her aching leg propped on the cushions, she wondered if Jenna had swallowed the explanation. Her friend tended to be suspicious even at the best of times.

Well, she thought miserably, at least Jenna's call had brightened her day a little. She wondered why King had darted off to Australia—of course, he was a busy man, and the ranch was his life. Ranches, she corrected herself. Her eyes closed. How was she going to avoid him at Jenna's wedding? That was thinking a long way ahead, of course, and she'd had years of practice at dodging him.

She'd think of something. No matter how much it hurt, she was going to have to find some way of never seeing him again. It would make the long years ahead a little more bearable, without the sight of him to taunt her with things that might have been.

The doorbell clanged loudly and she put down the magazine she was leafing through and hobbled to the door with the help of the walking stick. She'd ordered some more groceries from the store. It was probably the nice delivery boy back again.

She opened the door and stared wide-eyed at the tall, gray-suited man scowling down at her.

"Hello, Teddi," Kingston Devereaux said quietly.

She felt herself freezing, and all the hurtful things he'd said and done came back in a rush. She stared up at him with darkening eyes.

"I…I'm not dressed for visitors," she said. "Thank you for stopping by, but…"

He eased past her, closed the door, and scooped her up in his hard arms. The walking stick fell from her fingers as he carried her back to the sofa, and she succumbed for an instant to the need to be held, touched by him.

"Only a scratch, is that how the song goes?" he growled, staring at the bandage on her cheek and the one on her leg, the scratches and bruises visible where the sleeves of her robe fell away from her forearms.

"Will you put me down?" she asked, struggling.

He eased her down onto the sofa and let her go with obvious reluctance, seating himself close beside her.

"How bad is it?" he asked, indicating the bandage on her leg.

She shrugged. "I'll heal."

"How bad is it?" he repeated curtly.

"Some torn ligaments and a nasty scar," she grumbled. Her hand went to the bandage, and her lips trembled betrayingly as her eyes fell. "The stitches come out next week."

"What else?" he persisted, his eyes dark and stormy.

"Concussion. Some bruises."

He drew in a deep, slow breath. "Why the hell didn't you call me?"

Her eyebrows arched, her eyes widened. "Wouldn't that be a bit like having a scratched chicken call the fox for first aid?" she burst out.

"I suppose it must seem that way, after what I did to you," he agreed gently. His eyes searched hers, as if he were inspecting a beloved painting he hadn't seen in years. "But I would have come, all the same."

"From Australia?" she asked.

"From hell," he replied, "if I'd been there. And it felt as if I were, if you want to know. I haven't slept a full night since you left, remembering the way you looked…. Teddi, for the love of heaven, why didn't you tell me years ago?"

"How would I have gone about it?" she hedged, looking down at the tiny buttons on her satin gown. "We were worlds apart all those years, and you wouldn't have cared anyway." She laughed. "You'd probably have accused me of leading the man on in the first place—"

"Stop it," he ground out, running an irritated hand through his thick hair. "Don't you think I feel enough like a heel, as it is?"

He was the picture of a man tormented by regret eating him alive, and Teddi's compassionate heart was touched. But she didn't want his guilt. She only wanted his love, and that was out of her reach forever.

"It's all right," she said quietly, toying with a button on the flared skirt of the gown.

"Have you been here all alone, since the accident?" he asked.

She nodded. A tiny smile touched her mouth. "The delivery boy brought me a few groceries and made me some soup."

She heard his harsh intake of breath and looked up to see torment in his gray eyes.

"You're coming home with me," he said. "If I have to carry you out of here kicking and screaming, I'm taking you where you'll be properly cared for."

"You've made a habit of that lately," she said coldly.

He nodded. "I'll concede that point, I've been unjustifiably cruel to you." He stuck his hands into his pockets, stretching the material of his trousers across his flat belly, his powerful thighs. "I had a totally distorted picture of you from the beginning. I cultivated it," he added with a strange half smile. "It was my last line of defense. When I finally admitted the truth about you to myself, all the walls went down." He glanced at her. "I haven't taken more than a drink or two in years, but the day you left I took Joey into Calgary with me, and we came home at three in the morning singing 'Waltzing Matilda' at the top of our lungs. Mother was shocked. The next day I took off for the Australian property in a daze, and I feel as if I've stayed in it ever since. Teddi, I know there was nothing between you and Billingsly."

She stared quietly into his eyes. "Did Bruce call you?" she asked.

He shook his head. "He didn't have to. Jenna told me everything. Not that it would have mattered, once I came to my senses. You couldn't have been the way you were with me in the woods that day if there'd been another man.

And no money-hungry woman works the way you work to earn your keep."

It was nice to be believed at last, but was it guilt making him say these things?

"It...it was kind of you to come all this way to tell me," she murmured, confused.

"I came for more than that," he said. "I want to touch you. Are you going to let me, and not back away this time?"

Her breath almost stopped as she looked into those soft, quiet gray eyes, the face that she'd loved for an eternity.

"Not out of guilt, King," she pleaded unsteadily.

"Not out of guilt, darling," he said, his voice deepening with emotion. His fingers brushed her neck, her chin, the soft hollow in her throat.

"Your heart's trying to climb out," he murmured, watching the wild pulsing under his fingers. His eyes dropped to the silk over her taut breasts and he stared at it with a burning gaze. As if he couldn't help himself, his fingers began to trail down to that tautness, his knuckles brushing over her gently.

"No." She caught her breath, gripping his hair-covered wrist with cold, nervous fingers.

"I've lain awake nights remembering," he ground out, holding her eyes. "The way you felt, the way you looked.... I don't imagine it's going to be easy, but from now on, I'm going to handle you like priceless porcelain."

Her heart began to throb wildly at the light in his eyes, the deepening tone of his voice. Watch it, girl, she told herself, he's a master at teasing women.

"You aren't going to handle me at all," she said with a wobble in her voice.

"You're going to want me," he whispered, leaning over her with his big hands on either side of her head. "You already do, but you've put all the old walls back up because of what I did to you. I'm going to knock them down, Miss Whitehall," he promised softly. "One by one, day by day, until you're as hungry for me as I am for you."

Her cheeks flushed. "Never," she breathed. "I don't… I don't want that with you."

"Darling," he murmured, bending, "of course you do."

His mouth brushed against hers teasingly, tracing the outline of her full, soft lips, lightly pressing, nudging, until they parted helplessly. She felt his own lips parting and tasted smoke and coffee and mint as she gave in to the long hunger for him, the loneliness and heartache and sleepless nights when she would have given anything to touch him.

Her fingers went hesitantly to his shirt, and he caught them, lifting them to his face, moving them caressingly against his cheek.

"Yes," he whispered huskily, "like that. Soft little fingers, I could feel them when I closed my eyes, tracing patterns across my face…on my body."

She caught her breath as his mouth eased between her lips intimately.

"You've never touched me," he whispered tormentingly. "Don't you want to feel my skin, to touch it the way I've touched yours?"

She moaned, hating what he could do to her with words, hating the images that were flashing through her mind.

"Come here, darling," he whispered, lifting her gently against him to lie across his legs while his mouth took more and more from hers. Her fingers dug into his shoulders through the expensive fabric of his jacket, her mouth trying to match the expertness of his, trying to give what he was demanding. What she lacked in experience, she made up for with pure love, but that was something he'd never know, because she'd never have the courage to tell him. He'd think it was desire, like what he was feeling for her, a purely physical thing.

"I love the way you feel in satin," he murmured gruffly, letting his hands mold the soft curves of her body.

"You shouldn't...touch me that way," she managed.

"Nothing we do together is wrong, if we both want it," he said, lifting his disheveled blond head to look down at her. "Teddi, would you ever let another man touch you like this?" he asked solemnly.

She looked frankly horrified, and he nodded, his eyes watchful. "And I know that," he continued. "I'm not going to hold you in contempt for wanting my hands on this sweet young body, for letting me see it. I don't play bedroom games with virgins, surely to God you know that by now?"

Her eyes widened curiously. "What do you want, then?" she whispered.

He drew in a steadying breath. "Honey, you're not that naive, surely?"

"You...want me?" she asked shyly.

"Desperately," he replied quietly.

"But—"

He touched her mouth with a silencing finger. "I'm not going to seduce you. I could, very easily. But that's not what I want. I'm going to teach you how to trust me again. Then," he murmured, bending to kiss her very gently, "I'm going to teach you how to make love."

"I won't have an affair with you," she told him.

He smiled. "Won't you?"

"King..."

"Not now." He smoothed the hair away from her cheeks, sketching the soft lines of her face with eyes that blazed with curbed hunger. "Still nervous of me?"

"A little." She looked up at him, feeling as if all her dreams had suddenly come true. It couldn't be real; he must be the product of her insane longing for him. She reached up hesitantly to touch his hard face. "You're stronger than I am, and I know now how it is when you…when you want a woman."

"No, you don't," he replied, holding her hand against his cheek. "I was half out of my mind with jealousy. That wasn't lovemaking, it was pure revenge. Don't confuse the two." He searched her eyes slowly. "Teddi, men can be animals, but I could never be one with you past a certain point. Even that day in the den, when I looked at you, I could feel myself melting inside. Another minute, and you would have had no reason to be afraid of me. Not one." He touched her hot cheek and smiled faintly. "Despite what I did, I'm a gentle lover, darling. I'd be endlessly patient with you."

The flush got worse, but she didn't drop her eyes, she couldn't seem to look away. She was aware of the warmth and scent of him, the strength in his arms, the softness in his eyes as he looked back at her.

"You'd have to teach me…how to please you," she heard herself say.

"You already please me," he said, his fingers moving gently on her softness, the sound of them stroking the satin like the whisper of the wind. "Where are you bruised?" he breathed, looking down. "Here?" he asked, letting his hand linger over her heart as he caught her gaze.

"A…little," she whispered.

As she watched, he bent his head and she felt the hot press of his lips even through the fabric, in a caress she'd never shared with a man.

She moaned, catching his head with hands that didn't seem to know whether to push or pull.

Before the pleasure fully registered on her, he sat up, pulling her with him. "Someday," he breathed huskily, "I'm going to do that when there's no material in my way."

Just the thought of it made her heart run away, her breath catch in her throat.

She looked at him, her fingers on the buttons of the gown, and her gaze was full of hunger for his eyes, his lips.

He caught the expression in her eyes and drew in a sharp breath. "Don't," he cautioned, getting to his feet. "I want you too much already."

She stared, puzzled, her hands stilled as she tried to understand what he wanted.

"Teddi, I haven't felt like this since I was sixteen years old," he ground out, ramming his hands into his pockets as he turned away from her. "And that being the case, I think you'd better go and put on something that's a little more concealing. The whole world may have gone permissive, but I have a few things in common with my Victorian ancestors, and I don't want to take you into my bed on an impulse."

"I don't understand what you want," she murmured, rising.

"You will." He turned, moving close to brush a tender kiss across her forehead. "Now go and dress and throw something into a bag. I didn't come all this way to be turned down."

"Did anyone ever tell you that you have a Julius Caesar complex?" she asked, holding out her hand for the walking stick he'd picked up from the floor.

"Only where you're concerned, darling," he drawled with a wicked smile. "I do admit, in that respect, to an infatuation with the idea of conquest."

She hurried away before he could see the redness in her cheeks.

TEDDI COULDN'T REMEMBER ever being so much a part of a family. Miss Peake, thin and tart and motherly, hovered like a good fairy, trying to tempt Teddi's appetite with soups and delicate little pastries.

"But I'm perfectly able to get up," Teddi had protested the day King brought her home.

Miss Peake had looked down her hatchet nose with a sniff. "After a concussion?" she asked haughtily. "With that leg? Bruised from head to toe? You get out of that bed, Miss Teddi, and I'll carry you back in here myself!"

And that had been the end of it. Teddi had no doubt at all that Miss Peake was capable of making good on her threat. Mary and Jenna had laughed at the confrontation, but not in front of their formidable housekeeper.

"I can see her now," Jenna whispered merrily, "hauling you over her shoulder…"

"She wouldn't have to," Mary laughed. "King would beat her to it. No, my dear," she told the invalid with a kindly pat on the hand, "you stay where you are until King and Miss Peake feel that you're able to wander about again."

She left, and Jenna stared after her with both eyebrows raised. "Poor Mama." She shook her head. "She hasn't been able to change the furniture or make a major decision since King and Miss Peake took over the property."

Teddi laughed in spite of herself. "You make them sound like an invading army."

Jenna smiled. "What a delightful analogy!"

"They do tend to stick together," Teddi said, grinning.

"Did I tell you what King said to Blakely, when Blakely told him we were getting married and to do his worst?" Jenna asked.

Teddi shook her head.

"He congratulated him. Not a word about anything. He even offered to give us a tract in the Valley!"

"That was nice." Teddi smiled.

"Nice? It was incredible! Blakely couldn't believe his ears." Jenna stretched lazily. "Well, I'd better get out of here and let you rest. If you need anything, yell, okay?"

"Okay. Thanks, Jenna. You're all so kind..." Teddi faltered, trying to find words.

"You're family," Jenna said simply. She smiled. "See you later."

King looked in on her from time to time, friendly, caring, and Teddi couldn't help wondering if she was in the right house. He seemed altogether different now, and despite her wariness of him, she began to warm to his new attitude. She could relax, listen to his plans for Gray Stag, to his sometimes amusing revelations about what was going on around the ranch while she convalesced. But he didn't touch her. Not at all, not once. It was as if he was intent on building friendship between them before he attempted to move any closer physically.

Among them, the family managed to keep her mind off her future. But she still found time to brood. And one day King caught her at it.

"First get well," he chided when he came in unexpectedly, and his gray eyes danced under the familiar wide-brimmed hat. "Then brood. One day at a time, darling, that's how it's done."

"Change places with me and try that," Teddi challenged.

He shook his head, smiling wickedly. "I won't change places, but I might be tempted to join you."

She averted her eyes. Ridiculous how he could make her pulse jump with mere words. "It's a twin bed."

"All the better," he murmured dryly.

She glared at him. "I told you I didn't want an affair with you."

"So you keep saying," he sighed. "I'll just have to pay more attention to changing your mind."

"No fair," she muttered.

He only laughed. "Everything's fair now," he corrected. "What would you like for a snack?" he asked, moving closer. He was wearing denim jeans and a shirt with dusty boots, and he looked like a working man. "How about some strawberries?"

Her big eyes lit up. "Strawberries?"

"I'm having Miss Peake bring them in a few minutes, along with some whipped cream."

"A week ago, I'd have refused the whipped cream," she sighed. "But now, I don't suppose a few extra pounds will matter."

"My thoughts exactly." He stared down at her thin body under the sheets with concern. "You're practically all bones now."

He sat down beside her, his hard, warm thigh touching her side. He leaned forward to brush her hair away from her cheek. He'd already taken off the bandage, and he put the medicine on her cheek and on her leg, every night himself, trusting it to no one else.

Her eyes went to his chiseled mouth and she stared at it with an intensity she wasn't even aware of. She couldn't help herself. It had been so long since he'd kissed her, held her. She wanted him to...

"Do you want to kiss me?" he murmured softly. He leaned down, within touching distance, holding her stunned eyes. "Come on, Teddi. Don't hold back."

Her lower lip trembled. "I won't beg..."

"Oh, the devil with begging," he growled, parting her

lips expertly with his. "What does it matter who starts it if we both want it?" His breath sighed into her mouth, his teeth nibbled at it tenderly while his hands tangled slowly in her hair. His heart pounded heavily over her breasts as he eased down against them.

"King…" Her hands moved up, dislodging his hat to smooth the silky hair at his temples. Her eyes closed, her body lifted, grinding up against his. It was heaven. Heaven!

"Touch me," he whispered, teasing her mouth with kisses that burned like fire.

"I am," she whispered, nibbling back at his mouth, eagerly learning all the sweet lessons he was teaching her.

"Not the way I want you to," he murmured. He found one of her hands and pressed it against the damp front of his denim shirt, where his heart was shuddering in his chest. "Men are like cats, darling, they like to be stroked, didn't you know?" he murmured.

Her hands smoothed the fabric in slow, hard strokes while he kissed her.

"Teddi," he groaned. He held himself poised over her, his fingers going impatiently to the buttons of his shirt, tearing them open. "Now," he growled, thrusting one of her hands inside it, onto the warm, damp skin of his chest. "Like that."

She stared up at him, feeling a new kind of hunger, aware of exquisite sensations as her fingers tangled in the thick, crisp hair. He looked sensuously male like this, his body half-bare, his hair ruffled, his mouth slightly swollen, his eyes narrow with undisguised ardor.

"Macho," she breathed, looking straight into his eyes. "Much, much man…"

His hands tightened on her sleek, dark head. "You're not bad yourself, kid," he whispered with faint humor.

"Harder," he added, watching her hands with a half smile. "Touch, don't tickle."

"I'm trying," she murmured, "but I'm having to fight my way through the underbrush…"

"You little vixen," he accused. His mouth crushed down over hers, parting her lips almost savagely as he took what he needed from her. She felt the velvety hardness of his tongue easing into the sweet softness of her mouth, invading, taking, and a surge of wild feeling welled up in her. Her long nails dug into his chest before she lifted her arms to cling to him, raising her body against his warm hands, hands that knew where to touch, how to touch, to hold. A wild little moan whispered from her mouth into his, shocking him.

He drew back a breath, watching her. "Too hard?" he whispered, his hands gentle where they rested over the soft upthrust of her body.

"Oh, no," she whispered back, trembling under his expert caresses.

His thumbs stroked tenderly and she gasped. "You fit my hands so perfectly…woman, you feel like silk and satin, and you make my head spin when I touch you like this. You're not afraid of me anymore, are you?"

She shook her head slowly, watching him with her heart in her eyes.

His hands moved again, and she arched helplessly, dazed at the newness of what he was teaching her. "All woman," he breathed. "Soft and wild and giving. This is what a woman should feel when her man touches her. Oh, yes, darling," he whispered, bending slowly. "Yes, just like that, come up toward me. Darling, darling, move just…like… that…." His mouth caught hers again, and with a sunburst of sensation she felt his fingers opening her gown to the waist, gentle hands, so gentle, touching her in new ways, tenderly awakening sensations she had never known until now.

Slowly, the whole warm weight of his big body eased onto hers. She felt every sinew of him, every male contour; she felt his breathing as if it were her own. She seemed to have become a part of him.

Her body melted into his, softness giving way to hair-matted hardness, her body bare to the waist as his was, her flesh under his. She clung, unafraid, loving him until it was like torture to be so close and yet still not close enough.

Trembling, she drew her lips just a whisper away from his, shifting sensuously under him as she sought to get even closer, and he groaned.

"Please," she whispered achingly. "Please help me."

He held her face gently in hands that trembled, his face tense, his body strung as taut as a rope as he stared down at her with tormented eyes.

"I can't," he whispered, easing his weight from her. He settled alongside her trembling body and gently drew her close, his hands soothing now, easing the ache from her body.

"King," she whispered against his warm throat. "King."

"Next time," he said at her ear, "we won't stop. I'll finish it."

"I couldn't have said no," she moaned.

He laughed softly, tenderly. "I wonder what Miss Peake would have said if she walked in and I had given way to my instincts?"

"Miss Peake?" she echoed, dazed.

"You do remember I asked her to bring you some berries and cream?" he asked.

She gasped, drawing back to look at him. "I forgot!"

He cocked an eyebrow, letting his eyes drop to her open gown. She caught the edges together, flushing as her eyes met his.

"Don't be shy with me," he chided. "You're lovely."

"You make me feel that way," she corrected, looking at him quietly. "King…why?"

"Why what?" he murmured, throwing his long legs over the side of the bed. He sat up and lit a cigarette while she fumbled with her buttons.

"What do you want from me?" she persisted.

"Everything," he replied quietly, towering over her with his shirt still unbuttoned.

She searched his eyes, confused. "For how long?"

He shrugged. "Who knows?"

"And how about what I want?" she replied softly. He wasn't offering commitment. He was agreeing to nothing more than a few nights together, with no strings on either side.

"I know what you want, darling," he murmured wickedly. "You want me."

"And is desire enough to satisfy you?" she challenged.

He gave her a strange, intent look. "I suppose it will have to be."

At that moment, Miss Peake came in, carrying a tray with iced tea and a bowl of fresh strawberries and cream.

"King picked these for you," Miss Peake told her with a quick, appraising glance at King's open shirt. "Thought you might like some whipped cream on them, too."

King ignored the disapproving glance and moved toward the door. "I've got work to do," he said without looking back at Teddi.

"Too bad the cattle won't herd themselves," Miss Peake remarked.

King turned, glancing quietly at Teddi. "Isn't it?" he murmured.

She glanced up at him. "Thanks for the therapy," she murmured wickedly.

He cocked an eyebrow. "Is that what it felt like?" he asked. "I'll have to work on my technique." And he turned and went out the door, leaving her puzzled and breathless.

For the next few days, King reverted to being polite, friendly, and nothing more. It was as if he were giving her breathing space, time to consider the final step, to decide if she could settle for the only relationship he was willing to offer.

She agonized over it. Loving him as she did, she didn't know if she could ever accept an affair. It would be even harder to let go afterward than it was now. Because she would have had the joy of belonging to him. And that would bind her to him in new ways, with strings that were impossible to break.

He'd practically admitted that desire was all he felt for her, when he'd said that desire would be enough to satisfy him. But would it be enough for her? The physical relationship would be wonderful, of course, but was it enough? She loved just sitting with him in the living room, watching TV. She loved watching him over the dinner table, riding beside him and talking on lazy summer mornings. She enjoyed him in ways that had nothing to do with desire. The newness of physical possession would soon wear off, and what would they have left? Teddi would feel like a cast-off shoe, and she didn't think she could bear it.

She made up her mind slowly, but irrevocably. And when she felt well enough to pick up her life, and the stitches had been removed by a local doctor, she decided to go back to New York. The scar, while still noticeable on her cheek, could be covered with cosmetics, and she could walk well enough to work. She would work, she told herself, because she had to. And perhaps her career would take the place of a brief affair with King. Perhaps it would at least help fill the empty space.

Tearing off a hand would have hurt less, but she knew she had to tell King what she was going to do.

She followed him out the door after breakfast, she had made up her mind. She closed the door behind them, leaving the family at the breakfast table.

"What is it?" he asked gently. "Something important?"

"Yes." She licked her dry lips, fascinated by the way his eyes followed the movement so intently. He looked sensuously masculine this morning, in his tight-fitting jeans and brown-patterned shirt, the wide-brimmed hat cocked over one brow, his face faintly smiling as he looked at her.

"Well?" he prodded.

It was all she could do to keep from throwing her body against his and begging him to carry her off someplace. She shook her head to dispel that notion.

"I'm going home tomorrow."

He looked as if somebody had hit him on the head with a length of steel pipe.

"What?"

"I said, I'm going home tomorrow," she repeated. "I need to get back to work, and the scars are fading fast, thank goodness. I can cover them with cosmetics…"

"You're leaving me?" he burst out. "Just like that!"

She faltered, shocked at the fury in his hard face.

"I…" she began.

"Is it that Lothario accountant after all?" he growled. "Or is it just that you can't force yourself to make a commitment?"

"Look who's talking about commitments!" she threw back. "Old Footloose and Fancy-Free!"

"What did you expect, a ninety-nine-year contract, for God's sake?" he growled.

"No, thanks," she returned, "I couldn't take ninety-nine years of you!"

"Scared?" he chided.

"Not of you," she retorted. "I just want more than you've got to offer, that's all."

"Like what?" he challenged, his eyes blazing. "Flashy fashion shows and leering men?"

"It's my career!" she cried.

His face froze over. "Then, if that's what you want, go back to it," he said with ice in his voice. "Go today. I'll have someone drive you to the airport this afternoon, in fact."

She gasped. "What?"

There were storms brewing in his cold gray eyes, and a livid fury that she didn't understand. "You heard me," he ground out. "Get packed!" He turned on his heel and stomped down the steps.

Tears poured down her cheeks as his words sank in. He was throwing her off the property! She could barely believe her own ears. Did he hate her so much that he couldn't bear the sight of her anymore? Or was it just his masculine pride, damaged because she wasn't the pushover he'd expected her to be?

She went wobbling up the stairs to her room in a daze and started packing, wondering how she was going to explain this to Jenna and Mary.

She grimaced. Well, she'd just let King explain it. He could tell them whatever he liked. She'd make up some story about an assignment or something, and let him take it from there. Arrogant beast!

It only took a few minutes to get her things together. King thought she preferred modeling to him, and perhaps it was better that way. She didn't want him to find out how desperately she was in love with him. Her pride would be crushed if he knew.

She closed the bag and picked it up, taking one last look around the bedroom to make sure she hadn't forgotten anything. She turned, closing the door quietly behind her. Above all, she must act as if nothing were wrong, she mustn't let him know how devastated she really was.

She walked down the staircase, to find King in deep conversation with Jenna at the front door. He looked up when he saw Teddi in her white linen pantsuit and the same pale blue wrap blouse she'd worn the day he took her to Banff.

Something flashed in his gray eyes at the sight of that blouse, but his face gave nothing away.

"I was just telling Jenna about your new assignment," he told Teddi curtly, daring her to deny it.

She cleared her throat and tried to look radiant, wary of Jenna's sharp eyes on her as she went the rest of the way down the staircase.

"Yes, I'm so excited I can hardly stand it," she told her best friend with a forced smile. "Imagine, two commercials…!"

King looked uncomfortable and Jenna narrowed her eyes. "I thought it was a trunk show in Miami," she said.

Teddi shifted the small suitcase from one hand to the other. "Uh, yes, that's what it is…a trunk show and two commercials in Miami," she murmured, her voice fading away.

"What," Jenna asked, looking from one to the other, "is going on?"

King took Teddi's arm. "We'd better go or you'll miss your flight," he said gruffly, drawing her out the door.

"Jenna, I'll be back in a couple of hours," he told his sister, and slammed the door before she could ask any more questions.

"You might have given me time to say goodbye to Jenna and your mother," Teddi said angrily as he put her in the passenger seat of the Ferrari.

"You can wave at them, can't you?" he asked tautly. He got in and started the engine with an angry motion, barely giving her time to wave at the two stunned women standing on the front steps before he roared away toward Calgary.

She glanced at his set profile. He hadn't even bothered to change out of his work clothes. His boots were dusty and his hat looked as if it had seen better days. But of course nobody paid any attention to clothing in a busy airport. Her eyes unconsciously worshipped him. It was only just dawning on her that by saying "no" she was banishing herself from him forever. She'd never see him again after today.

Tears formed in her big brown eyes and she turned her face away before he could see them. She'd been lonely before, and she'd survived. But having tasted his ardor, it was going to be worse now. The thought of the lonely years ahead hurt terribly.

She brushed at a tear inconspicuously and straightened in her seat. This would never do. She'd have to get hold of herself.

As if sensing her uneasiness, he turned on the radio. A constant stream of music and news filled the silence between them as his powerful Ferrari ate up the miles. He was pushing it even harder than usual, as if he couldn't wait to be rid of her.

He pulled up in the parking lot at the busy international airport a few minutes later and cut off the engine. But he didn't make a move to get out of the car. His big hands gripped the steering wheel hard for an instant, then he sat back in his seat and lit a cigarette.

"Did you have to wear that particular blouse?" he asked in a cold voice.

She avoided his piercing gaze. "It was the only clean one I had," she said quietly. "I was going to wash the others this afternoon."

"You'll have to buy a ticket," he said. "I didn't stop to make reservations for you." He studied her with stormy eyes. "Do you have the fare?"

She swallowed. "Of course," she lied. She had planned to borrow money from Jenna.

He took a sharp draw from the cigarette. "Of course," he laughed shortly, reading her like a book. "I'll put it on my charge card. You can pay me back when you start working again."

She couldn't refuse. All she had in her purse was a hundred dollars. She'd spent every other penny on the hospital bill and food. But having to accept charity from him was the final indignity. A single tear made a path down her cheek, but she turned away before he saw it.

"Thank you," she said, composing herself.

He took another quick, jerky draw from the cigarette. "Will you be able to work?"

"I think so," she said proudly. "I'll have to, if I want to enroll for the next semester. I should be able to do trunk shows at least, the scars don't show at a distance. And I can cover them now with cosmetics. I'll be fine. Just fine."

He made an impatient sound and turned to stare out the window. His hat seemed to bother him. He ripped it off and tossed it onto the back seat, running a hand through his thick blond hair.

"It was your idea," he said accusingly, glaring across the seat at her with fierce gray eyes.

She blinked. "What was?"

"Going back to New York," he growled. "Back to your fabulous career, isn't that how the song goes?"

She bit her lower lip. It would only take a word, just one word, to get his arms around her. But she couldn't say it. She couldn't give in now, she couldn't sacrifice her pride, her self-respect, for just a few nights with him....

She stared out the window, hating the departing jets, hating the very sound of the engines as the huge planes swept up to touch the clouds. One of those would take her out of King's life forever.

As she brooded, she felt his fingers lightly touch her hair. She turned, aching, and looked up into his eyes.

Time seemed to stretch like a violin string between them while they searched each other's faces.

"Come here and kiss me goodbye," he growled huskily and reached out to draw her against him.

With something between a sob and a moan, she let herself be tugged over the console and into his big arms. He leaned across to put out his cigarette before he gathered her close and bent to touch her mouth with his.

Breathing unevenly, she parted her lips, giving him back the kiss as gently as he gave it, tracing his hard face with fingers that trembled and went cold as they eased over his skin, into the thick, cool strands of hair at his temples.

"Don't nibble me," he whispered huskily. "Kiss me properly."

"I can't," she moaned, hiding her face in his warm throat. "I can't. Oh, King!" His name was a cry of anguish, and he reacted to it in an unexpected way.

His arms contracted, lifting her higher against his taut body. "Teddi, do you want to go?" he asked intently.

"I have to," she said simply, her voice muffled against his collar.

"Why?"

"You know why," she whispered, closing her eyes. It was heaven to be held like this, crushed against his big body, feeling his breath, his heartbeat, as if they were her own.

"I thought I did," he agreed. "But you aren't any more anxious to get out of this car than I am to let you. It isn't the philandering accountant, it never was. It isn't your damned career, either." He lifted her face and searched her eyes quietly. "I think you'd better tell me the truth, little one," he said softly, "before you destroy both our lives."

Her heart jerked in her chest. "Both?" she whispered incredulously, aware of a new note in his deep voice, a new light in his eyes.

A sob broke from her lips. "Oh, King, I don't want an affair," she wailed brokenly.

"Neither do I," he said quietly. His big hands smoothed the blouse away from her collarbone, easing under the fabric to almost, but not quite, touch her high, firm breasts. When she tried to pull away, he brought her gently back. "Don't fight me, darling," he said softly. "There's no need for it anymore. I'm only touching what belongs to me. You do. You always did."

Her eyes closed and she moaned. She was going to give in, she knew it, and she was going to hate both of them. Tears welled in her eyes. "I should go home," she breathed.

"Home is where I am," he said. His eyes searched hers. "I told you that once, and you thought I was kidding. I wasn't."

"King...?" she whispered, aching for more than the light, teasing play of his fingers on her skin.

"I took one look at you when you were fifteen years old," he said in a voice too tender to be King's, "and hated you on sight because you were years too young. By the time you were seventeen, I was in torment. That night during the storm, when I walked in to check on you—I found you lying there in that transparent gown, and I wanted you so much that I ached like a boy. But I had to walk out and leave you, because you were a virgin and I was afraid of what I might do." His eyes searched hers. "I wanted you to the point of madness that night, and it's only been a little less consuming since." As he spoke, his hands eased down under the loose blouse and gently took the weight of her soft, bare breasts, and she cried out with the sudden stab of pleasure.

"It's all right," he breathed, bending to kiss her trembling mouth. "I feel the same way when you touch me. Waves of blinding pleasure, washing over my body like fire…"

She lifted her arms around his neck, yielding her body completely to his slow, tormenting hands, trembling at the newness of allowing him to touch her, caress her this way. Her eyes looked straight into his, her teeth catching her lower lip to stifle the moans that welled up behind them.

"I had to let you think I hated you," he whispered gruffly, watching her. "It was the only protection I could give you. If I'd touched you like this even once, there would have been no stopping me. I was obsessed with you. It was agony to have you at the ranch, because I spent all those long days and nights forcing myself not to look at you, not to come too close." He expelled a harsh breath, and she read the torment in his eyes with a sense of wonder at what he seemed to be saying. "Then, at Easter, you started playing up to me, and I all but left the country. I taunted you, but I had to, can you understand that? I had to run you off before we got in over our heads, until I could get a grip on myself. And Billingsly had been filling my head full of lies… I was so jealous of you that I could have killed him!"

She searched his darkening eyes. She had to know—she had to know!

"King, do you care?" she whispered shyly.

"Care?" His eyes closed and opened again, gray flames rising in them. His hands moved to her face, cupping it, caressing it, and they began to tremble. "I love you," he breathed. "I love you so much that I feel as if I'm starving to death for you. I want to have you all my life. To share with. To laugh and cry with. To love with. You're my whole world, little one, didn't you know?"

Tears poured from her eyes like rain on the desert. She couldn't stop. Trembling fingers traced his face, her eyes openly adoring him, loving him.

He caught his breath at the emotion in her face, and his own eyes closed for an instant. "My God, I've been blind, haven't I?" he asked huskily. "You're in love with me, aren't you?"

She nodded, her lower lip trembling, her eyes washed with tears as she tried to smile. "I can't remember when I didn't love you," she admitted brokenly. "But I thought you just wanted an affair…"

"I do," he teased gently, his eyes devouring her. "Sixty years' worth, and a few sons and daughters to love, and you in my bed every night, even the nights when we're too tired to make love." His eyes burned with emotion as they searched hers. "I want you in ways that go far beyond anything strictly physical, although," he added, easing the blouse off one shoulder to smooth his lips along her silken flesh, "I could make a meal of you right now."

She nuzzled her face into his throat with a joyful sigh.

"I love you," she whispered, "and I want you. But, darling, all our children will be illegitimate."

He laughed softly. "Then perhaps you'd better marry me before we discuss how many we're going to have."

"Did you say marry?" she asked, drawing back, confident enough to tease, seeing everything she would ever want or need in his worshipping eyes. "Old Footloose and Fancy-Free Devereaux actually proposing?"

"Do I recall your saying that you couldn't take ninety-nine years of me?" he countered.

"Was that before or after you threw me out of the house?" she retorted.

"I couldn't help myself," he confessed. "Having you around would have done me in if you hadn't cared. I thought you were telling me that I mattered less than your career, that you couldn't see a future with me. I was devastated."

"You're my career," she said very quietly. "You and the children I'm going to give you. That's all I've ever wanted."

He seemed to have a hard time getting his breath. His eyes narrowed. "And college?"

"There's a college in Calgary," she reminded him. "And I've got all the time in the world to finish school now."

He leaned down and kissed her softly. "In that case, you'd better go ahead and enroll, hadn't you, before we're married. Then maybe you'll have time to finish. Although, I don't know what their policy is toward pregnant students...."

Her eyes held his. "That soon?" she whispered.

He drew her back down, easing her head into the crook of his arm. "Very soon," he breathed, as his mouth opened and parted the soft line of her lips. "Will you mind?"

Her only response was a soft cry that was lost in the hunger of his kiss, and for a long time the only sounds were of heightened breathing, wild, sharp moans and cries. When he finally let her draw a breath, her cheeks were flushed and her eyes were bright with excitement.

"We'd better go home before we get arrested," he said unsteadily. "You see what you do to me? I touch you and lose what little mind I have left."

She touched his mouth with soft, loving fingers. "It's always been that way for me."

He pressed her fingers to his lips and let them go reluctantly. "We're going to have a lot of explaining to do when we get back, I'm afraid," he sighed as he let her ease back into her own seat.

She laughed. "I won't mind. Will you?"

He shook his head. "Fancy a double wedding, do you?" he asked with a cocked eyebrow.

Her face brightened. "Oh, King, could we?"

He caught her hand as he started the car and put it in gear. "We'll talk to Jenna and Blakely about it. Let's go home, darling."

She clung to his hand as they left the airport, her eyes full of dreams. In the distance, the Rockies were welcoming, and the sun shone down in a clear blue sky. Teddi smiled up at her fiancé with a warm, possessive gaze. He was right. Home was where he was. She leaned her head on his shoulder and closed her eyes.

* * * * *

HQN

To gain her rightful inheritance, Gaby Dupont takes a job with attorney Nicholas Chandler. She's shocked when sparks fly with the infuriating lawyer, but can Gaby risk her legacy for forever love?

Read on for a sneak preview of
Notorious,
by New York Times *bestselling author Diana Palmer.*

He gave her a long-suffering look. "I want to know if you have entanglements that will interfere with the work you do here," he returned. "I also need references."

"Oh. Sorry. I forgot." She handed him another sheet of paper. "And no, I'm not involved with anyone. At the moment." She smiled sweetly.

He ignored the smile and looked over the sheet. His eyebrows arched as he glanced at her. "A Roman Catholic cardinal, a police lieutenant, two nurses, the owner of a coffee shop and a Texas Ranger?" he asked incredulously.

"My grandmother is from Jacobsville, Texas," she explained. "The Texas Ranger, Colter Banks, is married to my third cousin."

"And these others?"

"People who know me locally." She smiled demurely. "The police officers want to date me. I know them from the coffee shop. The owner…"

"Wants to date you, too," he guessed. He stared at her as if he had no idea on earth why any male would want to date her. The look was fairly insulting.

"I have hidden qualities," she mused, trying not to laugh.

"Apparently," he said curtly. His eyes went back to the sheet. "A cardinal?" He glowered at her. "And please don't tell me that he wants to date you."

"Of course not. He's a friend of my grandmother's."

He drew in a breath. Her comments about men who wanted to date her disturbed him. He studied her in silence. He was extremely wealthy, not only from the work he did but from an inheritance left to him by a late uncle.

"You don't want the job because I'm single?" he asked bluntly.

Now her eyebrows lifted almost to her hairline. "Mr...." She glanced at the paper in her hand. "Mr. Chandler," she continued, "I hardly think my taste would run to a man in his forties!"

His dark eyes almost exploded with anger. "I am not in my forties!"

"Oh, dear, do excuse me," she said at once. She had to contain a smile. "Honestly, you look very much younger than a man in his fifties!"

His lips made a thin line.

The smile escaped and her pale blue eyes twinkled.

Don't miss
Notorious *by Diana Palmer,*
available July 2021 wherever Harlequin books
and ebooks are sold.

HQNBooks.com

HARLEQUIN
SPECIAL EDITION

Believe in love. Overcome obstacles.
Find happiness.

Save **$1.00**

off the purchase of ANY
Harlequin Special Edition book.

Available wherever books are sold,
including most bookstores, supermarkets,
drugstores and discount stores.

Save $1.00

off the purchase of ANY Harlequin Special Edition book.

Coupon valid until May 31, 2022.
Redeemable at participating outlets in the U.S. and Canada only. Limit one coupon per customer.